The Fourth Assassin

ALSO BY MATT REES

The Bethlehem Murders: An Omar Yussef Novel
The Saladin Murders: An Omar Yussef Novel
The Samaritan's Secret: An Omar Yussef Novel

The Fourth Assassin

An Omar Yussef Novel

Matt Rees

Atlantic Books
LONDON

First published in the United States in 2008 by Soho Press,
Inc., 853 Broadway, New York, NY 10003.

First published in trade paperback in Great Britain
in 2010 by Atlantic Books.

1 3 5 7 9 8 6 4 2

A CIP catalogue record for this book is available from
the British Library.

ISBN 978 1 84887 203 5

Printed in Great Britain by the MPG Books Group

Atlantic Books
An imprint of Grove Atlantic Ltd.
Ormond House
26–27 Boswell Street
London
WC1N 3JZ

www.atlantic-books.co.uk

For my brother Dominic
and my sister Melissa

Chapter 1

As he left the R train and came up the narrow, gum-blackened steps from the Fourth Avenue subway in Brooklyn, Omar Yussef glanced around for armed robbers and smiled. He recalled the secretary of his school in Dehaisha Refugee Camp warning him that New Yorkers would gun you down for a dollar. The scattered pedestrians stooped, as if beneath some invisible burden, scuttling over the wide sidewalks of Bay Ridge Avenue. Their heads lowered to the cold wind, they dropped into the subway without looking at him. He thought of the response he had given his worried co-worker: "I'm a Palestinian. Brooklyn will be a vacation from the dangers of my life in Bethlehem."

The sky was a blank, featureless gray above the three-story row houses. To Omar Yussef, the upper half of the landscape appeared to be missing, as though it had been concreted over. He checked his wristwatch and wondered if he had miscalculated when he set it to New York time. Its champagne-colored dial told him it was noon, but he couldn't remember ever having seen the sun so absolutely obscured at its zenith, even during blinding desert sandstorms.

He came to the corner of Fifth Avenue. From his pocket

he withdrew a slip of paper. With freezing fingers he lifted it close to his face and read the address scrawled across it. This, it seemed, was the right place. He sniffed and frowned at the tawdry shops along the block. He shambled past a jeweler's which bore the name of a famous Ramallah clan in Arabic characters on its purple awning and a café named for Jerusalem, *al-Quds*, the holy. Across the street, a doctor whose family Omar Yussef knew in Bethlehem had his office and, beside it, a sign proclaimed the offices of the Arab Community Association.

Omar Yussef shuffled along the broken sidewalk, skirting piles of dirty snow shoveled against battered newspaper-vending boxes. He squinted against a freezing gust and pulled his thin, fawn windbreaker around the slack skin of his neck. Drops of water blown from the tainted snow spotted his spectacles. He wrinkled his nose and pursed his lips.

This was his son's home, the section of Brooklyn where his countrymen lived. Little Palestine.

Except for the Arabic signs above the shopfronts, the avenue appeared archetypally American to Omar Yussef. Pristine cars, polished to a luminous finish he had only ever seen in Bethlehem on a government minister's sedan, nuzzled the brown snow at the curb. The Stars and Stripes rattled against the lampposts in the wind. For some puzzling reason, the gray, leafless trees along the sidewalk were adorned with large red ribbons tied in bows.

A Muslim woman hurried out of a *halal* butcher. Her head wrapped in a cream *mendil*, she puffed out her dark cheeks against the cold and hunched her shoulders beneath a coat that appeared to have been made for the Arctic. She caught Omar Yussef's eye and, looking demurely to the ground as she passed, muttered, "Peace be upon you."

"Upon you, peace," Omar Yussef replied. With these words, the first he had uttered in Arabic since his Royal Jordanian Airlines flight had touched down at JFK, he felt suddenly homesick and filled with regret that he had arrived too lightly clothed for the New York winter. At home, snow came every two or three years and swiftly melted. Despite his son's warnings, he had felt sure that New York's weather couldn't be so much worse. With his combination of extreme orderliness and dandiness, he had brought only a small half-filled suitcase, intending to add a few tasteful purchases of fine clothing before he returned to Palestine. Anticipating that he would buy a new hat, he had even left behind his favorite tweed cap. As he watched the woman haul her purchases along the block, Omar Yussef felt the white hair he combed over his bald crown lift on the raw wind.

At a door beside a boutique selling the traditional embroidered robes of the Palestinian villages which, in Arabic, confided that it was the establishment of someone named Abdelrahim, Omar Yussef checked the address once more. Then he shoved through the cheap black door and mounted the grubby staircase toward his son's apartment.

The corridor at the top of the flight of stairs was dark and silent. Omar Yussef paused to catch his breath and to let his eyes adjust to the dim light filtering up from the ground floor. A bus pulled away on the avenue, and a car briefly sounded its horn. Someone was cooking in one of the apartments. He inhaled a smoky undertone of eggplant beneath the thick, fatty odor of lamb and recognized the dish as *ma'aluba*. No one slow-cooked the meat and eggplant so that their flavors rose through the pot, infusing the rice, quite the way his wife Maryam did. Once again he felt the sense of isolation that had come over him with those first Arabic words spoken on the strange street, as though the tongue, which tasted and talked, were the natural seat of loneliness. He pulled himself up straight. He reminded himself that his son, whom he hadn't seen for more than a year and whom he loved, was waiting for him in one of these rooms, and he recovered a little of the excitement he had felt as he left the subway. He smoothed his gray mustache, smiled briskly to be sure that the chill outside hadn't frozen his features, and scuffed along the narrow, sticky strip of red linoleum toward the door of apartment number 2A.

It was open.

Omar Yussef halted. An inch of iron-gray light groped past the door into the corridor. He knew little about Brooklyn, but he knew that it was not a place where people left doors unlocked, let alone ajar. He stilled his breath and listened. Another car honked on the street. The apartment was quiet. He knocked twice and waited.

"Ala," he called. "Ala, my son. It's Dad."

Above the number, a strip of paper was taped to the door. On it, in a florid Arabic script, were written the words: *Castle of the Assassins*. Omar Yussef's lips twitched in a nervous smile. *Nizar always had good penmanship*, he thought. *That's a nice joke.*

He noticed a button in the center of the door. When he

pushed it, a dull bell sounded, but the pressure of his finger also swung the door back on silent hinges. He stepped into the living room of his son's apartment.

Once more he called his son's name and added those of his roommates. "Rashid, Nizar? Greetings. It's Abu Ramiz."

The room was shabby, furnished with a dilapidated sofa and three dining chairs, one of which was missing its plastic backrest. On the far wall hung a cheap, yellow prayer rug woven with the image of the *kaba*, the black stone at the heart of the Great Mosque in Mecca. Beside it, a page torn from a magazine had been taped to the wall. It bore a photo of the Dome of the Rock in Jerusalem. On a low table by the door sat a model of the same shrine made of matchsticks, the size of a football, painted gaudy yellow and turquoise. *The kind of art our boys make in Israeli jails*, Omar Yussef thought.

He crossed the room, with a wariness born of unfamiliarity and anxiety, and smelled the heavy, vinegary homeliness of *foule* coming from the tiny kitchen. He looked inside, noticed a grimy pot on the stove and a few brown smears of the fava-bean mash at its bottom. He held his hand over the pot and felt some warmth. A magnet advertising a Muslim community newspaper clamped a sheet of paper to the door of the refrigerator. It was a photocopy of the prayer times at a mosque called the *Masjid al-Alamut*.

Omar Yussef raised his eyebrows. *Alamut*, he thought. *The real castle of the Assassins. These boys didn't forget my history lessons.*

He knocked at a bedroom door and looked in. The shades were closed. He reached for a light switch. The bed was unmade. In the small room, a free-standing closet obscured most of the window. A calligraphic rendering of the opening lines of the Koran in gold on black hung above the bed. On the windowsill, there were two framed pictures of Rashid. The first showed him with his parents. The second had been taken when he was a high-school student, posing with his three closest friends and his history teacher, a grinning Omar Yussef. He shook his head. The photograph reminded him of how quickly he had aged. Maybe it was only that the smile seemed out of place in his current life, so full of misery and death had his hometown become since the days when he had taught the boys who now lived in this apartment.

He went to the next room. One curtain was open. The window cast a dim light, enough only for Omar Yussef to make out that someone was there, lying in the shadows on the bed furthest from the door.

"Ala, my son? Wake up." He knocked lightly on the door-jamb. "Nizar?"

The form on the bed didn't stir. In the sickly light from the window, Omar Yussef could see a pair of legs clothed in well-pressed black slacks and shiny black ankle boots. He approached, squinting into the shadows. He reached out to shake the sleeper's arm, touched the sleeve of a silk shirt, and found it was wet. He recoiled and yanked back the second curtain.

Omar Yussef stumbled, dropping onto the other bed. His pulse was suddenly overpowering. He pressed his hand to his heart as though to keep it from beating right through his rib cage and fleeing the apartment.

The man on the bed was dead. Where his head should have been, the darkness of blood soaked the pillow. A light gauzy piece of fabric had been laid above the ragged flesh of the neck. Blood covered the man's shirt and was splattered across the wall. The corpse's hands were bloodied too. Omar Yussef's cheek twitched. His eyes blinked and teared up.

Is this my son? he thought. His shoulders shook and he went down onto his knees, crawling toward the bed. His hands slopped through the blood on the floor by the nightstand. He whimpered and a burst of acid vomit burned out of his mouth. *It can't be him.* He wiped his sniffling nose and his lips with his wrist, staring at the body. The dead man had been short and slight, with a slim waist and delicate hands. *He has Ala's build. Do I recognize this shirt? Is it Ala's?*

On the nightstand, he saw a letter in his own careful hand. It lay unfolded beside the alarm clock, on top of a book of poetry by Taha Muhammad Ali. He picked it up. *My dear son, Your dear mother sends her love, and your niece Nadia encloses a short story she wrote about something mysterious that happened in Nablus. Here are my travel details: If Allah wills it, I shall arrive for the UN conference on the morning of February 11 and shall come immediately to see you in Brooklyn. As we have discussed so many times and with such anticipation, you will show me around Little Palestine. . . .*

He crumpled the pages in a bloodied fist and laid his shaking hand on the corpse's chest. His pulse palpitated so strongly in his palm that his hand seemed to rise and fall, as though the dead man's ribs still lifted with breath. The pooled blood seeped into his trousers, chilling his knees. *May the King of the Day of Judgment forgive me for all my transgressions,* he thought, *and find it displeasing that this should be my boy*

7

before me. As his joints stiffened in the cold gore, he knew that he lacked the faith that might will this body back to life. He was not a believer. His prayer only made him feel more desperate and isolated. He shuffled backward, away from the bed, and wept.

Chapter 2

In his shock, Omar Yussef sat with the terrified, expectant
stillness of a hunted animal. Eventually he wondered
how long he had been on the floor of the bedroom. He
watched his wrist lift like a corpse floating up through
water. There was blood on the face of his watch. He rubbed
it away with his thumb. Beneath the brown smear that
remained, the dial showed one o'clock.

He heard a footstep in the living room. He waited. Three
more steps, soft yet decisive. He sensed someone was just
beyond the open door of the bedroom.

Maybe it's Ala, he thought. *He's alive.* He opened his mouth
to call the name of his son, but then he glanced at the body
on the bed. *Or the murderer has returned.*

He shoved himself to his feet, feeling as though all his muscles
were encased in plaster. He was unsure if he intended to confront
the killer or find a place to hide. His knees shook. His brain
seemed to lurch into the backs of his eyeballs. He braced himself against the door frame as he stepped into the living room.

The front door was swinging and Omar Yussef glimpsed
the back of a man clad in a black padded coat, black pants and
shoes, and a black woolen cap. The man had bumped the

edge of the matchstick model as he passed, and it toppled to the floor. Omar Yussef made for the door, but by the time he reached it the man was down the stairs and gone.

His neck spasmed with adrenaline. *It could've been a thief who happened to see an open door and decided to try his luck*, he told himself. But he was sure he had seen the killer. He felt isolated and vulnerable. What if the murderer realized that he had no need to flee from the feeble old man trembling in the bedroom?

On the floor by the sofa, he noticed the telephone. *I have to get the police*, he thought. He picked up the receiver, then halted. *What's the number for the emergency services in this country?* He recalled reading an article which had explained why the deadly date had been so evocative for Americans, and he dialed.

A woman's voice answered. "Nine-one-one emergency."

Omar Yussef cleared his throat and spoke in his precise English. "I wish to report a death."

"What is the mode of death, sir?"

Omar Yussef strained to comprehend the woman on the other end of the line. The operator's voice had the impenetrability of poor diction forced to cope with a pre-scripted, elevated grammar. "I mean to say, it's a murder."

"How do you know it's a murder, sir?"

The phone shook in Omar Yussef's hand. "He has no head."

"You have a dead person there with no head, sir?"

Omar Yussef nodded at the phone.

"Sir? That is the situation?"

"That's correct," he stammered. "No head."

"What's your location, sir?"

Omar Yussef looked around for the slip of paper with his son's address. He checked his pockets, but it was gone. "I don't remember the address. It's in Bay Ridge. On Fifth Avenue. Above a boutique."

"The name of the boutique, sir?"

"Abdelrahim. But that's in Arabic. In English, it just says *Boutique.*"

"What's your name, sir?"

"Are you sending the police now?"

"Yes, sir. What's your name?"

"Sirhan. Omar Yussef Sirhan. From Dehaisha Refugee Camp."

"Where, sir?"

"Ah, Bethlehem, in Palestine. I'm not American." As he added that final, unnecessary information, Omar Yussef felt he had spoken from some kind of shame. It sounded to him like an admission of complicity in the murder of the man in the next room and those other murders infamously committed by his people in this land, a confession that he was an outsider not bound by the decency and trust that Americans believed they shared.

"Do you know the identity of the victim, sir?"

"Not absolutely." Omar Yussef sensed the pressure behind his eyes again. He dropped to the sofa and put his hand to his forehead.

"Sir?"

"It might be my son."

"Remain where you are, sir. The police are on their way."

"If Allah wills it, let them come. Meanwhile, I'll stay here, with him."

"Sir?"

Only after Omar Yussef had hung up did he realize he had spoken his last words to the operator in Arabic.

He picked up the matchstick model. The golden dome was caved in on one side, where it had landed on the floor. He tried to poke it back into shape, but his fingers smeared brown over the matches. He stared at his sticky hands, went to the kitchen, and ran the hot water, rubbing the blood off his palms. On the back of his hand, a liver spot dappled his olive skin. He felt aged and frail. His body was decaying—but still it lived. He gasped, thinking that his son might never grow old.

When he turned off the water, he heard footsteps on the stairs. He went into the living room, fearing that the man in the black coat had returned. But the steps were casual and loud. *It must be the police*, he thought. Looking down at his brown trousers, he wondered if the bloodstains at the knees were obvious. He became suddenly afraid that he might be blamed for the murder. His hands may have left blood on his face before he washed them, so he removed his glasses and rubbed at his brow with the cuff of his windbreaker.

He put his spectacles back on and saw Ala in the doorway.

"Dad, peace be upon you." The boy smiled, opened his arms, and approached Omar Yussef. The immobility of his father's face stopped him. "What's that on your trousers, Dad?"

"My boy, you're alive." Omar Yussef stroked the light curls

of Ala's black hair and felt the thin bristles of his mustache. At five feet seven, Ala was only an inch taller than his father, but he seemed to tower over the nervous, hunched man before him.

"Thanks be to Allah." Ala grasped his father's elbows and kissed his cheeks. "But what do you mean? Are you making a joke? Some parts of Brooklyn are dangerous, but Bay Ridge isn't such a bad neighborhood."

"My son, there's a body in your bedroom."

Ala gripped Omar Yussef's arms harder. "What? Dad, be serious. What's happening?"

Omar Yussef gestured toward his son's bedroom and lowered his head. The young man stepped into his room.

"May Allah have mercy upon him," Ala mumbled. "It's Nizar."

"My son, I thought it might be *you*." Omar Yussef shuddered as he came to the doorway.

"That shirt." Ala's voice, edged with tears, broke. "Those shoes, he was very proud of them. He called them his 'Armani boots.' They're expensive. It's Nizar." He took Omar Yussef's hand, still pink and warm from the scrubbing, squeezed it with tremulous fingers, then turned back to his dead friend with glassy eyes.

Omar Yussef let himself fall to the sofa and tried to find a way to sit that would hide the blood on his trousers. He covered his lap with a cushion. It was embroidered red on black with the geometric tribal pattern customary in Bethlehem. He ran his forefinger over the thick stitching and wondered if Maryam had made it for her son. He closed his eyes and tried to visualize his wife, but Nizar's face came to him instead. *My old pupil*, he thought. *My dear boy.*

Ala came out of the bedroom. The tears and the trembling were gone. His face was stern. Omar Yussef thought he detected pity and hate in his son's narrowed, hazel eyes.

"The son of a whore," the boy said. "Rashid. He finally did it. He killed Nizar."

"No, he was his best friend."

Ala shoved the front door hard. While its slam still echoed, he shouted, "Things have changed since we were all together at the Frères School, Dad."

"Even so, murder? What could've driven Rashid to something like that?"

"You don't want to know."

"I won't believe it. You can't be sure of a thing like that."

Ala turned to the window, pulled back a corner of the net curtain, and looked down at the gray street. His jaw stiffened, and his voice was sharp when he spoke. "He made it as clear as he could."

"What do you mean?"

The young man rubbed the thin curtain between his fingers. "The Veiled Man."

"What?"

Ala's eyes stayed on the window, furious. "That bit of material placed over the pillow, where Nizar's head would've been. It's a veil. Like the veil worn by a woman."

"But a veiled man?"

"You know as well as I do, Dad. You taught us about it in history class."

"The veil worn in the messianic stories by the traitorous man, the enemy of the Mahdi."

14

"That's it. When our messiah, the Mahdi, comes, the man who opposes him is supposed to wear a veil, and the Mahdi will battle him and kill him."

A siren sounded nearby.

"What does that have to do with Rashid?" Omar Yussef asked.

Ala shook his head. "Rashid and Nizar—"

The siren drew closer.

"Little Palestine isn't as I've led you to believe, Dad," Ala said. "America is very harsh. No one cares about my computer degree from Bethlehem University. I couldn't find a decent job. It's been the same for Rashid and Nizar. We're just another gang of Arabs to the Americans, terrorists or supporters of terrorism, anti-American bigots who deserve bigoted treatment in return." He slapped his hands against his hips and let his shoulders drop. "I'm not a programmer. I work as a computer salesman in a shop run by another Palestinian guy. To make ends meet, I drive a cab a few nights a week. Rashid and Nizar drive for the same company. I share this apartment with them because I can't afford a place of my own."

"What does that have to do with this? How does that prove that Rashid killed Nizar?"

"I've been here with them, close to them. I know how difficult life was for them here in America, and I know what went on between them."

"Which is what?"

Ala rubbed his hand across his eyes and let the curtain drop over the window. "The police are here," he said.

Chapter 3

The crime-scene technicians called out details about the body, its position and condition, its distance from the objects surrounding it. Their vowels were nasal and their tongues slapped distorted consonants into their front teeth, so that it was hard for Omar Yussef to understand them. Slumped in the corner of the couch, he wondered how he might explain to them why the dead boy had fled Bethlehem for Brooklyn. His hometown seemed distant and would surely be alien to these detectives. He feared they might misinterpret whatever he said for the worse, as those confronted by foreign situations usually do.

At the other end of the couch, Ala no longer appeared to be listening to the police. He stared at the scratches on the floorboards with his jaw clamped angrily. *What is it that he knows?* Omar Yussef thought. *How can he be so sure this killing was the work of his roommate?* He fought a resentful urge to lash out at someone for causing this disturbance to his visit. Despite himself, he blurted out, "Ala, what've you become involved in?" He instantly wanted to apologize, but Ala's eyes were bitter and forbidding.

Omar Yussef tugged at his spectacles and sighed. "Do you

remember," he asked, "how Nizar used to tease Father Michel at the Frères School? How he used to imitate his accented Arabic?"

Ala touched his fingertips to his brow, covering his face and refusing to engage his father. But when Omar Yussef mimicked the shrug and pout of the Catholic priest who had taught the boy French as a teenager, his son giggled and joined in. "The Father used to say, 'My boy, if I wished to offend you, I would call you a heretical Protestant, but instead I will stick to the facts and say you are merely a stupid child, eh?' Nizar impersonated him perfectly."

"Nizar was always the funniest boy." Omar Yussef's gaze was distant, lost in enchanted memories.

"When Father Michel was sick one time, Nizar took him a pot of his mother's *mouloukhiyeh* to warm him," Ala said.

"Yes, his mockery was always loving."

Their laughter subsided, both of them drifting through their reminiscences of the man whose body lay in the next room.

A short, dark-skinned woman with straight black hair spraying across her narrow shoulders hurried through the front door. She pushed a headband back from her forehead and adjusted her round glasses before she unbuttoned her long blue overcoat.

Behind her, the doorway filled with the heavy shoulders of a tall Arab man. His features seemed familiar to Omar Yussef. Bulky and jowly above a thick neck, his head tapered to a small crown, the hair shaved almost away. His lower lip drooped, and he breathed through his mouth. He wore a trim black goatee, and his eyes were dark, languid, and hard.

"They sent the token Arab cop to handle the dead Arab," Ala said.

Omar Yussef looked at the boy, appalled by his disrespect and hostility. *He's had a terrible shock*, he thought, *but there's something more that's eating him. He's covering it with a shield of aggression.*

"Not just an Arab cop," the big man said in a voice that was low and rasping. "I'm Palestinian, and I'm not here to handle the dead Arab, as you put it. We have specialists in the dead, Arab or not. I'm here to handle *you*."

He'll understand our language and recognize the nuances in our statements, Omar Yussef thought. *I hope that'll make him forgiving of my son's anger.*

"What're we looking at?" the woman called to the nearest uniformed officer. Her voice was high-pitched and sharp.

"The victim is back in the bedroom there, Lieutenant," the officer said. "Should we, you know, inform the FBI?"

"The Feds?" She stared at him.

"The victim's Arab," the big detective said. "That's what he means."

"Yeah, that's it." The patrolman nodded.

"You think he's some kind of suicide terrorist?" The Arab detective fixed him with the mirthless sneer of an imam at an orgy. "Did he cut off his head and throw it at someone? Maybe he kept a stockpile of illegal hand-grenades in his cheeks and one of them went off by accident."

The patrolman scraped his foot back and forth on the linoleum in the entrance to the kitchen. "Ah, Jesus, Lieutenant," he muttered, appealing to the other detective.

She shook her head and beckoned to the Arab detective. "Come on. Let's see what we've got back there."

The big detective followed her into the bedroom. As he went, he let his eyes linger on Ala. They had a drowsy intensity that made him look like a wrestler gathering strength between bouts.

Through the open door, Omar Yussef heard the Arab carry on a low conversation with someone already in the room. The other detective's sharp voice described the location and condition of the body. She came into the doorway and glanced at Omar Yussef, still talking into a small voice recorder.

As he listened to her catalogue of Nizar's visible features, Omar Yussef wondered how the detective might have described him, had he been the subject of her investigation. *Victim appears to be over the age of seventy, though identity documents show him to be fifty-eight. Hair: white, combed over liver-spotted bald scalp. Eyes: brown. White mustache. Gold-rimmed glasses, Gucci brand. Shoulders and chest show general lack of physical activity. Clothing expensive and good quality. Blue shirt, monogrammed OYS; fawn cardigan and windbreaker; brown pants, bloodstained.* As he mused, Omar Yussef looked up. The lieutenant was still in the doorway. She held her recorder to her chin, but she had stopped speaking. He saw that she had noticed the blood on his knees.

The Arab detective moved past the woman and stood above Omar Yussef.

"Greetings, *ustaz*," he said, in Arabic. His voice was lighter than it had been, as though he were greeting a friend.

"Double greetings." Omar Yussef stood.

"The other officers tell me you're visiting from Bethlehem. That's my hometown."

Omar Yussef smiled and looked at Ala. "Did you hear that, my boy?" His son twitched his cheek and sneered at his hands.

"I'm Hamza Abayat. I grew up just down the hill from the Nativity Church."

"I know the Abayats," Omar Yussef said. "You're from the Ta'amra clan."

Hamza grinned broadly. "Welcome, welcome to New York."

"Unfortunately, this is quite an unwelcome welcome." Omar Yussef choked out a bitter laugh. He was surprised at how warmly he felt toward the policeman, simply because they shared a hometown. *I must be feeling even more lost in this city than I suspected*, he thought.

The lieutenant came out of the doorway and looked at Omar Yussef. "The victim's Palestinian?"

"That's correct," Omar Yussef said.

She addressed herself to the Arab detective. "Here's what we found in the victim's pockets." She held up a transparent plastic evidence bag containing a blue passport. "Jordanian passport, identifies holder as Nizar Fayez Khaled Jado, born Bethlehem, West Bank, April 18, 1984. How does this guy have a Jordanian passport if he's Palestinian?"

"Palestinians don't have a state, so they don't have passports of their own," Hamza said. "Not the kind that're worth anything, at least."

The lieutenant waved the Jordanian passport. "You were born in Bethlehem, Hamza. Do you have this kind of passport?"

"I have an American passport, Lieutenant."

"Right, right." The woman smiled and brandished another clear bag. "Wallet containing New York State driver's license, bank card, Social Security card, all in the name of the said Nizar Fayez Khaled Jado, resident at this address. A couple of ticket stubs from the Cyclone at Coney Island and some paintball thing out that way, too—a thrill-seeker, this guy. Then there's this one other bag. What does this say, Hamza? It's in Arabic, right?"

"What's paintball?" Omar Yussef asked.

"Killing for fun," Hamza mumbled, reaching for the last plastic bag. Spread inside it was a sheet of pink writing paper covered in delicate script. Omar Yussef noticed Ala look up, as the detective read.

"It's a letter from someone named Rania. She's writing to this Nizar," Hamza said.

"What does it say?" the lieutenant asked again.

Hamza cleared his throat. "It's a love letter."

"Come on, bashful. Translate."

"'I want to be with you again, to feel you close—'" The big detective stopped. "It's not decent to read it here. It's very—detailed."

Ala sucked in his breath.

The lieutenant took the letter. "Okay, fine, we'll go back to the precinct house and dim the lights, and you'll read me Romantic Rania's letter over a nice bubbly flute of Chateau

Budweiser." She turned to the bedroom, halted, and pointed at the smaller room. "Whose room is this?"

Ala mumbled, "My roommate, Rashid."

"Rashid? Get his full details, Hamza." She went back to the corpse.

The Arab detective took out a narrow notebook, small in his thick hand. He rubbed his chin and lifted his eyebrows at Ala.

The boy dropped his eyes to Hamza's tan boots. His lip rose as though he felt nauseous. "His name is Rashid Takrouri," he said.

"Where is he?"

"Perhaps he's working. He drives a taxi. So did Nizar. They were like brothers."

"That'd make him a prime suspect—it's a specialty of us Palestinians to kill our brothers." Hamza wiggled his fingers. "His description?"

Ala shrugged like a surly teenager. "Rashid's about my height, a bit shorter. All three of us used to share clothes, except for some of Nizar's better items; he was very particular about *them*. Anyway, Rashid's slim and has dark hair that he wears brushed back. He's clean-shaven. He smokes all the time, and he's very jumpy."

"Does he have a black coat?" Omar Yussef asked.

"Yeah," Ala said.

The detective stared at Omar Yussef, even as he posed his next question to Ala. "When did you last see him?"

"Yesterday evening, when I went out to do my night shift in the taxi."

"Anything unusual? Did he seem especially nervous or excited?"

Ala folded his arms. "Especially nervous? Since he came to New York, Rashid has always behaved like there was someone around the next corner who might want to kill him. He's constantly terrified of being mugged or shot or stabbed or pushed under a subway train."

"Why?"

"He thinks Americans are all blood-crazed street hoodlums who hate Arabs." Ala stuck out his jaw and sneered. "What do *you* think of Americans?"

"Stick with Rashid, okay?"

"He's perpetually terrified."

"And that's how he seemed last night?"

"No more than usual."

Hamza turned to Omar Yussef. "What's your name, *ustaz*? Where in Bethlehem does your family live?"

"I'm Omar Yussef Sirhan, from Dehaisha Refugee Camp."

His eyes on the notepad in his hand and his voice quiet, the detective said, "You're the schoolteacher called Abu Ramiz. From the UN Girls' School in the camp?"

Omar Yussef looked in surprise at the policeman. "How do you know?"

Hamza rocked his head from side to side on his thick neck. "I don't seem familiar to you?"

Omar Yussef swallowed. "You do look like someone with whom I had a run-in a couple of years ago."

"Hussein Tamari."

"The gunman. The head of the Martyrs Brigades in Bethlehem."

23

"He was my uncle, may Allah have mercy upon him."

"May his lost years be added to yours by Allah to lengthen your life," Omar Yussef mumbled. "Your uncle and I—"

"It's in the past, *ustaz*."

Omar Yussef examined the damp, dark eyes of the big detective and wondered if his conflict with the man's uncle was truly forgotten.

"I hadn't seen him for years, anyway," Hamza said. "My father brought me to Brooklyn when I was barely a teenager. All those things, the intifada, the Israeli occupation, they seem so far away."

"Lucky for you."

Hamza sucked his back teeth and tapped his fingernail against his notebook. "If you don't mind, *ustaz*?"

Omar Yussef gestured with his open palm for the detective to continue.

"What time did you arrive at the apartment?"

"It was noon. I checked my watch, because I couldn't believe that the sun would be so obscured at that hour." Omar Yussef glanced at his wristwatch and noticed that Nizar's blood still smeared its face. He took out his handkerchief and rubbed it away.

"Where were you before you came here?"

"My hotel in Manhattan. I'm here for a conference at the UN."

Hamza raised an eyebrow.

"I'm not so important," Omar Yussef said. "It's a conference on the 'situation in Palestine.' I'm supposed to give a talk on the UN school system in the refugee camps. I dropped off my bags at my hotel and came here to see my son."

"And before you got to the hotel?"

"I took a taxi to Manhattan from the airport," Omar Yussef said.

"What time did your flight land?"

"About half past nine."

"Do you have anything from the flight? To verify your statement." The detective shrugged an apology.

Omar Yussef produced the stub of his boarding pass from his jacket. Hamza took it and said, "I'll have to check this."

Is that flight my alibi? Do I really need an alibi? It was as though by being drawn this far into the case, Omar Yussef had assumed some of the murderer's guilt. "What time was Nizar killed?" he asked.

Hamza glanced at the stub. "About the time you say your plane touched down, as far as we can tell at this stage," he said. "What about you, sir?"

Ala raised his eyes, keeping his jaw tight.

"Where were you at nine-thirty?" the policeman said.

"I was somewhere else."

Hamza worked his tongue around his mouth and lifted his chin.

"That's all I can tell you," Ala said.

"It's not enough."

"My son, you have to give the policeman an alibi," Omar Yussef said. "Weren't you with someone who could verify where you were?"

"Yes, but I can't say who." Ala's stern face became momentarily desperate and childlike. "I just can't, Dad."

"It isn't your Dad who's asking you," Hamza said. "If you can't give me an alibi, we're going to have to take you in."

"You can't arrest him," Omar Yussef stammered.

"Calm down, *ustaz* Abu Ramiz. This isn't Palestine. If your son has to come to the station with me, he'll have all the rights that are due to him."

"But he's innocent."

"He's guilty of hiding something, and I want to know what that is."

"Ala, tell him where you were. This is serious."

Ala clasped his hands, but Omar Yussef saw that they were shaking.

"You won't tell Mama about this, will you?" the young man said.

Chapter 4

An officer put his palm on the crown of Ala's head, guiding him down into the patrol car. When he took it away, the boy's curls fell across his eye. Omar Yussef stepped forward to smooth the hair back, but the policeman slammed the door. As the car turned the corner onto Bay Ridge Avenue, Omar Yussef shivered.

"You'll need a better coat if you're going to walk the streets of New York, uncle." Hamza came to Omar Yussef's side, pushing his big hands into the pockets of his blue parka. "It's colder than a water-carrier's donkey, as they say back home."

Omar Yussef was about to tell the detective that his shivers were for his son, but a sharp gust of icy wind stopped him. His hands trembled as he tried to zip the front of his wind-breaker. "I'm going to the police station," he said. "I don't need a coat."

"Not a good idea. You won't be able to see your boy for a long time, unless he changes his mind and decides to talk."

"I'll wait."

"Even if he isn't the perpetrator—"

"That's ridiculous. Of course he's not."

"—he's hiding something. The killer may know that and want him out of the way, in case your boy decides to spill. Could be he's safer in custody than out here. Maybe that's why he clammed up."

Omar Yussef spun around, as though the killer might lurk behind one of the stark winter trees. He shuddered.

Hamza stared south along the avenue, away from the direction in which the patrol car had disappeared. "This isn't the magical, exciting New York you see in the cinema," he said. "This is just a quiet neighborhood of Brooklyn. But there are many astonishing things even here, uncle—things we could never imagine back home in Palestine."

Omar Yussef closed his eyes and breathed deeply, willing his frozen hands to stop shaking. *He's giving me a chance to fumble with the zipper on this jacket without embarrassment. He's also switched to calling me* uncle *from the more formal* ustaz. *He wants to charm some kind of information out of me. Perhaps I can lead him away from the idea that Ala could've had anything to do with this. Maybe that'd be more use to my son than waiting in a corridor at the station.* "The neighborhood looks very ordinary to me, but I'm ready to be impressed," he said with a smile.

"Look all the way beyond the end of the avenue, uncle. What do you see?" Hamza stretched out his arm. Perhaps two miles away, past the signs for the Korean bodegas and Arab cafés, the Italian pizzerias and American ice-cream chains, stood the enormous piers of a suspension bridge. Its gray towers loomed with the arrogant symmetry of a Manhattan skyscraper. "That's the Verrazano-Narrows Bridge."

"It's so big, it's terrifying." Omar Yussef finally succeeded in pulling the zipper of his windbreaker up to his chin.

"The engineers had to factor the curvature of the earth's surface into the design, because it's so massive. It expands and contracts with the heat of the season so that in the summer the road hangs three meters lower than in winter." Hamza shook his head in wonderment. "Think of that. Can you imagine our people building something like that in the Arab world? This is an amazing place, uncle."

"Is it just big bridges and tall buildings that you like about New York?"

"The Arabs in this neighborhood, Bay Ridge, are mainly Palestinian. In the direction of Manhattan, you'll find Atlantic Avenue, where there're a lot of Yemenis. Then in Queens you have the Moroccans. Whenever any of them makes enough money, they cross that bridge to Staten Island, and they buy a nice big house." Hamza turned and swept his arm along the avenue. "Bay Ridge used to be Norwegian and Irish, until about a decade ago. Then our people came, and soon it turned into Little Palestine. Eventually all the Palestinians will have become prosperous and crossed that bridge. This place will be taken over by some other poor immigrant group. Little Palestine is destined to die young." He looked closely at Omar Yussef and raised an index finger. "But in big Palestine, you'll still be living in the same dirty refugee camps. There's no alternative back home, no way up. That's why I like it better here."

Omar Yussef jerked his thumb over his shoulder. "Unfortunately, your colleagues weren't taking my son across the bridge to prosperity. They went in the opposite direction."

"Don't worry about him, uncle. He'll be safe at the station. My colleague Lieutenant Raghavan isn't one of these Americans who believe the Arabs are capable of all evil."

"What about you? Are you 'one of those Americans'?"

"If you think I'm being tough on your son because he's an Arab, you're wrong."

"You're tough on everyone?"

"I'm just tough."

"You don't really believe Ala killed that boy upstairs, do you?"

"There's a snack bar a few blocks down run by a fellow from Beit Hanina," Hamza said. "Come and let me buy you the best *sfiha* in Brooklyn."

He took Omar Yussef's elbow in his fist. The schoolteacher gave a last look in the direction in which the police car had vanished, whispered the name of his son, and let himself be dragged away.

They went along the avenue, passing a basketball court enclosed by a chain-link fence. In the corner, six Muslim girls played handball against a tall gray wall. They wore their black *mendils* tight around their heads and with the ends tucked inside their collars.

"Even if a girl wasn't religious, she might cover her head against the cold here," Omar Yussef said.

"When the summer comes and they start to sweat, they can't wait to go home and take them off." Hamza waved to one of the girls, who blew him a kiss in return. "My daughter," he said.

"You live here? You didn't make the trip across the bridge to a bigger house?"

"For the same reason, I would guess, that you didn't move out of the refugee camp, though you don't dress like a poor man. I like to live where people know me."

Omar Yussef observed the detective's steady gait. The man looked heavy, with shoulders that sloped powerfully to a bulky back, but he balanced easily on the balls of his feet. His body, like his facial features, mirrored that of the dangerous relative Omar Yussef had tangled with back in Bethlehem.

"Your uncle Hussein wasn't as bad as I at first believed, Hamza," he said, cautiously, keeping his eyes on the detective's face. "But under his command the Martyrs Brigades did terrible things in Bethlehem."

"You think he'd still have been that kind of man if he hadn't been born into the violence of Bethlehem?" The detective turned back to watch his daughter celebrate victory in the handball game and run for her coat.

Omar Yussef remembered the way Hussein had swaggered around Bethlehem with his massive machine gun on his hip. *I'm quite sure he'd have been a gangster wherever he had lived,* he thought. *Bethlehem only offered him easier opportunities.* He recalled the lawlessness of the intifada, the beatings and extortion and murder, and he wondered how much of the viciousness with which Hussein had administered his gang had been passed on to Hamza in his genes. Those had been violent times, but he had never before seen a man's body with its head cut away.

His shoe slipped on a smear of snow, and Hamza caught his elbow, supporting him in a grip so tight it seemed as strong as the jaws of an animal.

Chapter 5

An awning ran above the slick, gray sidewalk outside the Suleiman snack bar in red, white, and green stripes. "I expect they bought it from the same company that makes all the signs for pizza joints in the colors of the Italian flag," Hamza said. "Fortunately for them, those also happen to be the colors of the Palestinian flag."

Omar Yussef squinted at the awning. "They've missed a color. There should also be black."

"The little cartoon is black." Sketched beside the name of the snackbar, a slim waiter wearing a fez and a waxed Turkish mustache lifted a tall coffee pot. "So they have the correct colors, after all. Since you mention black, why did you ask your son if Rashid wore a black coat?"

"After I found the body, someone else entered the apartment. Whoever it was, he fled as soon as he heard me. I only saw his back as he went out of the door. He was wearing a black coat."

Hamza scratched his eyebrow. "Yeah," he said.

Omar Yussef didn't like the skepticism in the detective's tone. "You think I made that up to divert suspicion from my son?"

"As soon as we sit down, I'll take out my notebook and write 'black coat.' Let's go inside."

Hamza edged past three young men in the doorway. The youths were exchanging elaborate handshakes with each other, snapping their fingers and touching knuckles, then wishing each other courtly Arabic farewells. Hamza guided Omar Yussef to one of the five small tables beside the food counter and went to order.

Omar Yussef peered into the display case, examining the wide dishes of oily vine leaves stuffed with rice and the pyramids of baklava, chopped pistachios green in their nests of phyllo pastry. He was suspicious of changes that might have been made to traditional Arab cuisine in America. But he found nothing wrong with the appearance of the food and, though he remained dubious, he was surprised at how much he wanted to taste it.

Hamza set down a cheap plastic tray laid out with a *mezzeh* of small spreads and salads. After the stress of the morning, Omar Yussef was calmed by the sight of the hummus, pooled with olive oil, and the *sfiha* flatbread with its coating of pale ground beef and pine nuts. He picked up the *sfiha* with both hands and took a bite.

"To your doubled health," Hamza said.

Omar Yussef mumbled his gratitude as he chewed. He dipped a corner of the bread into a plate of *labaneh* and scooped the white paste into his mouth. He had been expecting the inferior, mild flavor of strained cow's milk, but this had the sharpness of goat's yoghurt particular to the best *labaneh*. He savored the taste of his home as though he had been absent a year rather than a single day. *Am I a child, that I should be so homesick?* he thought.

Hamza called to the heavy, mustachioed man behind the food bar. "Abu Hisham, we'll have some *kousa mahshi*, please. My friend here has had nothing but airline food for a day. He needs to recover." He rubbed the back of Omar Yussef's hand affectionately with the pad of his thumb.

A plate of zucchini stuffed with ground beef, rice, and diced tomato came over the counter. Omar Yussef cut into one and chewed. It was hot on his tongue. "Your double health, *ustaz*," Abu Hisham said.

Omar Yussef felt himself warming and he shared a smile with Hamza. "You're not eating?"

"Abu Hisham will bring me some chicken in a minute." The detective checked his watch. "I'm careful about my diet. It's time I ate some protein." He took a dull green squash ball from his pocket and squeezed it between his thick fingers.

"Do you have a health problem?"

"I'm competing next month to be Mister Arab New York."

Omar Yussef wiggled his hand, palm upward—a question.

"I'm a bodybuilder," Hamza said. "I'm training for the bench press and the clean and jerk. But my specialty is the dead lift."

"A good exercise for a homicide detective."

Hamza ran his thumb over the keypad of his mobile phone and turned the screen toward Omar Yussef to show a photo of himself smiling in tight trunks, his massive body oiled and hairless, his biceps riddled with thick veins, like a map of the Nile Delta. "That's me winning another competition a couple of months ago," he said.

Omar Yussef squinted at the heavy muscles and recalled the strong grip on his elbow. "Excuse me if I don't wait for you to eat. I'm training for nothing more strenuous than lifting a pile of exercise books filled with essays on the history of the Fatimids in Egypt."

"That sounds heavier than my dead lift. Enjoy the food. To your doubled health."

The *kousa mahshi* stuck in Omar Yussef's throat, and he coughed. He knew why. "What's the food like in the cells at the police station?" he asked.

Hamza rolled the squash ball from hand to hand across the tabletop. "How was your flight? You departed from Amman?"

"I see the food in the jail is too disgusting to talk about."

"The food is fine. It's the cells that I prefer not to discuss."

Omar Yussef's mouth was dry. "The plane was almost empty," he said, "except for a troop of New York National Guardsmen returning from a tour in Iraq. They were thin and stiff, like ghosts draped in desert fatigues."

Abu Hisham brought over a plate of grilled chicken that appeared to be plain except for a little lemon juice. Hamza tore a strip from a breast and stuffed it into his cheek. "They must have seen some terrible things over there."

Omar Yussef thought of Nizar's headless body and wondered if the image would let him sleep when he closed his eyes. "Excuse me," he said.

He went into the bathroom at the back of the snack bar, removed his glasses, and splashed water over his face. He felt the water dribbling from his brows and nose, but when he looked in the mirror his myopia blurred the image and it appeared as though his face were melting. He gripped the sink and yanked at it, as though he might pull it from the wall, and he let his forehead drop against the mirror. "Ala, my little Ala," he whispered.

When he returned to the table, he pulled a wad of napkins from their metal dispenser. He tore them absently into strips, laying them next to his plate.

Hamza watched the arrangement of the shredded napkins, then drew a long breath. "How does your son come to know these roommates of his?"

Omar Yussef balled up the napkins in his fist. "He was in their class in school."

"High school?"

"All the way through. He's known them since he was three years old."

"The Frères School?"

"How did you guess?"

Hamza lifted one side of his mouth into a grin. "I can't imagine you letting your son go to a crappy UN school in the camp."

"Be careful. You know I'm the principal of one of those UN schools. I have some professional pride."

"What's the quality of the education where you work?" The detective smiled with one side of his mouth again and lifted his chin knowingly.

Omar Yussef tapped his plate with a stiff crust of *sfiha*. "Funds are very limited." He looked at Hamza. "Ala studied at the Frères School because, at the time, I was a history teacher there."

"Why did you leave?"

I was fired because the government schools inspector believed I was too much of a free-thinker, too critical of the fight against the Israelis, Omar Yussef thought. *How would that sound to this man? He's an American now, but he's also the nephew of a dead resistance leader.* "It's not important," he said. "The boys were all in my class. They were very close. They even had a little gang."

"A gang?"

Omar Yussef flicked his fingernail against his plate. Its ring sounded like the distant echo of an alarm bell. "Gang" had been the wrong word.

He took another bite of the *sfiha* and chewed it without enthusiasm. When he looked up from his plate, he caught Hamza glaring at him with hard, narrow eyes. The detective's expression quickly reverted to affability. Omar Yussef watched the thick fingers pulsing on the squash ball.

Hamza waited while Abu Hisham placed two coffees and a plate of baklava on the table. A young Arab woman in a black headscarf and a pink fur coat entered, greeting the staff and smiling at Hamza and Omar Yussef. Hamza tested the heat of the small coffee cup with his fingertips. "What kind of gang was it that these boys formed?"

"It was more of a secret society. They called themselves The Assassins."

The detective raised an eyebrow.

"When the boys were fourteen, I taught them about the medieval order of the Assassins in my history class. They named their club after that sect. It was an intellectual society, an innocent little secret."

"These three roommates were the members?"

"There was another boy. But he doesn't live in New York."

"What about that sign on the door of the apartment: *The Castle of the Assassins*?"

Omar Yussef remembered what Ala had said about the Veiled Man, the betrayer with the disguised features who would battle the Mahdi. *He was an essential part of the historical Assassins' beliefs. Is Hamza right to wonder about this connection?*

"Why are you frowning, *ustaz*?" the detective asked.

"If you want to cheer me up, release my son." Omar Yussef pushed his chin toward Hamza and saw instantly that aggression had no effect on the detective. Hamza ran his tongue along his bottom lip and stared at Omar Yussef with eyes as blank as a funeral shroud. *He's tough*, Omar Yussef thought. *Even if I were the type to bully people, I'd have no success with this man.* "The sign about the 'Castle of the Assassins' is just some sort of nostalgic joke. The apartment is hardly a castle."

"If this little gang was secret, how do you know about it?"

Omar Yussef lifted his coffee cup by its delicate handle and sipped. He grimaced at its sweetness. *Son of a whore, I forgot to ask for mine bitter,* he thought. He rattled the cup into its saucer petulantly. "I was a part of the club. Well, in a sense."

"You were one of The Assassins?" Hamza gave a deep, slow giggle. "Forgive me, *ustaz*. But I would more likely send that girl over there in the pink coat to be an assassin than you."

"I told you, it was an academic joke. No one was actually going to be assassinated." The boys had given him the name of the medieval chief of the Assassins, the Old Man of the Mountain. He had still been young enough that it hadn't offended him to be called an old man. He polished his glasses with a napkin. "We used to go on picnics to ruined Crusader castles."

"Castles?"

"We pretended they were Alamut. That was the name of the biggest Assassin fortress."

"Alamut?" Hamza said, stroking his beard. "What does that mean?"

Omar Yussef replaced his glasses and squinted at Hamza. *You're not the simple muscleman you'd have me believe you to be,* he thought. "The Death Castle. That's the most likely meaning in Arabic and Persian."

"The Death Castle, eh? But the note on the door about the 'Castle of the Assassins' is just a nostalgic joke, as you put it? The body inside the apartment spoils the fun, don't you think?"

Omar Yussef spun his coffee cup slowly on its saucer. "There's a prayer schedule for some place called the Alamut Mosque in the kitchen of the apartment. Maybe it's connected."

"So now an entire mosque is in on the joke?" Hamza scratched gently at his goatee. "I remember reading that when these medieval Assassins went off on their suicide missions, they were high on drugs."

"That's a myth. They seemed so unafraid of death that others thought they must have taken hashish and so called them the *Hashishine*. 'Assassin' is a corruption of that word. But in reality they were like the people from Hamas and Islamic Jihad and al-Qaeda today. They did insane things because they believed they would be rewarded in Paradise."

"The virgins, the dark-eyed *houris*, and all that?"

Omar Yussef bit into a piece of baklava and crunched the

pistachios between his back teeth. "Everything isn't always about sex, Sergeant Abayat."

Hamza waved his hand. "Sure, they receive a seat next to Allah, and they get a free pass into Paradise for their relatives too. But I think most young men are more interested in the virgins, no matter how much they love the Master of the Universe or their mama's cooking."

"I see that you're no sheikh."

"And I see that you're no Assassin."

"Neither is my son."

"Nizar probably wasn't killed by someone looking for the rewards of Paradise. Most of the killings around here are simply related to the drug trade."

Omar Yussef stiffened. "My son isn't involved in such things. How dare you?"

"Even if it wasn't true, the reputation of the Assassins was that they were stoned on hashish. Maybe these boys revived the name of their teenage gang as a joke, as you say. But perhaps the joke was a private reference to the fact that they were dealing drugs."

"You're trying to provoke me. That's crazy."

"Forgive me, but even in Brooklyn we don't see headless corpses every day. *That* is crazy." Hamza leaned over the table, and Omar Yussef pressed himself back against his chair. "It also happens to be a craziness that involves you somehow, *ustaz*."

Omar Yussef struggled to hold Hamza's gaze. He worried that he had been too open with the policeman, and he felt panic chill him. *Maybe he'll use this information about the Assassins to pin the killing on Ala, or even on me as revenge for what happened between me and his uncle back in Bethlehem*, he thought.

"They were intelligent boys. That's why they based their little club around their interest in history. They didn't go out to throw stones at the Israelis. Study was their reward, not Paradise." Omar Yussef played with the triangle of baklava on his plate. In Bethlehem, the intifada turned people who had previously seemed peaceful to violence and martyrdom. *But not these boys*, he thought. *I'm sure of it.*

A police siren approached. Hamza watched the blue and red lights streak past the window, then looked hard at Omar Yussef. "After Nine-Eleven, the FBI woke up to the fact that Bay Ridge had turned into Little Palestine. They sent agents to investigate all the community leaders. They found a few who were married to people whose cousins back in Ramallah were neighbors of someone who was in jail for being in Hamas. That kind of nonsense. But it made people very suspicious here. It made the cops suspect Arabs, and it made Arabs resent the cops and the FBI and ultimately America itself. One day that's going to result in something bad, *ustaz.*"

"Do the people here resent you, too?"

"The police brass is suspicious of all Arabs. The INS, the FBI, everyone in law enforcement is down on the Arab community, and that goes for Arab cops too. And the Arabs on the street see me as a traitor working for their persecutors." Hamza struck the table with the side of his heavy fist. "I'm not scared of any of them. My only fear is that someone from Palestine will come here and use this place as a base for terrible acts. If that happens, the Feds will come back, and then, may it be displeasing to Allah, they'll stomp Little Palestine into the ground."

The syrup in the baklava coated Omar Yussef's esophagus, and for a moment he felt smothered. He sipped from his water. "Thank you for this meal," he said. "It was very good."

"May you enjoy it with double health deep in your heart." Hamza took a business card from his wallet and handed it to Omar Yussef. "My cell-phone number. In case you think of anything important, *ustaz*."

Hamza walked Omar Yussef back along the avenue toward the subway station. The clouds remained featureless and uniform, blanking out the sky, but the fawn bricks on the side-street row houses looked bright. The detective gestured down a street lined with trees. "The homes on these streets are expensive," he said. "There're a lot of Greeks on that block. The Arabs mostly live here on the avenue, above the shops, where the apartments are cheap."

"Where do *you* live?"

"The end of that block. For my wife to be near the church."

Clad in dark granite, the square tower of a church cut across the flat gray sky.

"She's a Christian?"

Hamza grunted and pulled some chicken from between his teeth.

"What did your tribe back in Bethlehem have to say about you marrying a Christian?" Omar Yussef asked.

"It's better than marrying a refugee from the camp where *you* live." Hamza pointed to the red ribbons on the trees. "It's

Valentine's Day this week. You remember the Christians in Beit Jala used to celebrate it back home?"

Omar Yussef nodded. "You're supposed to give a card to your wife or your fiancée."

"In America, the whole thing is commercialized, *ustaz*. In the schools, the children give Valentine's Day cards and little bags of chocolate to everyone in their class."

"And everyone has to put a red ribbon on the tree outside their house?"

"Not everywhere, but the neighborhood association organizes it here. It's better than graffiti about dead martyrs, isn't it?" Hamza smiled. "What about the unfortunate Nizar's Valentine? Who's Rania?"

Omar Yussef remembered his son's anxious glance at the love letter, the recognition he seemed to show at the sight of the pink stationery in the evidence bag. "It's a fairly common name. Rania could be anyone."

"I don't think it was a letter from the Queen of Jordan." Hamza frowned. "Here's your station, *ustaz*."

"I want to go and see my son."

"If Allah wills it, you'll be able to talk to him tomorrow. But not now."

"Don't hide behind Allah. Why don't *you* will it?"

"I may be an American, but we're speaking Arabic and it'd be rude of me to come right out and tell you that the answer's no."

Omar Yussef lifted his jaw in anger. "You said yourself that this isn't the Middle East. My son has rights, and so do I. I'm asking you as an American to give me the right to see my son."

The detective grinned mirthlessly. "If Allah wills it."

"Damn it, Hamza. I want to see him."

"Take the R train one stop and change to the N," Hamza said. "It'll get you back to Manhattan quicker."

"Do you think I'm so eager to escape Brooklyn?"

As Omar Yussef descended the grimy steps beneath the subway-station sign, he heard Hamza's voice, slow and deep: "No, *ustaz*. In any case, you certainly can't escape me."

At the bottom of the steps, Omar Yussef considered that he might have to make a number of trips out to Brooklyn to see his son. He decided to buy ten rides. He pushed a twenty-dollar bill into the tray of the token booth and received a yellow-and-blue ticket in return. There was something familiar about the ticket clerk, who dropped his eyes when Omar Yussef wished him a good day.

Omar Yussef swiped the card at the turnstile. As he pushed through to the other side, he noticed the little electronic screen read "$2.00/$16.00 Bal." The machine had deducted the two-dollar fare, but there were only sixteen dollars remaining on the card. Omar Yussef stopped and looked back at the clerk in his booth. The man held Omar Yussef's glare. He was in late middle age with a pinched sour face and a thin, mean mouth. He wore thick, black-framed glasses, and his gray hair was slicked back. *He looks like the man who used to be the American Defense Secretary,* Omar Yussef thought, *the one who blew the war in Iraq.*

He went back through the turnstile. The clerk made a show of counting bills as he approached the booth.

"I bought a ticket for twenty dollars, sir," Omar Yussef said, "but you gave me a card worth only eighteen."

The clerk spoke, but Omar Yussef heard nothing. He

repeated his complaint, and the clerk lifted his head to his microphone. "Sold you a twenty-dollar card, sir." His voice drawled through the speaker as though it were cut roughly from metal.

Omar Yussef decided to be generous. "Then there has been a computer error, because the machine says I only have sixteen dollars remaining."

"Sold you a twenty-dollar card, like I said."

"You took my twenty and kept two dollars for your pocket." Omar Yussef had the familiar feeling of his heartbeat quickening, drowning all sense of moderation and leaving him full of anger. "This is a damned outrage."

"Watch your mouth, buddy," the clerk said.

"You cheated me, sir."

"I'll make you a deal. I'll give you another ticket for nothing."

Omar Yussef took a long breath. "Very well."

"One-way, non-stop back to Baghdad, Osama." The clerk sniggered, as he licked his thumb to count a pile of twenties.

Omar Yussef brought his fist down beside the change tray. The quarters jumped on the clerk's desk. "You may keep my two dollars," Omar Yussef said. "I don't wish to sell my dignity as cheaply as you do."

The clerk sneered.

Omar Yussef swiped his card in the turnstile again and followed the signs for the Manhattan platform.

Chapter 6

The windows of the N train were scratched and daubed in an ugly paste graffiti, the translucent letters dripping like a sugar glaze on a cake. The floor was black and speckled to disguise the dirt, but pink smears of vomit and red chewing gum and the explosions of dropped soda cups stained it.

As Omar Yussef rattled toward Manhattan, fewer than half the slippery, unwelcoming seats in the car were taken. Encased in voluminous coats, the passengers hunched their shoulders, crossed their arms, and coughed into their collars, though it was warm in the train. Omar Yussef let his eyes drift across the smiling faces in the advertisements just below the ceiling of the car. The ads pushed training courses for paralegals and court reporters, the services of doctors who would give you better skin or allow you to commute on the train without hemorrhoid pain. He imagined the ads might have been there to torment the riders with the Siberian gloom of their journey, allowing them to glimpse the mediocre extent of the improvements they might pursue. Enclosed in plastic, strip lights flickered over the ads and across the immobile faces of the passengers. Their glow gave the train the somnambulant aura of a midnight bus station.

He felt a rush of loneliness. He missed his wife and wondered if he ought to have insisted on waiting for his son at the police station after all, despite Sergeant Abayat's dissuasion. On the wall beside him, the N train snaked its yellow trail across a subway map. To distract himself from his worries, he lifted a finger to the map and tried to trace his path to his destination, but he lost track of the route in the mess of different lines converging on lower Manhattan. He realized that he'd forgotten Abayat's instructions and was unsure if he needed to change trains again to make it back to his hotel. The variegated twirls on the map made no more sense to him than the wires in a diagram of an electrical appliance. He glanced nervously around the train. To ask directions might, he feared, invite a mugging.

A fur-lined hood bracketed the face of the girl on the bench opposite Omar Yussef. She was slight, even in her quilted brown coat, but her cheeks had an Andean broadness. Omar Yussef heard a jangling pop tune, and the girl pulled a mobile phone from her pocket. When she flipped it open, to his surprise she answered the call in Arabic. She squirmed in her seat with enjoyment as she whispered into the phone, smiling to reveal a row of teeth imprisoned behind heavy orthodontic apparatus.

"I'm on the train," she said, giggling. "I might be cut off in the tunnel, so I'll call you back."

Despite the relentless thundering of the train and the quietness of the girl's hurried voice, Omar Yussef detected the soft consonants of the educated Palestinian. When she returned the phone to her pocket, he smiled at her. "Where in Palestine are you from, my daughter?" he asked.

She opened her eyes in surprise. *Is it, perhaps, so odd for a stranger to talk to another on this train?* Omar Yussef wondered. *Or did she simply not take me for an Arab, just as I mistook her for a South American?*

"Jerusalem, *O Hajji*," the girl said.

I look so old, youngsters assume I must by now have fulfilled the obligation to go on the pilgrimage to Mecca, he thought. "I'm not a *Hajji*, my daughter, though may it be the will of Allah to grant you the honor of such a journey to the holy places in Arabia."

"If Allah wills it, *ustaz*."

Allah might will it, Omar Yussef thought, *but I'd no more go on the Hajj than I would enter a mosque to pray in Brooklyn.* He recalled the page on Ala's refrigerator with the prayer times for the Alamut Mosque. He wondered which of the boys worshiped there. He didn't remember any of them being religious. Maybe it was only the name—with its connection to their old Assassins gang—that had led them to display it.

"Which neighborhood of Jerusalem?" he said.

"Sheikh Jarrah."

It had been many years since Omar Yussef had visited that quarter north of the Old City where the leading Arab families had their mansions, dilapidated now that their owners no longer were the power in the town. "How long have you lived in New York?"

"I was born here, *O Hajji*." She corrected herself: "Sorry, I mean *ustaz*. My parents came when my mother was carrying me. And you, *ustaz*?"

"I'm—visiting my son in Bay Ridge," Omar Yussef stammered. "I'm from Bethlehem, from Dehaisha Camp."

"May you feel as if you were in your own home and with your family in New York."

"You don't look typically Palestinian." Omar Yussef stroked his own cheekbones to demonstrate what was different about her appearance.

"My great-grandfather came to Palestine from Libya, *ustaz*," the girl said with a grin. "My mother says I inherited the cheekbones of a North African tribeswoman."

"May Allah bless you." Omar Yussef paused as the train rocked across the points and the lights flickered. "How is life here?"

"It's all I've known, *ustaz*," the girl said. "My dear parents love Jerusalem, but I've only visited once. The city seemed full of frustration."

"This subway car is very far from Jerusalem."

"It's also far from the fears people experience there, *ustaz*."

Omar Yussef thought of the desperation in his son's eyes when the police took him away, of the headless body and the strange reference to the Veiled Man. Did Palestinians have to take trouble with them wherever they went? Couldn't they be more like Americans, engaged in their financial struggles, but unburdened by politics? "Far away, my daughter? It seems to me that fear tracks our people faster than they can flee it."

"May it be displeasing to Allah, *ustaz*." The girl rose as the train came into the Pacific Street station. "This is my stop. May Allah grant you grace, *ustaz*."

Omar Yussef remembered why he had spoken to her in the first place and lifted his hand to catch her attention. "For 42nd Street—?"

"Stay on this train, *ustaz*. Peace be upon you."

"And upon you, peace. May Allah lengthen your life."

He watched her slip into the crowd on the platform and lost sight of her as the train picked up speed again. The subway car had felt comforting while they spoke, but she had taken all that warmth with her and left him feeling more bereft and alien than before.

As the train carried him through the tunnel, he had the feeling that he was trapped like an African crammed below the decks of a Yemeni slave ship. Whenever he tried to divert his thoughts from the arrest of his son, he knew that he was like the slave dragging his chains over the inert bodies of those packed beside him, hoping that his efforts took him in the direction of home. But he was being stolen quicker than he could struggle toward freedom. He felt himself transported beneath a world that was outlandish and dangerous and imprisoning. *You've been here less than a day, and already you're so gloomy*, he thought. *Remember how excited you were to arrive here, to see your son.*

He left the train at Times Square, squinting along the busy platform as he sought the EXIT sign. He made his way through a series of wide, low-ceilinged tunnels. Passengers passed him swiftly, dodging between those hurrying in the opposite direction until their movement made Omar Yussef dizzy. He came to a stretch of tunnel quiet enough that he could hear his own steps over the rattle of the trains, rounded a corner to a flight of stairs, and found the exit barred by a locked gate. *No wonder no one was around*, he thought.

As he turned back, he heard someone moving stealthily

along the tunnel. His breath quickened. He held himself close to the cream tiles on the wall and peered around the corner. The footsteps halted. He saw no one. A fluorescent light flickered over the dirty concrete floor with a stuttering buzz.

He would have headed back toward the crowds, but his fear filled the empty corridor with the image of the man in the black coat he had glimpsed fleeing Ala's apartment. He went further along the tunnel, quickening his pace.

Before he had gone twenty yards, he was panting, and tension lanced through his chest. He stopped to catch his breath and heard a single set of footsteps behind him.

"Rashid?" he said. The name of his former pupil, the boy his son believed had become a killer, echoed in the tunnel. Omar Yussef heard the quaver in his own voice. "Rashid, my dear one?"

Water dripped from a short-circuited light fixture. The steps sounded again, as though someone were moving with fast, short paces. But Omar Yussef saw nothing. He recalled his secretary's warning about New York muggers and wondered if he were about to be robbed. *It'd be preferable to a murder,* he thought.

At the end of the tunnel, another exit seemed to be barred and he whimpered in self-pity. He advanced on the gate in desperation and discovered that, while the entry was blocked, a one-way turnstile allowed him access to the stairs. As he scrambled up the steps, he heard someone running along the tunnel behind him, but no one came through the turnstile. The cold on the street chilled his scalp, and he realized that he had been sweating with tension.

He hurried along 42nd Street toward his hotel, watching the crowd over his shoulder as darkness overwhelmed the blank light of the winter's day. He tried to pick out a man in a black coat, but the dour dress of the commuters making for Grand Central melded into an indistinguishable mass. In Bethlehem, where he had lived since infancy, he recognized all the faces in the street, even when the *souk* was busy with market stalls and hawkers. But in New York he could be on personal terms with a million people, and there would still be seven million strangers around him. His teeth chattered, and his eyes teared in the wind.

Outside his hotel, he reached into his pocket for the conference schedule and read from the first page: *5:30 p.m. Welcome tea and coffee for conference delegates and UN staff, Room 3201, Secretariat Building.* He was too nervous to be alone in his room. He folded the pages neatly, put them in his pocket, lifted his shoulders against the cold, and went east, toward the UN tower.

Chapter 7

The Saudi delegates in their long, white *jalabiyyas* would have been happier with whisky, but the consideration of the UN for their country's Islamic proscriptions restricted them to coffee. They floated past Omar Yussef, their pure white robes falling around lumpy paunches, their cheeks seeming dark and unshaven despite the reek of expensive cologne that followed them through the overheated air. *Like angels gone to seed*, Omar Yussef thought. He surveyed the bright African costumes and the somber gray suits mingling in the shabby reception room. *Perhaps this was a mistake. I don't know if I can put on a sociable face and chatter with these people.*

A man with a blond beard came smiling across the thin institutional carpet. He rubbed Omar Yussef's fingers with both hands. "Abu Ramiz, you're freezing," he said. "As your boss, I'm responsible for your health while we're in New York. Don't you have a proper winter coat?"

"I left it at the hotel, Magnus." Omar Yussef played with the zipper of his windbreaker. After his disconcerting day, he was unsure of his ability to get a lie past even this credulous Swede.

"Let's find something to warm you up." Magnus Wallander

led him to a counter where a smiling West African woman in a colorful wrap poured him a cup of lemon tea. "To your double health," Wallander said.

Omar Yussef sensed the raggedness of his smile. "Your Arabic is much better in New York than back in the office in Jerusalem, Magnus."

"At least here no one suspects me of being a spy just because I speak Arabic." Wallander's skin became rosy beneath his trim, fair beard. He sipped his soda water. "Your president will address the conference the day before you do, Abu Ramiz. But frankly I'm looking forward much more to your talk. There're delegates here from all over the Arab world, and I don't believe they ever hear the real story of Palestine."

"You think they're ready for reality?" Omar Yussef said.

Wallander reached into his pocket and handed Omar Yussef a laminated UN identity card. "Here's your pass for the week. You didn't send me a photo, so I had to use the one from your personnel file. The card gives you access to all the delegate areas of the UN buildings."

Omar Yussef regarded the photo with regret. It showed him more than a decade younger, his hair only receding a little and his mustache its original black. He detected sadness and shame in the tired eyes—the weary guilt of the habitual drinker.

"The picture's a bit old, but it still looks like you," Wallander said.

Omar Yussef slipped it into his pocket. "I may have some other commitments this week, Magnus."

"You mean your son?"

Omar Yussef coughed.

"How's Ala?" Magnus asked.

Omar Yussef sipped some tea to settle his throat. "Busy. He's very busy." He looked around the room for a man in a black coat. *Could he follow me here?*

Magnus reached out to snare the elbow of a man in his mid-thirties. "Laith, come here," he said. The man's black hair waved under apple pomade. His chubby face bore a three-part beard—the thick mustache dropped over a triangle forking like a black tongue beneath his bottom lip, and a full growth jutted from his chin like a brush. Magnus introduced him as the head of the Lebanese delegation to the conference.

"Abu Ramiz is from Bethlehem," the Swede said.

"Bethlehem?" The Lebanese smiled. "One of my delegation was born there."

"What's his name? Perhaps I know him," Omar Yussef said.

Before the man could reply, a tall delegate, whose collarless shirt buttoned to the top suggested that he was from Iran, hooked his hand into the crook of the Lebanese's arm and took him away with a quick smile of apology.

The Iranian's diplomatic leer depressed Omar Yussef. It seemed as meaningless as the statements he felt sure he'd hear at the conference. Every delegate would have to declare how much he loved the Palestinian people and supported their right to freedom. They'd call on Israel to do whatever they knew the Israelis weren't prepared to do, and they'd congratulate themselves for protecting ordinary Palestinians whose lives would, in fact, remain untouched by their deliberations.

"*Ustaz* Abu Ramiz, what a pleasure to see you here."

Omar Yussef shifted his spectacles and turned them upon Haitham Abdel Hadi. He wore a limp gray suit, a cheap cream shirt, and a brown polyester tie. When Omar Yussef grasped Abdel Hadi's languid handshake, a spark crackled in his palm from the static electricity surrounding the man like a pricklish force field.

"And Mister Magnus, how happy I am that you brought Abu Ramiz all this way," Abdel Hadi said, with a nasty grin. "I'm very contented that the conference will provide a showcase for his talents."

"Of course you must have met him on one of your school inspections," Magnus said.

Omar Yussef looked sourly at the dandruff on Abdel Hadi's lapels. "This gentleman and I have often had cause to discuss the future of our schools together," he said to Wallander.

Since Abdel Hadi had forced Omar Yussef out of his job at the Frères School for refusing to teach government propaganda, the schools inspector had risen in the Education Ministry in Ramallah. Even though Omar Yussef had been consigned to a school for the poorest of refugees, Abdel Hadi still seemed to want to punish him for his independent thought.

He bowed toward Omar Yussef. "I trust that you will recognize the importance of this conference for the Palestinian people, *ustaz*," he said.

"Is it so very important? I'm worried it'll be just talk."

"Then why did you come? For a free flight? So you can visit your little son in Brooklyn?"

Omar Yussef sensed his face coloring. His anger confused

him. He was unsure if he had been provoked by Abdel Hadi, or if it was just that his bewildering day had left him eager for a fight. He switched from English to Arabic, lowered his voice, and felt the bile burn off the end of his tongue. "Listen to me, Honored Deputy Director-General Abdel Hadi. I've had a difficult arrival in New York already. Don't try to embarrass me in front of this foreigner."

Abdel Hadi grinned coldly at Wallander. "Excuse me," he said to him in English. Then, in Arabic, he spoke with a deceptive smoothness to Omar Yussef: "This week you'll appear on the biggest stage you'll ever have. I'm going to make sure everyone's ready to see you fail. When you get back to Bethlehem, you'll pervert no more children with your dangerous ideas."

Omar Yussef's teacup rattled in its saucer. "I'm proud that the children in my class would see you for the hateful fool you are."

Abdel Hadi took a quick step toward Omar Yussef.

Magnus laid a hand on Abdel Hadi's shoulder and edged himself between the two men. Omar Yussef heard the static from Abdel Hadi's cheap suit crackle against the Swede's fingers.

Omar Yussef let Wallander guide him back to the counter, where he deposited his teacup. "I apologize, Magnus. It's been a hard day," he said.

"It's all right, Abu Ramiz. I've had a couple of meetings in the past with Doctor Abdel Hadi, and I must admit he's a disagreeable fellow. I expect you're also tired after your journey."

His angry interaction with Abdel Hadi had convinced Omar Yussef that he ought not to have come to the reception.

Ala was too much on his mind. "Perhaps I should rest. Good evening, Magnus."

In his hotel room, Omar Yussef double-locked the door and dropped heavily onto the edge of his bed. Dry, warm air rumbled out of the heating duct, and sweat stood on his scalp. The image of Nizar's headless corpse returned to him, and he remembered the boy's family. He took out his diary and turned to the neat page of phone numbers at the back. Reaching for the telephone, he read the dialing instructions encased in a plastic stand beside the phone and tried to obtain an outside line. His call went through to room service, which only reminded him that he didn't want dinner. He read the instructions once more and this time heard a dial tone. While the phone rang at the other end of the line, he checked his watch and calculated that it would be 2 A.M. in Bethlehem.

A sleepy, irritable voice answered.

"Greetings, Abu Khaled," Omar Yussef said. "I'm sorry to call you so late. This is Abu Ramiz. I'm calling from New York."

The voice brightened. "Double greetings, Abu Ramiz. Don't worry about the time. It's always a blessing to hear from you. How's your health, my dear sir? How's the health of your family?"

"May Allah be thanked, everyone's well."

"We must thank Allah. May Allah bless you, my dear one."

Omar Yussef coughed lightly. "But, Abu Khaled, I have bad news for you."

The man on the line seemed once more to grow sleepy. He grunted a low, wary syllable of acknowledgement.

"I went to visit my son today at the apartment where he lives with your nephew Nizar." Omar Yussef's mouth was dry. "I'm sorry to say that I found your nephew dead, may Allah be merciful upon him."

"There is no god but Allah, and Muhammad is his messenger," Abu Khaled whispered.

"The New York police are investigating."

"What is there to investigate? Do you mean it was a murder?"

"It would appear to be—suspicious."

"Did they arrest anyone?"

Omar Yussef felt his pulse shooting faster as he thought of his son in a cell in Brooklyn. "They have no suspects yet." His untruth came out strangled and stumbling.

"How was he killed?"

The schoolteacher was silent. *I should have waited to make this call until my own shock had abated,* he thought. He took a breath. "I can't say exactly."

Abu Khaled sighed and the exhalation turned into Nizar's name. "Death can play terrible games with a family, dear Abu Ramiz."

Omar Yussef leaned toward the minibar and took out a bottle of water. He opened it and wet his mouth, but his throat still felt tight and raw.

"My poor nephew," Abu Khaled murmured. "When he was only a little boy, five years of age, his dear father was assassinated. Right there in New York."

"Yes, yes," Omar Yussef commiserated. "I join you in your sad mood." Nizar's father had been notable for his writings, political fables and heroic resistance tales, which had appeared in magazines across the Arab world. Like most Palestinian authors, he had also held ideological posts in one of the PLO factions. Omar Yussef recalled a rumor in Bethlehem that the man had been killed by the Mossad to silence someone whose words were a powerful weapon against Israel.

"It's as though he were born to die this way. My dear nephew Nizar, it's so tragic."

As Abu Khaled sobbed and mumbled a prayer, memories of the life that had been lost came to Omar Yussef: Nizar walking on his hands along the high parapet of a ruined Crusader castle in the Galilee. Weeping with laughter at the farting cushion he hid on Omar Yussef's chair in class and, when he was alone with his teacher, crying because he wished for a father above all other things. The kitten he gave to Omar Yussef's favorite granddaughter Nadia when she was only a few years old, and how he had shown her the way to feed it milk from a doll's bottle. His energetic grin at the door of Omar Yussef's home, a taxi idling in Dehaisha Street behind him, as he waited for Ala to bring his bag, leaving for America. Had all the good times been mere delusions? Had Nizar's life truly been as tragic as his uncle claimed?

"When did you speak to him last, Abu Khaled?" Omar Yussef asked.

"About a week ago. He was very happy. O my grief. He said soon he would tell me good news."

Omar Yussef thought of the love letter. "What kind of good news?"

"He was very secretive about it. I hoped perhaps he would be coming home to be with us again here in Bethlehem. Perhaps he had found a wife. He mentioned a girl, but only very briefly."

"Dear Abu Khaled, I will give your phone number to the police so that they can contact you—about the body, I mean. Will you want it returned to Bethlehem?"

"The body? I don't know—I'll have to think. . . . Thank you for alerting me to this sad news, Abu Ramiz."

"May his lost years be added to your life," Omar Yussef said.

"May you receive blessings from Allah."

Omar Yussef hung up. He put his small suitcase on the bed and opened it. His pale blue pajamas were folded neatly on top of his other clothes. He took them out and placed them on the quilt. The scent of his wife's lavender perfume rose from the case, and he closed his eyes for a moment. He laid his hand on a box six inches long that Maryam had given him. It was a gift for Ala, an expensive pen, a Mont Blanc like the one he himself carried. He had told Maryam it was a ridiculous gift for a computer programmer, but she had wanted to give her boy something special. He slipped the box into the pocket of his jacket—he would hand it to his son when next he saw him. *What are you feeling now, my little Ala?* he thought. He sat beside his suitcase on the bed and put his face in his hands. He wept hard until he fell asleep in his clothes.

Chapter 8

A sharp thumping like the fire of a heavy machine gun brought Omar Yussef awake with his heart racing. His glasses were cutting into the bridge of his nose. He righted them and looked around, blinking. His panic persisted a few seconds until he realized he was lying across the bed in his hotel room, his arm draped over his open suitcase, pulling it close as though the scent of lavender within could substitute for the comforting presence of his wife.

He pushed himself upright and rolled his neck with a groan. On the nightstand, the clock showed almost 7 A.M. The hammering started again. He heard a cough in the corridor and realized that someone was out there knocking. He tucked his shirt into his pants and opened the door.

"Do the windows in your room open?" Khamis Zeydan shoved past Omar Yussef.

The schoolteacher blinked at his old friend, the Bethlehem police chief. He felt dull and slow. "What're you doing here?"

Khamis Zeydan reached behind the curtains, feeling for a catch on the window frame. "I told you half a dozen times I was coming. There's no point explaining anything to you," he said. "You only pay attention to Ottoman history and medieval Andalusian poetry. Our president's visit? You remember? His speech at the UN and consultations with the Americans? I'm advising him on security issues."

Omar Yussef shut the door and took a swig from the half-empty bottle of water on the bed. "I'm a little sleepy."

"What're you talking about? You're already dressed." The window slid back, and a strong gust of chilly air cut through the heavy warmth of the room. The cunning lines around Khamis Zeydan's blue eyes deepened, and the ends of his nicotine-stained white mustache rose. "May Allah be praised. My windows won't unlock. I've already set off the smoke alarm in my room twice this morning." He took out a Rothmans and lit up with relish.

Omar Yussef looked around for an ashtray to give to his friend.

Khamis Zeydan shook his head. "They don't allow it here, Abu Ramiz. In America, you have the right to carry a gun wherever you want, but you're banned from flourishing something as lethal as a cigarette."

Omar Yussef shivered. "Does the window have to be open quite so wide? It's February, and this city is almost arctic. When did you arrive?"

"We landed in the middle of the night." Khamis Zeydan shoved the window until it was open only a few inches and brushed some ash from the lapel of his navy-blue trench coat with annoyance. "Son of a whore," he muttered.

"Why aren't you with the president now?"

"He has meetings in his suite all morning and a lunch with

some Arab diplomats. I told him that if I had to listen to all the shit they'll talk, I might whack one of them. He sent me away to be a tourist." Khamis Zeydan rattled phlegm in his throat, opened the window wider, and expectorated out of it. He watched the wind whip his spit along the street toward the turquoise glass of the UN building. "By Allah, we're high up here, aren't we?"

Omar Yussef was comforted by the arrival of his old friend. He went to the window and looked down. His head spun a little as he watched the yellow taxis threading past the double-parked black limos twenty floors down. He wondered if one of the tiny figures below was waiting for him, tracking him. He shivered. "I'm happy to see you, Abu Adel," he said.

The habitual boldness of Khamis Zeydan's voice receded as he reached for Omar Yussef's hand. "Something's wrong, my dear Abu Ramiz."

The schoolteacher rested his forehead against the cold glass. "I found a dead man yesterday," he murmured.

"Allah is most great," Khamis Zeydan said. He slapped his knuckles into the gloved prosthesis he had worn since a grenade took off his left hand in the Lebanese civil war. "This is a violent city. Even so, what're the odds that you should find yourself a bystander?"

"Not just a random body. It was Nizar Jado, one of Ala's roommates. The police took Ala."

"Took him? Why? Surely he's not a suspect?"

"He refused to give an alibi. He may be in danger. He hinted that he knows about something that went on between

Nizar and their other roommate, Rashid. I can't believe Rashid is the killer; but if he were, he might try to get at Ala—to keep him from talking."

"Nizar, eh?" Khamis Zeydan flicked his cigarette out of the window, and the wind carried it away in a brief flurry of orange sparks. He shut the window and shivered. "Where are they holding Ala?"

"At the police station, I think. I can check with the detective." Omar Yussef took Hamza's business card from his pocket. He sat by the phone a moment, until he remembered how to obtain an outside line, then dialed.

Immediately, Hamza picked up: "Abayat."

"Greetings, Sergeant, this is Abu Ramiz speaking, the father of Ala Sirhan."

"Morning of joy, *ustaz*."

"Morning of light, my dear sir."

"Did you pass a good night?"

"Fine, fine, may Allah be thanked."

"May merciful Allah bless you."

"Sergeant, I would like to talk to my son."

"If Allah wills it, *ustaz*."

"Yes, if Allah wills it. You told me it would be possible today."

"If Allah wills it."

Omar Yussef wasn't sure if he had heard irritation or merely fatigue in the detective's voice. "Where is he?"

"He's at the Brooklyn Detention Complex."

"He's not at the police station?"

"It's easier for us to keep them at the Detention Complex

and bring them to the station for questioning when we need them."

Them. The criminals, Omar Yussef thought. *The suspects, the guilty, the people who cut off heads. But my son?* "Where is this Detention Complex?"

"Atlantic Avenue."

"That's in Little Palestine?"

"It's not far away. You can visit your son for up to one hour, provided the lieutenant okays it."

Omar Yussef spoke quietly. "Hamza, my son."

"Yes, uncle." The detective responded to the emotion in Omar Yussef's voice.

"Has my boy been charged?"

"No. He was questioned through the night by myself and Lieutenant Raghavan." Hamza sighed. "You understand that we need to work very intensively on a murder case. If we don't have a suspect within forty-eight hours, it's likely we might never have one."

"Have you been up all night?"

"This is the city that never sleeps, *ustaz.*" The detective laughed wearily. "I can't follow the short and unpredictable office hours of the Middle East here."

"If you come to a village where they worship a calf, gather grass and feed it."

"As they say back home." Hamza spoke quietly in English to someone in the room with him. Omar Yussef heard the yipping voice of the female lieutenant in the background, then Hamza came back on the line. "Lieutenant Raghavan agrees that you can talk to your son, *ustaz.* She'll contact the

Detention Complex. They'll be expecting you. And, *ustaz*, please try to talk some sense into him. He isn't helping anybody by clamming up."

"Thank you, Hamza." Omar Yussef hung up the phone.

Khamis Zeydan had gone through another Rothmans while his friend talked. He looked at Omar Yussef. "Something else on your mind?"

"I think I was followed. On the subway yesterday, coming back from Little Palestine." He stared into the dark glass of the building across the street. Though it was early, he saw the outlines of office workers at their computers. "I'm nervous about returning to Brooklyn."

Khamis Zeydan exhaled smoke from his nostrils. "I always knew we'd end up in jail together one day. I don't fancy the observation deck on the Empire State Building in this cold weather, anyway. Let's go to Brooklyn."

As they walked along the corridor, the smoke detector whined out its electronic siren in Omar Yussef's room.

Chapter 9

A pockmarked Latino with a hoarse voice and a thick accent brayed over the chatter and rumble of the D train. "When the kingdom comes, you're going to be there," he bellowed, his head back like a market tradesman to project through the crowded car. "He'll tell the world, and you're going to teach what He says. Only Jesus Christ can save all of you."

Khamis Zeydan fingered his pack of Rothmans. "I ought to remind him that only the believers in Allah will be saved," he mumbled.

"Allah is most great, Honored Sheikh." Omar Yussef poked his friend's chest. "Jesus is a prophet named in the Koran. Maybe this guy is a Muslim after all. Anyway, of those believers who will be saved, how many will be former PLO hit men with a fondness for Scotch whisky and cursing? I expect the answer is none."

"You may be right. Ah, then, fuck the believers."

"If it is the will of Allah." Omar Yussef smiled.

"I entrust myself to the protection of Allah." Khamis Zeydan rubbed his palms together as though he were washing his hands. "But if Paradise is a no-smoking zone like America, I want to go to Hell."

"For a Palestinian, that's the easiest of wishes to grant. One doesn't even have to leave home to get there."

They approached the Grand Street station as the Latino finished his message: "All the people who will be saved will be saved by Jesus Christ. All of you are chosen to be saved. Thank you for listening, and have a beautiful day."

"May Allah grant you grace," Omar Yussef whispered as the preacher left the car.

The train rumbled at low speed onto the strangely terrifying superstructure of the Manhattan Bridge. Downriver, beyond the massive girders and the mesh of electric lines, the Brooklyn Bridge arched over the water. Its famous towers sprayed thick cables along its span. Omar Yussef felt as though he were flying out of control through the air, high above the river and the tangle of highway along the shoreline. An old Vietnamese man screamed into his cell phone over the noise of the train. The wheels rang like the slow beating of a giant steel kettledrum until the train slipped back under the earth, jumped to a different track, and picked up speed. "This is an unnatural way of traveling," Omar Yussef whispered.

"There's a daily caravan between Manhattan and Brooklyn, if you prefer." Khamis Zeydan leered. "Next time we'll rent a camel and join them."

Omar Yussef shook his head and wondered if he ought to buy some nicotine gum for his irritable friend. "Maybe you shouldn't have left your work today. I'd prefer the president had to deal with your rotten temper, rather than me."

"My brother, I have a bad feeling about his visit. Some danger that I can't predict."

"Surely there's plenty of security at the UN?"

"America used to be the last place you'd expect any kind of attack." Khamis Zeydan rubbed the knuckle of his prosthetic hand against the sharp edge of his front teeth. "Not anymore."

"May it be displeasing to Allah."

"It makes me nervous to be stuck on a subway train when someone might be planning a strike against my boss right now."

Omar Yussef, too, wished to be elsewhere. He wondered what lies Abdel Hadi would be telling the other delegates at the UN conference about him in his absence. He needed to sort out Ala's problems and return to the UN before any plots could play out against him. He had given little thought to the speech he was to make, but now it seemed he had almost no time to prepare. His nervousness made him bitter. "May Allah curse this train," he said. "I feel trapped like a bound man in a pit of scorpions."

They left the subway at Atlantic Avenue and emerged at a big intersection that received traffic from five directions. Omar Yussef covered his ears with his hands as the lights changed and a troop of shiny SUVs bellowed past.

Khamis Zeydan lit a cigarette and lifted his head to the deepening gray in the sky. "Rain's coming," he said. He pulled a tweed cap from the pocket of his trench coat and covered his short white hair. "You're not exactly dressed for this weather, are you?"

Omar Yussef approached an elderly Arab who was resting on his cane by the traffic light, his red-and-white-checkered *keffiya* wrapped under his chin. "Peace be upon you," he said.

"And upon you, peace," the man responded.

"The Detention Complex, which way is it?"

The old Arab looked Omar Yussef up and down. *He wonders who I'm visiting at the jail*, Omar Yussef thought. *He's suspicious of my criminal connections.*

"It's a long walk," the Arab said, pointing with his cane. "That direction. Six blocks."

"Thank you."

"But they're long blocks. Atlantic Avenue is a long street."

It's not my criminal ties that make him look at me so dubiously. It's my frailty. "We'll be fine, sir."

The old man laughed, coughed, and spat. "You don't live in New York, do you? You thought that just because you were going to an address on Atlantic Avenue, you ought to go to the station with the same name. You don't look like peasants to me, but sometimes you can't tell the real hicks by sight. You should've taken a different subway line altogether and you'd have come up much closer to the jail. Anyway, you ought to take a bus now."

Omar Yussef resented the old man for pointing out his mistake. "I think we'll walk."

The man gave Omar Yussef a doubtful look. "If you don't get tired from the long walk, you're certainly going to freeze. You ought to have a hat. This isn't the Naqab desert, you know."

"Didn't I tell you?" Khamis Zeydan said, patting the warm cap on his own head.

"I'll buy a hat then," Omar Yussef said, impatiently. "Over there."

Across Fourth Avenue, they came to a stall hung with *keffiyas*, baseball caps, and woolen hats. The vendor stood beside it, leaning against the wall of a red-brick Gothic building that housed a mosque, his hands so deep in the pockets of his thick quilted coat that his elbows were locked.

"Take this one," Khamis Zeydan said, pointing at a woolen cap emblazoned with a white skull and crossbones. "That's your style. It ought to appeal to your interest in history."

Omar Yussef felt his cheeks reddening with irritation, but his scalp was numb with cold. Some of the hats bore only a few colored letters, so he reached out for the first one that came to hand and gave the vendor three dollars. When he pulled the hat over his head, the lancing pain of the freezing wind on his baldness left him, and he sighed with relief.

Khamis Zeydan read the letters on the hat. "*NYPD*? The design's not quite up to your usual standard of elegance, but it might get us into the Detention Complex a little quicker."

Beyond the mosque, they passed a row of Arab mini-markets stocked with buckets of sumac and cardamom, the price of *halal* meat advertised in the windows. Outside a store selling greeting cards and bumper stickers, Khamis Zeydan stopped to read aloud: "*Hatred is not a family value—Koran 49:13*. The Koran says *that*?"

"In that verse, Allah says he 'made you into nations and tribes, so that you might get to know each other,'" Omar Yussef said.

"So this is the dumb American version?"

"What do you want from them? It's only a bumper sticker." Omar Yussef tried to pick up their pace. "Did you ever meet Nizar, may Allah have mercy upon him?"

Khamis Zeydan shook his head. "Only briefly. He was out walking with Ala near the Nativity Church. They were with those other two boys who were always close to them."

"The other members of The Assassins."

The police chief grimaced. "I don't know why you encouraged them with that name."

"It was just a historical interest, a little bit of fun."

"I don't see that there's so much fun to be found in a bunch of medieval drug addicts."

"History was never your strong subject when we were together at university, Abu Adel."

"Screw your sister, schoolteacher. I majored in women and whisky."

"With a minor in cursing. The Assassins weren't drug addicts. Their leaders used the promise of Paradise to train fanatical killers."

"So not drug addicts, but insane murderers."

"Their leaders weren't insane. They were ruthless and manipulative. They used the men they sent on suicidal missions to eliminate political enemies and to protect their particular strain of Islam."

Khamis Zeydan picked at his back teeth. "Even so, a bunch of kids named 'The Assassins' is the kind of thing people take seriously in the Middle East. If the Israelis had found out there was a group with that name in Bethlehem, they'd probably have assassinated them."

Omar Yussef took a sharp breath. *Could that be what happened to Nizar?* he wondered. *People believed it was the Mossad that killed Nizar's father, after all.*

"They were very important to me, all those boys," he muttered.

"I don't know why you get so close to your pupils. Emotional involvement only causes trouble."

"There you see the difference between a teacher and a professional killer."

Khamis Zeydan clicked his tongue.

Omar Yussef hurried across Third Avenue, stepping aside for a pair of stout Arab women, their *mendils* tight beneath their plump chins. "Maybe you knew Nizar's father. He was a PLO guy back when you were running around on missions for the Old Man."

Khamis Zeydan cupped his hands to light another cigarette. "Yeah, I knew Fayez."

"What was he like?"

"*Arrogance is a weed that mostly grows on a dunghill*, as they say. The PLO was a real dunghill, and that's how all those assholes were—arrogant as cockerels, every one of them." The police chief hunched his shoulders against the wind. "Fayez ran off to study in Baghdad and joined the PLO there. He prospered on the dunghill. He had his own little commando group within the PLO for a while and used to write heroic essays about their exploits against the Israelis."

"I've read some of his political essays. I seem to remember they were mainly critiques of the Arab nations."

Khamis Zeydan sneered. "When he merged his fighting unit with the main PLO forces, the Old Man rewarded him by making him a special ambassador."

"What did that involve?"

They crossed another side street. "We're being followed," Khamis Zeydan said.

Omar Yussef spun around in surprise, but his friend grabbed his arm and pulled him along.

"A man in a black coat."

"Where?" Omar Yussef turned his head.

"Stop it. If he knows we've seen him, it might force his hand."

"Force his—You mean, he might try to—"

"Steal your new hat." Khamis Zeydan took Omar Yussef's arm more casually, linking their elbows so that he could watch over his shoulder.

"Can you see him?" Omar Yussef whispered.

"His face is covered by a scarf." Khamis Zeydan's eyes glittered with intensity.

"It's him, isn't it? The one I saw at the apartment, and I'm sure he followed me back to the hotel, too."

"Well, he's gone now. He went down the side street."

"Should we follow him?"

Khamis Zeydan shook his head. "He might be armed."

"We have to get away."

"I don't expect he'll follow us into the prison. Keep walking."

The police chief seemed to enjoy exercising his old skills from his time as an undercover operative. He became expansive. "You asked about the special ambassador? It sounds like a bullshit title, but the Old Man actually sent Fayez on secret diplomatic missions. He stationed him here in New York for a while."

Omar Yussef remembered the lieutenant holding the plastic evidence bag with the dead boy's passport. "But Nizar wasn't born in exile."

"Fayez sent his wife to his parents in Bethlehem whenever she was pregnant, so that the kids would be real Palestinians, as he saw it, born on the land. That's why she was able to get permits from the Israelis to live there with them, after the—when Fayez died."

Khamis Zeydan pulled Omar Yussef to a halt in front of the display window of a lingerie store.

"What're you doing?"

A skinny mannequin in high heels and thigh-high stockings pushed her lacy ass toward the two men. Khamis Zeydan squinted into the glass. "I'm checking to see if there's anyone across the street," he said.

Omar Yussef looked at the figures reflected in the window. A line of people waited at a bus stop with an appearance of innocent boredom.

"How did Fayez die?" he asked.

"Assassinated."

"He really was murdered?"

"You sound shocked. Come on, you're a history teacher. Without assassination, history would be a dull subject. Murder is your business."

A group of teenaged boys stopped to giggle before the store window.

"Was it the Mossad?" Omar Yussef glanced over his shoulder, but Khamis Zeydan grabbed him and led him along the sidewalk. "Did they kill Fayez?"

76

Khamis Zeydan threw his cigarette into the gutter and retched a wet cough from the bottom of his lungs.

"That's what people said in Bethlehem. Is it true?"

"Sure, the Mossad," Khamis Zeydan snorted.

The bitterness in his friend's voice made Omar Yussef suspicious. "Tell me?"

"While he was in New York, Fayez made contact with a couple of prominent Jews. They introduced him to some left-wing Israeli politicians. Together they came up with a peace plan."

"I don't understand. The Mossad killed him to cut off those peace talks?"

Khamis Zeydan made his eyes wide and sarcastic. "Yes, and they also blew up the Twin Towers so that the U.S. would invade Iraq. But they called all the Jews who worked in the buildings first and told them to stay home that day. Oh, and they also exported special chewing gum to Egypt to make all the single men unbearably horny and, thus, destroy Arab morality. Those Israelis have put together quite an amazing organization, you know."

"So who killed him, if it wasn't the Mossad?" Omar Yussef shivered and pulled up the collar of his windbreaker.

"We Arabs managed to knock off quite a few of our own during that time." Khamis Zeydan watched a massive kebab turning on a spit in the window of a restaurant, dribbling fat. "You didn't have to step much out of line to be dead meat."

"You yourself—" Omar Yussef halted when Khamis Zeydan turned his glare upon him.

"I myself?"

"Carried out a few such missions. Why are you looking at me like that? Well, you did, didn't you?"

The police chief stared along the avenue with a malevolent concentration. "It's going to rain, and it's already so fucking cold," he said.

"Did Fayez have the approval of the Old Man for his peace talks?"

"The Old Man never approved anything until it was done. That way he could take credit for it if it succeeded and be absolved of blame for any failure."

"Did the Old Man rub out Nizar's father?"

"Don't you have enough to worry about, with your son in jail?"

"All this could be important to my son's case." Omar Yussef spoke quickly. "If Nizar's father was killed by the Old Man or by another PLO faction or, I don't know, by the government of some Arab country, maybe the same people wanted Nizar dead. Maybe it was they who cut off his head."

"Maybe this time it *was* the Mossad."

Omar Yussef cursed and marched ahead. His thighs ached with fatigue. He damned the Arab man at the subway station for having recognized that he was too weak to make this walk in comfort. He paused for breath, leaning against a battered yellow newspaper-vending box, then stepped out to cross the street.

He heard the splashing first, then the heavy, threatening groan of a big engine accelerating. A blue Jeep with tinted windows came through the intersection fast, rushing over the puddles. Instinctively Omar Yussef put one foot back on the curb.

The Jeep veered toward him. Khamis Zeydan grabbed him, throwing him backward. He fell in the snow piled around a lamppost. His head struck the ground with an impact like the kick of a donkey's hoof.

The Jeep jumped onto the curb, its bumper knocking the newspaper box across the sidewalk. A pile of tabloids spilled into the wind. The Jeep disappeared quickly down the side street. A copy of the *Daily News* blew into Omar Yussef's face. He pushed it away. Khamis Zeydan helped him to his feet.

"By Allah, that must've been the bastard who was tailing us," Khamis Zeydan said.

"Did you see him?"

"The windows were too dark."

A middle-aged black woman in a camel-hair coat came across the side street. "You're lucky to be alive," she said to Omar Yussef.

"Think again, dear lady," Khamis Zeydan said. "My friend's a Palestinian."

When the police chief laughed, the woman gave him an affronted stare and walked on.

"If you couldn't see him, how do you know that was the man who was following us?" Omar Yussef felt the back of his head where it had hit the snowy ground. It was wet and tender, but the skin hadn't broken.

"He was out of sight just long enough to get into his vehicle and line us up."

"Why does he want to kill me?"

"As far as he knows, you might've seen his face at Nizar's apartment."

Omar Yussef's jaw trembled. Anyone in the crowd on the sidewalk might be tracking him. All the cars thundering through the traffic lights were potential instruments of his death. He covered his face with his hands and felt his pulse jumping behind his eyes.

"My brother," Khamis Zeydan said quietly, "let's go to your son."

The Arab food stores and cafés dwindled as Atlantic Avenue rose into a gentle slope. The Islamic bookstores with pamphlets on Muslim marriage and gold-inlaid copies of the Koran in their windows were replaced by the unsightly offices of bail bondsmen, encased behind bars like their clients. The bondsmen hung gaudy signs above their doors painted with glib slogans, as though temporary release from jail were a purchase no more worthy of deep consideration than that of a slice of pizza.

Across the street, a nine-story tower rose in pink stone. The windows were composites of thick glass bricks molded around a mesh of iron bars that caged the entire building. The branches of the trees along the sidewalk had been cut back to their gray trunks, so that they looked like men with their hands cuffed behind them. The sign above the blacked-out glass in the entrance read: *Brooklyn Detention Complex*.

Omar Yussef lifted his head, following the bars up through the glass bricks to the top of the jail. His spectacles spotted with water. The rain had started.

Chapter 10

A guard patted Omar Yussef down and ushered him through a chipped metal door painted the soapy blue of swimming-pool tiles. Behind him, the guard found Khamis Zeydan's cigarettes and took them away. The Bethlehem police chief cursed under his breath and rubbed the back of his prosthetic hand nervously.

"You don't like being in somebody else's jail for a change?" Omar Yussef said.

"My station house only has a few cells," Khamis Zeydan muttered. "It's not much of a jail. This place is the real thing. You can smell it."

Omar Yussef inhaled a rough undertone of body odor, clashing with the chemical scent of disinfectant. It bore the disconsolate heaviness of mass sanitation, as though the inmates were bugs or bacilli to be exterminated with industrial acids from a bucket.

A bulky guard awaited them beyond the metal door, his shoulders filling the corridor. Omar Yussef caught a trace of cheap cologne emanating from the guard's dark blue uniform. He seized upon it to block out the disinfectant, but it came with a hint of the dried sweat it was intended to disguise. He sniffed the French toilet water he always placed on the back of his hand to counter unpleasant odors.

The guard reached for a clipboard passed through the doorway by his colleague. He looked it over with the sleepy eyes of a man who has eaten heavily, and belched. "You're here to see Sirhan?"

"You're quite correct, my dear sir," Omar Yussef said, standing as straight as his little paunch allowed and speaking with a formality born of nervousness.

The guard's eyes flicked up from the clipboard, as though he thought Omar Yussef were mocking him. "Related to the guy who killed Bobby Kennedy?"

"I see you know your assassins," Omar Yussef said. "Sirhan Sirhan was from an entirely different clan. I'm sure that the actions of the senator's killer would be shocking to my son. He's never been a violent boy."

The guard rolled his tongue under his bottom lip and turned the clipboard toward Omar Yussef. "Sign here," he said, "both of you."

As Omar Yussef handed the clipboard to Khamis Zeydan, he noticed a pin on the guard's breast pocket. It bore the date of the infamous attack with the digits of the "eleven" thickened and topped by a radio mast so that they resembled the Twin Towers. The Stars and Stripes ran along the bottom of the design.

"My son would never have approved of that attack, either." Omar Yussef pointed at the pin.

The tall guard came close enough to Omar Yussef that his big, hard belly touched the schoolteacher's diaphragm. "I lost a brother in the Trade Center. He was a cop, and he was try-ing to save people from what you Arabs did to us."

Omar Yussef breathed slowly. "I'm sorry about your brother."

"You going to tell me the Nine-Eleven terrorists weren't 'really Muslims'? Like all those stories in the papers making excuses for the Arabs?"

"No, they were Muslims, and it's true that many Muslims approved of what they did." Omar Yussef looked up at the guard's double chin, pale, shiny, and smooth. "But I was not among their supporters, and neither was my son."

"Sure about that?"

"As sure as you are that your brother was a hero."

The double chin quivered, and the guard stepped back. With the clipboard, he gestured toward an open door down the corridor. "In there," he grunted.

Behind a Plexiglas screen, Ala leaned his elbows on a counter. Tiredness seemed to have spread from his red eyes through new lines in his face, sucking the color from his skin. He had the desperate drowsiness of an insomniac after another failed night of sleep, a long day of terrible fatigue ahead of him. He lifted the handset beside the screen, as Omar Yussef sat down.

"Morning of joy, Dad." His voice was cracked and dry. He smiled weakly at Khamis Zeydan. The police chief folded his arms and inclined his head.

"Morning of light, my son." Omar Yussef noticed that Ala wore the same dress shirt in which he had been arrested. He had half-expected to see the boy in an orange jumpsuit and thought perhaps it was a good sign that he hadn't been forced into the anonymity of a prison uniform. "How've you been?"

"I was at the precinct house for a long time with the Indian lieutenant and that meathead bastard, the Palestinian sergeant." Ala's eyes darted about urgently, as though he were being hunted. "Then they brought me here."

Omar Yussef was surprised at the force of his son's anger toward Hamza. "What's it like?" He lifted his chin. "In there?"

"I'm in a small cell with a lot of other men. Everyone tries to stay close to the bars, staring down the corridor, waiting for someone to come and release them. They look like the people on the street watching anxiously for a bus. Everybody is nervous and irritable and talkative. They all want to describe how they were arrested and keep telling the others they're sure someone will bail them out. Everything stinks and something in the air is making my asthma act up." Ala wheezed and scratched the stubble on his face almost vindictively. "And I'm itching all over. It's driving me crazy."

"My boy, you can end this now," Omar Yussef said. "Tell the police where you were when Nizar was killed."

"I can't do that, Dad."

The bruise on the back of Omar Yussef's head throbbed.

"Don't you think the police have been asking me that all night?" Ala continued. "That bastard Sergeant Abayat thinks I killed Nizar."

"Surely not."

"He's badgering me to confess. 'Tell us the real story; tell us how you did it; you went out to get rid of the murder weapon, and when you came back your father was there, so

84

where did you hide it?' America's full of Arabs like him. They want to show their American patriotism, so they make out that other Arabs are all bad guys. Why not hang the murder on me? I'm just a stinking Arab, after all."

"You're letting your animosity toward that man obscure what you ought to be focusing on. You need to reveal your alibi."

"I'm sorry to try your patience, Dad, but there's somebody I must protect."

"By Allah, you mean that you really know who committed this murder?"

Khamis Zeydan leaned forward and took the second handset. He lifted an eyebrow to indicate that Ala should continue.

"That isn't what I mean by protecting someone." Ala rocked his head from side to side. "I was with a woman when the killing happened. I'm worried about her reputation."

"Her good name is worth more than your freedom?"

"I've already told the meathead detective that I waive my right to a lawyer. I don't want to have to admit where I was, and there's no other way out of this for me." Ala sucked his upper lip.

"Without a lawyer, they'll pin this murder on you. They could put you away forever." Omar Yussef slammed his palms onto the counter before him. The guard stuck his head around the door with a warning look.

Ala's voice softened. "I love her. I'm ready to sacrifice for her." His face was beatific, but his lower lip twitched.

"She'll surely be prepared to let you tell your story. She'll corroborate your alibi."

"She's an Arab woman, Dad. She can't just say, 'Sure,

I was with him.'" Ala scratched at his curly black hair and groaned.

He's worried someone will kill her. To punish her for besmirching the honor of her family by meeting alone with an unmarried man, Omar Yussef thought.

"Tell me who she is, my son. I'll persuade her to let you speak. Then you can go free. I'll appeal to her love for you."

"She doesn't love me, Dad."

"Why not?"

Ala snorted a tired laugh. "Am I talking to my father or my excessively proud mother? I'm not irresistible to women, you know." The boy fretted at his lips with his front teeth. The whites of his eyes were shaded blue and green and shot through with red.

She doesn't love me. Omar Yussef remembered the pink sheet of writing paper in the bony hand of the police lieutenant, the love letter from the corpse's pocket with the graphic language. He recalled the pain in Ala's face when the Arab detective read the name "Rania" from that letter. It must have been the same girl, the one Ala was with when Nizar was murdered. But it had been Nizar she had wanted. Omar Yussef felt his son's desolate loneliness through the Plexiglas. "You and Nizar were rivals for a woman's love?"

Ala looked up sharply, his haunted, unhealthy eyes wide and defiant. Omar Yussef recognized something of the strength and desperation that must have seen the boy through the long police interrogation. "You think I killed Nizar because he beat me in love, Dad?"

"Of course not. But I want to know the truth. Tell me."

The boy leaned back in his cheap plastic chair, gazing around at the whitewashed walls and the posters advising prisoners' relatives of their visiting rights. "You remember Nizar and Rashid as bright young students, Dad, but they changed."

"Why?"

Ala gave a vague wave of his hand. "You know, the intifada."

"I know about *your* intifada."

"It wasn't much, was it? Going out with the guys to throw stones at the Israelis. The Assassins, as we used to call ourselves, all four of us." Ala turned to Khamis Zeydan. "We stoned an army jeep at the edge of the camp."

"I don't know why you did it," Omar Yussef muttered. "It just wasn't like you, or the other boys."

"Everyone did it."

"Other kids at least would've run away before the second army jeep came up behind them and arrested them."

Ala bit the nail of his thumb. "Somehow I think we wanted to be arrested. So we could feel part of the struggle like everyone else. Throwing stones? Well, as you say, it wasn't like us."

Arrested and held in a tent on a cold hillside near Ramallah, Omar Yussef thought. *The cells here in the Detention Complex must seem like a hotel room with a mint on the pillow compared to the Israeli camp.* "It was a terrible time, my son. But you said that it changed Nizar and Rashid. How?"

"In the Israeli jail, they became close to a sheikh from Hebron. The Israelis had picked him up for running an Islamic Jihad mosque."

"The boys joined Islamic Jihad?"

"I don't know that."

But it's what you think. "It made them radical?"

Ala shook his head. "It made them religious. It was something else that made them radical."

"What?"

"Ismail."

Ala's classmate, my old pupil, Omar Yussef thought. *The fourth Assassin.* "I don't understand."

"The Israelis offered Ismail a deal."

"I see where this is going." Khamis Zeydan clicked his tongue.

"They told Ismail that if he informed on the sheikh, they'd let the four of us go free," Ala said. "You remember what Ismail was like, Dad. It was easy to sway him. He loved The Assassins. He'd have done anything for us."

Omar Yussef remembered Ismail as a shy boy who'd always been on the periphery of the class and of the games in the schoolyard, until he had come into the circle of The Assassins. He recalled the habitual trace of fear and nervous supplication in Ismail's eyes, even when he was smiling; the way he trained his attention on Nizar and Rashid, the gregarious leaders of the gang, laughing at their jokes a beat too late and just a little too loudly.

"So Ismail did what the Israelis demanded?"

"In prison, he talked with the sheikh every day," Ala said. "We all thought he was becoming religious too. Then suddenly the sheikh was gone. The Israelis put him on trial and sent him away for life."

"Using Ismail's evidence?"

Ala's nod was reluctant, as though he were acceding to a

sentence of death against his friend. "That's why the Israelis released the four of us."

"I can't believe this."

"After our release, Ismail confessed to us. He was ashamed, but he thought we'd understand. I hugged him and told him that it wasn't his fault, that the interrogators had put him under impossible pressure. But Rashid and Nizar called him dirty names and refused ever to speak to him."

"What happened to Ismail?"

Ala puffed out his cheeks and lifted his eyebrows. "I lost track of him when I came to New York."

"Did Nizar and Rashid ever forgive him?"

"They never mentioned his name again. They were too busy praying five times a day." Ala's eyes drifted to the damp-stained ceiling, struggling against his fatigue to keep track of his story. "But after a while Nizar changed."

"How?"

"He started dressing more fashionably. You remember the nice boots he was wearing when he—when he was killed?"

Omar Yussef recalled the luscious black of the leather on the dead body and winced.

"He stayed out late every night," Ala said. "Rashid was often angry with him and accused him of betraying his religion for a good time."

"A good time? What was Nizar up to?"

"He told me once, with great relish, that he was having sex with ladies."

Khamis Zeydan grinned. "That's more fun than praying, may Allah be praised."

Omar Yussef scowled at his friend.

"Then suddenly Nizar's bad behavior stopped." Ala's face bore a look of strain as though he had experienced the twinge of a forgotten pain.

"There's only one thing that can stop a young man wanting to have sex with everyone in sight," Khamis Zeydan said. "The poor slob must've fallen in love."

"At the Arab social club in Bay Ridge, Nizar and I were on the same *dabka* team," Ala said. "Some of the younger kids liked to inject break-dancing and other strange American stuff into the traditional Palestinian dances, but Nizar said we should keep our *dabka* slow, just the way we did it back home. There was a girl who liked that attitude, because she's also relatively new to the U.S."

Omar Yussef imagined the hunched, twitching boy behind the Plexiglas standing straight in a circle of dancers, performing the skipping, kicking, stomping motions of the *dabka*, lifting his hand to twirl a kerchief above his head. He wondered what it must be like to dance a traditional step in exile. *I imagine it might move me to tears*, he thought. *Lucky I don't have the breath for it*. Ala and his friend Nizar had danced with the same girl, and Nizar had won her. "Rania?" Omar Yussef said.

Ala's energy seemed to drain away, and his gaze was as dead as a Ramadan afternoon. "I used to visit her father's café. It's right next to our apartment building. I became friendly with her father, and he invited me to dinner. It was the beginning of our courtship."

"So you had the father's approval?"

Ala brightened, but his smile died quickly. "Nizar also

started to go to the café. He knew that I was courting Rania. He told me he wasn't interested in her. He was just glad to drink mint tea, smoke a water pipe, and talk to her father about Middle Eastern politics and the Koran and Egyptian football. I didn't object, because it kept him from his wild ways. But then I saw how he and Rania looked at each other. I couldn't compete with him. He's handsome. He has that long hair. He's so charming."

"My son, I don't wish to seem unfeeling, but Nizar is gone. Things have changed. You have your alibi, and perhaps you can still be with Rania after she has mourned for Nizar. Don't lose hope. You must tell the police where you were and leave this jail so you can claim her."

"She'll never be mine. I saw how it was between her and Nizar. In comparison, she felt nothing for me." Ala scratched his scalp with both hands. "When Nizar was being murdered, I was with her. But only to tell her that she should go with him. I intended to inform her father too. He was looking forward to meeting you and settling all the details of our engagement. I couldn't bear to break it off, so I delayed until the last minute, right before you arrived. Then I went to their apartment above the café and I told her that there would be no arrangement between us."

"How did she react?"

Ala sucked in a breath and was silent.

"Did Nizar ask to marry Rania?"

"I'm sure he didn't. Rania's father would've told me. I can't put my finger on it, but I think the friendship between Rania's father and Nizar was not entirely simple."

"Could Rania's father have found out about the secret relationship and killed Nizar for the sake of family honor?"

Ala shook his head. "I never heard bad words between them. With our roommate Rashid, on the other hand, Nizar argued every day, even after he stopped his bad behavior with girls and alcohol."

"What were the fights about?"

"They always spoke in urgent whispers. When I tried to ask them what they were talking about, they told me to mind my own business." Ala stared distantly beyond his father's shoulder, as though he were chasing through the permutations that might lie behind the murder, tracking each sign to a point where the death would make sense. "There's also the veil."

The Veiled Man, Omar Yussef thought. *The betrayer who must be killed by the messiah.*

"Rashid was fascinated by all the Islamic mythology of the Assassins. He read and reread those stories that we first learned in your class, Dad. He might have believed Nizar had betrayed him somehow. If he killed him, he could've left the veil as a sign."

"Knowing that only you would understand it."

"Or you, Dad. He knew you were coming to visit."

Omar Yussef's jaw shook. *A sign for me to interpret,* he thought. *But why?* "Could Rashid really kill a man?"

Ala winced. "I think that was what he and Nizar used to fight about," he said.

"Killing?"

"I didn't hear enough to know any more than that for certain. But I believe they planned to kill someone."

Chapter 11

Khamis Zeydan glowered at the Arabic signs above the shopfronts and the thick-set women bustling along the street, their round faces framed by cream polyester *mendils*. The rain was turning to a gelatinous gray sleet, and he spat on the slick sidewalk. "Little Palestine," he muttered, shaking his head.

"That's the café." Omar Yussef pointed out the smoked-glass window and heavy brown drapes. In English and Arabic, the purple awning announced the Café al-Quds. In Arabic, it promised tea, coffee, fruit juices, pastries, and *nargileh* water pipes. "We have to make this girl Rania go to the police. We have to make her provide an alibi for my son."

"*Make* her do it? Who're you, the chief of secret police?" Khamis Zeydan grinned bitterly.

"All right, then we have to—persuade her." Omar Yussef heard the sinister edge to his words. He evaded Khamis Zeydan's smile with a guilty flicker of his eyes. "Let's get out of the cold."

The air in the empty café was stale with lingering traces of apple-scented *nargileh* smoke. The control panel of the stereo behind the bar pulsed lurid pink and turquoise with the driving *baladi* rhythm of a famous song. Omar Yussef recognized the voice of a Lebanese singer a few years older than himself.

What happened to us, my love? she sang. *The love of my country still wails: Take me, take me, take me home.*

The music was loud, as though the staff didn't expect customers and had turned up the volume to listen to the song while they worked in another room. Omar Yussef went behind the bar to a door that leaked a dim light into the café. He knocked against the cheap wooden frame.

The Lebanese star sang on: *The breeze blew at us from where the river divided.*

A young woman answered Omar Yussef's knock in Arabic. Wiping her hands on a dishcloth, she came out of the kitchen, wearing tight jeans, a black T-shirt, and a short purple smock that dropped loosely from her breasts to her hips. Her black *mendil* was drawn around her face and folded under the collar of the T-shirt.

"Greetings, *ustaz*," she said. Her voice was quiet and husky, as though it had been worn out.

I'm afraid, O dear, to grow old in exile. . . .

"Greetings, my daughter," Omar Yussef said. "I'm Abu Ramiz, the father of Ala Sirhan."

. . . and that my home would no longer recognize me.

She put her hand to her breastbone. "You're with your family and as if in your own home, *ustaz*."

Take me, take me, take me home.

"You're Rania?"

Her eyes were deep and big, haughty and critical behind long lashes, but the whites were a blurred pink, tired and recently tearful. They closed slowly to indicate that Omar Yussef had been correct. A lick of hair so black that it seemed polished had escaped her headscarf. It stroked softly against her pale throat. She smiled briefly with her wide, shapeless mouth.

Take me, take me, take me home.

"I need to speak to you about Ala. He refuses to tell the police that he was with you when Nizar was killed." Omar Yussef saw the big eyes wince at the name of the dead man. "The police may blame him for the killing unless he reveals your meeting. Won't you go to the police station and confirm his alibi?"

The girl raised her eyebrows. "Excuse me, *ustaz*, but I only have your word that you're Ala's father."

"Of course I'm his father. Try to imagine my face thirty years ago." Omar Yussef removed his spectacles. "With more hair and better eyesight. I think you'll see the resemblance."

"Imagine he'd never developed a taste for whisky and blown his health on bad living." Khamis Zeydan laughed, beating his hand on the bar to the four-four time of the song. "Come on, my daughter. We need to be serious here. If you don't go to the police, the police will come to you."

The girl pushed out her lips, affronted by the police chief's bluntness.

"We're asking you politely," Khamis Zeydan said. "But do you think we're going to let Ala go to jail just to save your blushes?"

"I can't help you," she said.

Khamis Zeydan looked at her hard. "You have no choice."

Omar Yussef saw a flicker of fear on her face. Then came

an angry twitch of her long lips, and Rania blew out an exasperated breath. "A moment, *ustaz*," she said to Omar Yussef, and she went back into the kitchen.

Khamis Zeydan picked a green olive from a bowl on the bar and ate it with a nod of approval. "Reckon this place is a front?"

"What?"

He dropped the olive pit tinkling into a ceramic ashtray. "I know it's still not yet noon, but they aren't exactly fighting off the customers, are they?"

"A front for what?"

The girl returned with an older, shaven-headed man who wore a blue apron.

Take me, take me, take me—

He pushed the OFF button on the stereo, switched on the lights above the bar, and wiped his thick hands on the apron. He looked with narrowed eyes at Omar Yussef and rubbed the fleshy grooves that ran from his wide nose to the corners of his mouth. His lips were purple and pursed and disapproving, like a sybaritic pharaoh. When he turned to take in Khamis Zeydan, Omar Yussef saw that short black hairs grew in the fat fold where his scalp met the back of his neck, out of reach of his razor.

"Greetings, my dear sirs," he said. "I'm Rania's father, Marwan Hammiya. Please sit while we prepare coffee for you." Marwan muttered to his daughter and invited his guests to the table nearest the bar.

On the wall above the table, an Ottoman sultan and his courtiers chased a stag through a clearing, and six tall Corinthian columns rose over the ruins of Jupiter's Temple at Baalbek. Omar Yussef leaned forward to admire the prints before he sat.

"Forgive me," Marwan said, running his thick, hairy fingers over the chips in the Formica, "but may I see your identification?"

Khamis Zeydan opened his mouth to protest, but Omar Yussef halted him with a hand on his knee. He took his passport from the inside pocket of his windbreaker and handed it to Marwan Hammiya. The café owner bowed his head as he returned it.

"I apologize, gentlemen. Please understand the suspicion. During the last few years, the FBI has sent many people into our neighborhood pretending to be someone else. They were very keen to prove all kinds of bad things about us Arabs."

"If the FBI had half an hour with my friend here—" Omar Yussef waved at Khamis Zeydan "—they'd have plenty of evidence of the wickedness of the Arabs."

Khamis Zeydan spat another olive pit into the ashtray. "Maybe you'd be warmer in an FBI hat," he said.

Omar Yussef removed his NYPD cap, put it on the table, and straightened his hair.

"May it be displeasing to Allah." Marwan smiled. "I had hoped to meet you in happier circumstances, *ustaz*."

Rania brought a tray of *ajweh* cookies, then returned to the bar. Her face was tight, but something trembled around her lips. She blew her nose, wiped her finger beneath her eyes, and set to making coffee. Omar Yussef nodded his approval as he bit through the cookie's buttery shortcake and tasted the date paste within. "Excellent," he said. "Not too sweet."

"Rania knows exactly how much rose water to add to the filling." Marwan pushed the tray toward Khamis Zeydan. "She learned the secret from her dear departed mother, may Allah have mercy upon her, before we left Lebanon."

"Your daughter runs the café with you?"

"She's a counselor at the Community Association across the street. But she helps me, too."

From the bar, Rania called: "With sugar, *ustaz*?"

"No sugar," Omar Yussef said.

"And you, *ya pasha*?" she asked Khamis Zeydan.

"Sugar, please," he replied. "How do you know I'm a *pasha*, a military man?"

Marwan intervened quickly: "Rania grew up in Lebanon. There one learns early to recognize a fighter, even when he wears his civilian clothes. It can be dangerous not to do so."

Khamis Zeydan watched the girl closely as she poured the coffee. He took a sachet of sugar from the pot on the table and read the label. "The Maison du Café, Khaldeh Highway, Lebanon." He snorted a laugh. "I was shot in the shoulder once on the Khaldeh Highway."

"Israelis?" Marwan said.

"Shiites. Near the airport."

"The bad old days of Beirut."

"Where are you from, Marwan?" Omar Yussef asked. He tried to make his question sound friendly, but something sharp in his voice took the smile off Marwan's sensuous lips.

"Baalbek, in the Bekaa Valley, *ustaz*."

"So you're Shiite?"

Marwan directed a thin, apologetic smile at Khamis Zeydan and stroked his shoulder, as if to salve the police chief's old wound. "I'm not religious. I'm modern. Here we sit, with my unmarried daughter standing right next to us. I don't worry about keeping her out of the sight of men. We're no longer in the old country, are we?"

Rania set the coffee cups on the table.

Omar Yussef detected the scent of lavender water when she bent close to him. "May Allah bless your hands," he said, touching the saucer of his cup.

"Blessings," she murmured.

"Marwan, how long have you been in New York?" Omar Yussef asked.

"Since the end of 1998. Sadly I brought only my Rania, who was then barely a teenager. Her dear mother rests in Baalbek, may Allah have mercy on her, and I have no other children."

"You've had the café since then?"

"Only a year or two."

"It's not very busy."

"It's early. Later in the day," Marwan hesitated, "we have many clients. They come to hear Arabic spoken and to enjoy the tastes of their homeland."

Rania watched her father from behind the bar, her broad mouth turned down at the ends, her shining eyes impatient.

"What did you do in Lebanon?" Khamis Zeydan said over the rim of his small coffee cup.

"A merchant. Trade, business, different things."

"Business got bad in 1998, did it?"

Marwan looked hard at Khamis Zeydan. Omar Yussef was surprised by his friend's sarcastic tone. Khamis Zeydan winked at him. *That year means something to him,* Omar Yussef thought. He needed to break the tension between the two men, to turn the conversation to Ala's alibi. "I've been to see my son at the jail," he said.

Marwan's eyes were stern when they moved to Omar Yussef. "The jail?"

"He refuses to give the police an alibi. He won't tell them where he was when Nizar was killed."

"A terrible thing. The whole neighborhood is sad." Marwan shook his head. "Why won't he give an alibi?"

Omar Yussef stared at Rania. She polished the bar, her eyes following the cloth over the surface of the wood with great concentration.

"Rania?" he said.

She turned her deep, black eyes to the mirror behind the bar.

"Ala knew about you and Nizar." Omar Yussef stood and went to the bar. "That's why he met you yesterday. To release you from your arrangement, to set you free to be with Nizar."

Marwan scraped his chair as he came to his feet and spoke with a rough edge of assaulted authority. "Rania, is this true?"

"What does it matter? Nizar is gone." Her voice quavered, but it didn't quite break. She ran her hand along the shelf behind the bar and rubbed away the dust from her finger pads.

Marwan laid his heavy hand on Omar Yussef's wrist and led him to the door. "Let me persuade my daughter, *ustaz.*

She'll help Ala, I'm sure of it." He patted Omar Yussef's shoulder as he saw his visitors out.

Omar Yussef sheltered in the doorway of the boutique next door while Khamis Zeydan lit a cigarette and cursed the weather. As they walked along the sidewalk, his scalp chilled and the sleet dribbled into his eyebrows.

"I forgot my cap," he said.

They doubled back and entered the café again. The bar-room was empty, and Omar Yussef headed for the table where he had left his woolen cap. As he picked it up, he heard Rania's voice from the kitchen.

"Yes, I was with Ala yesterday morning. From about eight until half-past nine. He was—"

"Isn't that when Nizar was killed?" Marwan's words rumbled beneath his daughter's faltering voice.

"You ought to know." There was sudden hate in her tone. It seemed to free her, and she wailed a deep, hoarse moan.

"Rania, what're you saying?" Marwan brought a hand down hard on a metal surface.

"Nizar and I were in love," she cried. "I never had that with Ala, no matter what you wanted, Daddy."

"Silence," the man bellowed. "Ala is too good for you. He's a good Arab, not like that flashy bastard Nizar who had you under some kind of spell."

"And may Allah have mercy upon him, the dear boy," Khamis Zeydan whispered, with a sarcastic grin.

Omar Yussef gestured for quiet and crept to the kitchen door. He peered into the room.

Marwan leaned heavily over the steel kitchen counter, his

wide back to the door. "He made you love him, and then he took advantage of you, my darling. You followed him to places where it wasn't right for you to go, because he had made you love him."

Rania's black eyes were angry and beautiful behind their tears. "I loved him *because* he went with me to Manhattan. He helped me to experience a new life there. We were going to go away, anywhere away from here."

"Now you'll go nowhere." Marwan's fist came down on the counter. "You'll stay here and learn to behave yourself, or you'll pay a heavy price."

"I paid the highest price when my Nizar died."

Marwan snorted through his nose. "This is my reward for taking you away from Lebanon. For bringing you to this city."

The girl clicked her tongue dismissively and, in the same moment, dodged backwards as her father's hand swung through the air where her face had been. Her movement knocked a *nargileh* from the shelf behind her, and its water bulb smashed on the tiles.

Omar Yussef went through the door and grabbed Marwan's hairy wrist as he raised it once more to strike his daughter. "Enough," he grunted. The wrist jerked and Omar Yussef needed to lay his other hand across it, too, before he could still it.

Marwan pointed to the broken *nargileh* and growled at his daughter, "Clean that up." He staggered into the café and leaned over the bar with his palm on his shaven head. When Omar Yussef touched his thick shoulder, he realized the man was sobbing.

Rania came to the doorway with her arms folded and her jaw quivering and no more secrets to protect. "Can we suggest to the police that they come and talk to you?" Omar Yussef said to her. "To confirm Ala's alibi?"

As the girl bowed her head in assent, Omar Yussef couldn't help but think what a fine couple she and Nizar would have made. The girl's beauty was of the flaring, sensuous sort that would force most men into unhappy appeasement. She needed a lover who could laugh off her passions because he was daring enough to risk inflaming them still further. A man like Nizar.

Omar Yussef's glasses fogged when he left the café. He pulled his NYPD cap over his ears. "What's so special about 1998?" he asked.

Khamis Zeydan lifted the collar of his trench coat and cupped his hand around his cigarette. "That was the year the Lebanese government amnestied a thousand convicted drug traffickers. Marwan's from the Bekaa, the center of Lebanese narcotics production."

"You're saying Marwan was a drug trafficker?"

"He knew what I was suggesting, and he didn't like it. It was a shot in the dark, but I think I nailed him." Khamis Zeydan exhaled, and the smoke came to Omar Yussef damp on the cold air.

"Why would he leave Lebanon if he had been amnestied?"

"He might've had no choice. He could've been on the wrong side of the local bad guys."

"Gangsters?"

"Worse, maybe. Hizballah, Islamic Jihad. Perhaps he came here to get away from them."

"He'd have had to lie about his drug conviction on his immigration forms. Otherwise the Americans would've denied him a visa—amnesty or no amnesty." Omar Yussef crossed the road and walked close to the buildings, sheltering from the light sleet under the storefront awnings. "If Nizar found out about that deception, Marwan could've killed him to protect himself from blackmail."

"If Marwan murdered Nizar, it might just as easily have been to protect the reputation of his daughter," Khamis Zeydan said. "It was all the fellow could do not to call her a whore to her face."

"Just because she followed her heart." Omar Yussef shook his head. He wondered who was most pitiable: the girl who had lost the man she loved, or the boy who tried to protect her though she had rejected him. "Poor Ala."

A police patrol car glided slowly down the empty street, squelching through the rivulets of sleet. Khamis Zeydan pointed at the police department logo on Omar Yussef's stocking cap and gave a thumbs-up. The officer in the passenger seat touched the peak of his cap, and the car rolled on.

Chapter 12

I n his Iraqi dialect, the young man who gave them directions to the police precinct house cautioned that it was
ten blocks away. Omar Yussef stared through the rain and
clenched his fists. He was filled with apprehension about
the likely treatment of an Arab in the Brooklyn Detention
Complex, and every delay in passing on the information
about Ala's alibi extended his son's incarceration there. The
immensity of the city frustrated him, even as its rain mocked
his inadequate clothing and its justice system imprisoned
his innocent son.

"It's a long walk, *ustaz*," the young man said, looking Omar
Yussef up and down.

"You don't think I'm healthy enough to walk so far?" Omar
Yussef shoved his chin forward and edged his voice with
aggression. The Iraqi flinched. *All these things I'm having to
deal with have made me angry*, Omar Yussef thought, *and this
boy might just be the one to catch it*. He turned to Khamis
Zeydan. "I must look particularly frail today. Nobody thinks
I can make it to my destination."

"Cool it," Khamis Zeydan said.

"What do I have to be calm about?" Omar Yussef shoved

Khamis Zeydan's shoulder with the flat of his hand. "Am I the only one who wants my son to get out of jail?"

"You're being ridiculous. This weather has frozen your brain. You need a decent coat so you can warm up and start thinking straight."

"May Allah curse this rain." Omar Yussef stamped in a puddle. The cold water flooded his loafer and chilled his toes.

The young Iraqi stroked his thin mustache and flicked away the rainwater gathering there. "I wasn't referring to your health, uncle. It's just that the weather is so bad. Maybe you should take a bus."

"I'll freeze standing at a bus stop."

"The buses are frequent. You won't have to wait long. But if you insist, walk straight up the avenue. You'll find yourself underneath a raised highway on big concrete supports. Follow the street beside it and you'll reach the precinct house. May Allah give you his aid."

"May Allah turn you into a monkey."

Khamis Zeydan sniggered at his friend's ill humor and gave the young man a consoling pat on the shoulder. "Beg the pardon of Allah," he said to Omar Yussef.

As he stumbled along the roadside, Omar Yussef felt ashamed to have yelled at the youth. The longer he spent in this alien city, the further he veered from reactions he would normally expect of himself. Every circumstance seemed set against him, and he had nothing secure to fall back on, so cut off was he from the things he knew.

"You really ought to buy a better coat," Khamis Zeydan said, "and that woolen cap isn't much good in this wet weather."

"We don't have time. We have to get Ala out of jail."

"Did you bring your magic carpet to break him out?"

"We'll tell the detective about Rania. She'll give him the alibi."

"Don't be so sure the girl will play along."

"What do you mean?"

"I mean that Nizar was fucking the daughter—"

"Don't be so crude."

"—of a man who may have been in jail in Lebanon for a drug offense and who now runs a café with no apparent customers. The third roommate is still unaccounted for, too: remember that. It may not be as simple as it seems."

Sleet crackled against the shoulders of Omar Yussef's windbreaker with a sound like a fusillade. He felt his spine stiffening. After another block, he stopped and gave Khamis Zeydan a mournful look.

The police chief smiled. "Ready to make a new fashion statement?"

They went into a store that announced itself as "The Chic Bazaar." Khamis Zeydan approached a short Arab man with a belly like a watermelon, a receding forehead, and a thin gray mustache. "My friend isn't equipped for the New York winter," Khamis Zeydan said. "What can you do for him?"

"Quickly," Omar Yussef said. "We're in a rush."

The man simpered and rubbed his hands. He pulled a long black quilted coat from a rack and held it open for Omar Yussef. The schoolteacher removed his windbreaker and handed it dripping to Khamis Zeydan. His tweed jacket was damp and musty, like a sheep in need of shearing, so he removed it too. The walk had made him sweat, and a trace of steam rose from within the jacket.

When the storekeeper dropped the big coat onto Omar Yussef's shoulders and flipped the hood onto his head, he was surprised by its light weight. The zipper buzzed up to the end of his nose.

"It's perfect, *ustaz*," the storekeeper said, turning Omar Yussef toward a full-length mirror.

All his life, he had worn the finest clothes, European styles that made him feel as though he were a Parisian or a Milanese, not an inhabitant of a Bethlehem refugee camp. Now he was forced to dress himself in the outlandish garments of another kind of ghetto. "I feel ridiculous," he said.

Khamis Zeydan pulled the zipper down a few inches. "We didn't hear what you said. It was too muffled."

Omar Yussef looked in the mirror. The coat came to his knees, and his hands were lost in the enormous sleeves. He had to admit that he already felt warm. *If I do up the zipper and wear the hood, no one will even know it's me in this coat*, he thought. *I'll look like any New Yorker wrapped up against the elements.*

When they left the shop, they saw a bulky man in a wide-brimmed hat hurrying along the other side of the road, his arms flailing as he tried to propel himself faster. He noticed Omar Yussef and crossed the street.

"Is it you, *ustaz*?" Marwan Hammiya came close to Omar Yussef. "May Allah grant you grace, my dear sir."

Omar Yussef pushed the hood of his new coat off his head and ran a palm across his thin hair. "Greetings, Marwan."

The Lebanese gripped Omar Yussef's elbow and drew him

toward the curb. He leered with an awkwardness that exposed his crooked lower teeth and gave a brief wave to Khamis Zeydan, indicating that he needed to speak to Omar Yussef alone.

"I'm so happy to have caught up with you, *ustaz*. You're going to the police station?"

"With the news of Rania's alibi for my son."

Marwan's pressure on Omar Yussef's arm grew stronger, as though he intended to drag him in the opposite direction, away from the precinct house. "I followed you because I wished to apologize for the scene in my café. Don't be offended by my Rania. You know how girls can be?"

"It's nothing."

"After you left, she calmed down and agreed to my proposition. She consents to Ala."

"Consents?"

"To resume the engagement."

Omar Yussef blinked. "I'll see what he thinks once he's out of jail. Thanks to her evidence."

"In good time, *ustaz*."

Omar Yussef tried to pull his elbow away, but Marwan held onto it and his leer widened.

"You understand that I have fatherly feelings toward your boy, as we may hope that I will soon be his father-in-law. Fatherly, protective feelings. For that reason, I must say that now may not be the right time to free him, my dear Abu Ramiz."

"Rania can hardly marry him in jail."

"Maybe not." Marwan rubbed his face. "She certainly can't marry him if he's dead."

Omar Yussef ceased to resist the café owner's grip.

"If he leaves the jail, *ustaz*," Marwan said, "he may be an easier target."

"A target for whom?"

Marwan watched Khamis Zeydan smoking a Rothmans under the awning of the clothing store. "I can't—" He sobbed. "They have their teeth into me. I can't help Ala any more than this."

"Who're *they*?" Omar Yussef pulled the big man's collar. "Who?"

"Leave him where he is, *ustaz*. He'll make a good husband for my Rania. He'll look after her when I'm gone, and he's honest—"

"Gone?"

"—and he isn't involved in bad things."

"You mean, not like Nizar?"

"Leave him where he is."

"I can't do that."

Marwan's sobs had become steady tears. "I'm trying to survive; that's all," he said. "I'm not a bad man."

"Marwan, what is it that Ala knows? Why would anyone want to harm him?"

"He doesn't know anything. But *they* don't know that. It's possible they believe he knows everything. He could be next."

"Tell me who *they* are."

When Marwan lifted his brown eyes, Omar Yussef knew that the man was in the kind of danger from which there was no escape and that the more he struggled against it, the tighter it bound him. In Bethlehem, he had seen men drawn into collaboration for whom the first transactions with the Israelis had seemed harmless, a way to obtain a travel permit or a hospital bed, only to find that gradually they were sunk into an absolute immorality with no choice but to participate in the deaths of others. Who had that power over Marwan?

"I was the one who discovered Nizar's body," Omar Yussef said. "A boy I loved was slaughtered. I have to get the police to free my son so they can concentrate on finding the real killer."

"You were there, in the apartment?" Marwan said. "Then they'll be after you, as well."

Omar Yussef remembered the Jeep rushing at him, mounting the curb, and he shivered inside his new coat. "We're going to the police station. They'll protect you. Come with us."

"Leave the boy in jail, *ustaz*," Marwan said. He smiled, hopeless and resigned, like a man facing a math problem he knew to be beyond him. "Please come and talk to me. We will discuss the engagement. May Allah lengthen your life and the life of your son."

Omar Yussef watched Marwan hunch along the street toward his café. Khamis Zeydan flicked his cigarette butt onto the sidewalk and smiled through one side of his mouth. "It's tough to be a legitimate businessman in this city," he said.

Omar Yussef kicked the butt into the gutter and once again turned in the direction of the police station.

Chapter 13

O mar Yussef mounted the bare staircase to the detectives'
bureau at the 68th Precinct, trudging slowly in his soggy
shoes as patrolmen and plainclothes officers hurried past.
Breathless from the climb, he waved across the gray metal
furniture to Sergeant Hamza Abayat, whose desk was crammed
into a corner near a high window, and crossed the room.

Holding a phone to his ear, the Arab detective came halfway to his feet, shook Omar Yussef's hand, and touched his
palm to his heart in the traditional gesture of sincerity. From
a chair in front of his battered desk, he picked up a large tub
of whey protein with a ludicrously muscled man straining to
lift a pair of massive dumbbells on the label and motioned
for Omar Yussef to sit.

Next to the desk, Khamis Zeydan rested his foot on a pile
of bodybuilding magazines. Omar Yussef glanced at the thick
sinews in the tanned, oiled chest of the cover model by his
friend's shoe. Beside the magazines was a pile of community
newspapers. He read the main headline on the first tabloid:
"NY Youth 2nd in Int'l Koran Contest." *The murder of the
Veiled Man will push that off the front page of the Muslim press,*
he thought.

"I'll send a uniformed officer along to talk to them, Missus Pierre," Hamza said. He looked impatiently at the telephone in his hand. "Don't worry. Thank you for your call."

He put down the receiver and lifted his eyes to the ceiling. "By Allah, these people are crazy," he said. "May Allah preserve you, *ustaz* Abu Ramiz. How're you?"

"Thanks be to Allah, Hamza. This is my friend Abu Adel."

The sergeant rolled a chair from the next desk toward Khamis Zeydan. "Are you the Abu Adel who's the police chief in Bethlehem?"

With a nod, Khamis Zeydan folded his hands in his lap. "And you're the Hamza Abayat whose relatives run riot all over my town like a bunch of gangsters."

"Your town? I heard you arrived in Bethlehem only a decade ago when the Old Man brought you from exile in Tunis."

"It's my town so long as I'm police chief."

"Abu Adel, this is not the place." Omar Yussef touched his friend's knee.

Hamza gazed at the gray sky beyond the window. "Police work is never easy. We all have different challenges—and failures."

That's how a real policeman reacts, measured and considerate, Omar Yussef thought. *My friend is the Bethlehem police chief, but at heart he's still a guerrilla, surviving on his passion and bursting with indignation.*

Khamis Zeydan pulled out his cigarettes. Hamza wagged his finger toward a sticker on the wall that read *No smoking—it's the law*. Khamis Zeydan put the pack away. "You donkey's ass," he whispered.

Hamza cleared his throat. "I just got off the phone with a Haitian lady who says her neighbors are practicing voodoo against her. She claims they placed white powder on her doorstep as a threat. I'll have to send a patrolman around to tell the neighbors not to put powder on the lady's doorstep."

"That's ridiculous," Khamis Zeydan snorted.

"Sometimes a true threat can seem ridiculous, Abu Adel. Slander rolls off Americans like the rain off Abu Ramiz's fine new coat, but for us Arabs it's as hurtful as the blow of a Yemeni knife."

"If the gunmen in Bethlehem limited themselves to white powders and voodoo spells, I'd consider myself lucky," Khamis Zeydan said.

"You think it's easier to be a cop in Brooklyn than Bethlehem? We found a human fetus in a gutter last week."

"Did you find the owner? I mean, the mother?" Omar Yussef said.

"We followed a trail of blood to an apartment along the street. A Puerto Rican girl had miscarried on the sidewalk and left the baby there."

"Poor woman."

"She was only a girl. Newspapers didn't write stories about her the way they cover the mayhem in Bethlehem." Hamza leaned an elbow on the papers spread over his desk. "But I saw the girl's shame when she opened the door to us. Her case is no less important to me than a war in my hometown."

Khamis Zeydan rubbed his chin. "May Allah's curse fall on these times," he murmured.

"Let us rely on Allah," Hamza said.

They fell silent. Omar Yussef sat forward and, as he moved, the susurration of his quilted coat brought the two men out of their reverie.

"Hamza, we have an alibi for my son," Omar Yussef said.

"May it be pleasing to Allah."

"When Nizar was killed, Ala was with Rania Hammiya."

The detective lifted his eyebrow. "Marwan's daughter?"

Omar Yussef nodded. "Rania had an agreement with Ala that they would become engaged. But then she fell for Nizar. Ala realized this. He went to her to cancel their agreement."

"And just at the very moment he was doing this, someone happened to kill his rival?"

Omar Yussef extended a shaky finger toward the detective. "Skepticism is all very well, but your investigations have uncovered nothing. I'm giving you a lead which eliminates one of your suspects. I seem to have obtained more from my son with a few kind words than you were able to get out of him with an entire night of bullying."

Hamza rolled his tongue inside his cheek. His face was blank. "Provided the alibi is true."

"You'll find Rania at the Café al-Quds. Take her statement and release my boy."

Hamza took the squash ball from his pocket and worked his forearms. "So if Ala didn't kill Nizar—"

"You never seriously thought he did it, surely?"

"—who could be our killer?"

Khamis Zeydan spoke quietly. "You still have one other roommate to consider."

"Rashid?"

"Has he turned up?" Khamis Zeydan asked.

Hamza closed his eyes and clicked his tongue. *No.*

"Someone's been following us," Omar Yussef said. "I'm sure it's the same man I saw fleeing Ala's apartment after I found the body. He tried to run us down."

"The same man?"

"He's wearing black and driving a blue Jeep with dark windows," Khamis Zeydan said.

"You think it's Rashid?" Hamza rolled his tongue between his back teeth, thoughtfully.

Khamis Zeydan said, "What theories are *you* operating on?"

Omar Yussef lifted his finger. "Can we release my son before we go any further?"

"If Allah wills it, soon, *ustaz.*" Hamza turned to Khamis Zeydan. "There're fewer killings in Brooklyn than you might expect. In this precinct, we only had one murder last year. Those that do occur are mainly connected to turf battles between rival drug dealers. That's probably what's behind this, even though the PLO has cleaned up its act."

"The PLO?" Omar Yussef asked.

Hamza flexed his fingers on the squash ball. "A local street gang of Palestinian youths. They used to strut about looking tough. They sold drugs."

"That sounds familiar." Khamis Zeydan laughed. "Are you sure they aren't the *real* PLO?"

"What do you mean that they've 'cleaned up their act'?" Omar Yussef said.

"They came up against the Bloods, the Crips, the Latin Kings. In the neighborhoods around here, the black and Hispanic gangs are much, much nastier than the PLO was. Frankly, our boys were whipped. Eventually they just gave up the gang life."

"What became of them?"

"They're community leaders now, speaking out against drugs," Hamza said. "But they're still hard men. If they found a dealer in our community, they might put him out of action. They might even go too far and leave him dying. Maybe that's what happened to Nizar, may Allah have mercy upon him."

Only if the PLO gang also read up on the Assassins and the myth of the Veiled Man, Omar Yussef thought. *Otherwise they wouldn't have known to leave those clues.* "I can't believe it. What possible connection could Nizar have to the drug trade?"

"I didn't say for certain that it's drug-related, only that it's probable. If I had evidence that drugs were involved, I'd have to be in touch with the Drug Enforcement Agency. You'd find its agents less sympathetic to your son than me, *ustaz.*"

"There's no need to involve them, as you say." Omar Yussef tried an encouraging smile, but it came out as a blink of his eyes and a wince around the lips.

Hamza drummed the desktop. "Is that all now, *ustaz*? I have to get going."

"What're you doing to find Rashid?" Khamis Zeydan said. "He might have the answers."

Hamza stood and took his coat from the back of his chair. "If he's still alive, we'll find him."

Omar Yussef exhaled impatiently. "Will you release my son now?"

"I only have your word about that alibi."

"So check it." Omar Yussef slapped his hand on the arm of his chair.

Hamza rolled his heavy shoulders and headed for the frosted-glass door at the entrance to the detectives' bureau.

Khamis Zeydan touched his arm as he passed. "The drugs around here—where do they come from, mainly?"

"Just recently, from Lebanon."

Khamis Zeydan's mustache twitched. "'Just recently'?"

"The Lebanese army used to uproot the hashish crops in the Bekaa Valley. But since the Israelis fought that stupid war with Hizballah in 2006, all the Lebanese soldiers are in the south in case the Israelis try to drive to Beirut."

"And the drug trade in the Bekaa got back into gear?" Omar Yussef scowled.

"That's correct."

Omar Yussef followed Hamza to the exit, perspiring in the overheated detectives' bureau. "You aren't suggesting my son has anything to do with this drug trade? He's a computer technician."

"The heads of Hamas are all engineers and doctors," Hamza said. "The founder of Islamic Jihad was a medical man."

"We're talking about my son, not those hotheads. Ala is innocent." Omar Yussef lunged for Hamza's big fists and pressed them to his chest. "Let him go, please."

"If Allah wills it." Hamza started down the Spartan staircase, his heavy footsteps echoing off the whitewashed walls.

"Perhaps you can help me with a little background from back home. Tell me about Nizar's father."

Omar Yussef glanced at Khamis Zeydan. "He was a big shot in the PLO—the *real* PLO. He was killed here in New York because he wanted to make peace with the Israelis."

"Killed by whom?"

"Someone else within the PLO, maybe? I don't know. His family maintains it was the Mossad."

"The killing was never solved?" Hamza glanced at Khamis Zeydan, who rattled his cigarettes in their pack as they approached the exit, edgy at the prospect of lighting up. "So Nizar's family isn't new to intrigue and murder."

You knew already, didn't you? Omar Yussef thought. *With Nizar's family background, you won't believe that he was an innocent victim.*

"Where can we find the gang?" Omar Yussef said. "These 'PLO' people?"

"A basement mosque in an apartment building at the other end of Fifth Avenue," Hamza said. "A couple of blocks down from the restaurant where we ate yesterday, *ustaz*. When you get there, ask someone for the mosque."

"I'll find it. Where're you going?"

"To take Rania's statement. I'm at your command, after all." The detective buttoned his parka. "At the mosque, ask to speak to Nahid Hantash. He's the top guy. May Allah ease your path."

Chapter 14

The Arab men wished each other evenings of joy and light as they departed *Maghrib* prayers, pulling the hoods of their parkas over their white skullcaps. Omar Yussef leaned on the onyx balustrade by the sidewalk and looked down on the concrete staircase to the basement mosque. The last of the worshipers zipped their coats and shook hands at the door. As they reached the street, Omar Yussef called to one of them: "Peace be upon you."

"Upon you, peace, *ustaz*."

"Will we find the Honored Nahid Hantash inside?"

"He's always the last to leave after prayers, *ustaz*."

Omar Yussef descended past boarded-up basement windows and entered a short corridor. The wall was covered with posters of Palestinian children, hackneyed images of defiance and suffering, and political slogans that fatigued Omar Yussef with their posturing and sentimentality. He glanced over a photo of a burned-out car, three victims of Israeli helicopter missiles lying within, their bearded faces vaguely nauseous in death, empty eyes staring past the camera. *Is this meant to promote the correct frame of mind for prayer?* he thought.

He slipped out of his loafers and slid them into a wooden cubbyhole still wet from the last worshiper's shoes.

At the end of the corridor, a sheet of prayer times laid out the schedule of devotion like a dense page of logarithms. The time for every prayer advanced by a minute or two each day as the moon shifted over the course of the month. Khamis Zeydan rapped his knuckles against the notice. "I don't know how they have time to do anything else," he said. "I can think of only a few things that're worth doing five times a day, and praying isn't one of them."

Beyond the door, low stools surrounded a big circular water fountain tiled in fake jade and marble, where worshipers would sit to wash their feet, hands, ears, and nostrils before prayer. Khamis Zeydan turned on one of the shiny copper faucets and scooped water into his mouth. Wiping his mustache, he looked along the narrow mosque. "Do you think that's our man?" he said.

Omar Yussef peered into the dim light from the scalloped glass light fixtures along the wall. The basement was painted white, and its carpet was gray with diagonal green stripes. At its far end was a niche decorated with the same fake marble as the water fountain and the chair from which the imam would deliver his sermons. On the floor beside the niche, his head leaning back against the wall and his legs stretched out before him, sat a dark man in his early thirties.

As they came toward him, the man brought his palm to his heart and bowed his head. "Peace be upon you," he whispered, hoarse and calm, with the accent of Palestine.

"Upon you, peace," Omar Yussef said. "Are you his Honor Nahid?"

The man held up his hands modestly. He wore a light suede baseball jacket, baggy jeans, and white socks. A blue stocking cap was pulled low on his brow and over his ears. He had shaved his facial hair into a thin line along his jaw and around his mouth, as though it were the scaffolding upon which a beard would later be constructed. In one eyebrow, a small scar, pale and hairless, made his eyes look ready for a scrap.

"May you feel as though you were with your family and in your own home," Nahid Hantash murmured.

"Your family is with you." Omar Yussef sat on the floor in front of Hantash. "Brother Nahid, I'm the father of Ala Sirhan, a friend of Nizar Jado."

"Ah, Nizar, may Allah have mercy upon him."

"May Allah grant you long life."

"I've met your son."

"Here in the mosque?"

Hantash's smile was forbearing. "You don't need to pretend that your boy is religious, nor will you have to quote the Koran to make me like you, *ustaz*. If you're Ala's father, you must be from Dehaisha Camp. I know it well. You and I are linked by our struggle to liberate Islamic land from the Occupation. That's all that counts."

"I saw your posters in the corridor."

"We still must play our part, even if we're thousands of miles from home."

"It has more to do with playing a part than with reality."

Hantash twitched his head with puzzlement.

"Those posters have no place in a house of worship," Omar Yussef said. "Such images are no good for the soul. It's sick."

"O Allah," Khamis Zeydan sighed.

"They're the truth," Hantash said. "Facts."

Omar Yussef had vented his frustrations on the young Iraqi in the street, but he couldn't afford to be so harsh with Hantash. *Calm down, Abu Ramiz,* he told himself. *You need this man on your side.* "What would you expect an American to think if he saw your posters?"

"Americans don't come here." Hantash swung a languid arm around the basement. "They wish we didn't exist. We aren't even allowed to broadcast the call to prayer on loudspeakers, because of their noise laws. But if they did come, I'm sure these images of martyrdom would remind them of their Christian churches. They have a big model there of a man being tortured to death. They call it a crucifix. Some of them hang it over their beds when they sleep—and you say *I'm* sick?"

Hantash drew his legs up and linked his fingers around his shins. The knuckles were pink and white and scarred, like the skinned knee of a child, reminding Omar Yussef that the man had done battle with the gangs of Brooklyn.

"Americans aren't innocent of crimes against Muslims," Hantash said. "In Iraq, they kill thousands. The U.S. government's secret jails are full of men whose only offense is to have obeyed Allah. On the streets, Islam is mocked and hated. It's hard for us to live here."

Khamis Zeydan offered a cigarette to Hantash, who waved it away with a gesture that showed he didn't object to his guest smoking. "Where are you from, Brother Nahid?" the police chief said.

"I was born in Hebron. My family left the West Bank when I was a teenager."

Hard-headed and stubborn by reputation, the Hebronites, Omar Yussef thought, *and violent.*

"May Allah bless your town. Forgive my friend for his ill humor," Khamis Zeydan said. "His son has been arrested, and he's very nervous about him."

"Arrested?"

"He won't give an alibi for the time when his roommate was killed."

"He's a suspect? That's ridiculous," Hantash said. "Ala wouldn't hurt anyone."

Omar Yussef forgot his antagonism and warmed to Hantash with a desperate swiftness. "I want to find out more about Nizar and Rashid," he said. "My son tells me there was some sort of conflict between them."

Hantash was silent. His eyelids were low and lazy.

"The police also think Nizar's death may have had something to do with drugs," Omar Yussef said, "and that you might be able to give us some leads."

The young man's eyes flickered with hostility.

Khamis Zeydan whistled impatiently. "My friend means that, as a community leader, you know what happens on the streets," he said. "Certainly he doesn't mean that you're involved in drugs."

"No, of course." Omar Yussef cringed and wrung his hands.

Hantash focused hard on his scabbed knuckles. "The

police have been here already," he said. "We're accustomed to their harassment."

"Do they suspect you?"

"The Arab detective Abayat suspects all Arabs. You ought to remember that, *ustaz*. Don't trust him just because he calls you 'uncle.'" Hantash stroked his fingers across the carpet. "In truth, the police have no reason to suspect me. I used to be a gang leader. I led the PLO. We thought that was a good joke— to name ourselves after another gang of Palestinian hard men. But I put an end to it after the attack on the Twin Towers."

"Why?"

Hantash held up his index fingers, parallel to each other, almost touching. "*The hour of Doom is drawing near, and the moon is cleft in two*," he said, parting his fingers. "In the Holy Koran the splitting of the moon into two is a sign of the Day of Judgment. When I saw the two towers explode, they were like the sun and the moon, and their destruction was an image of the end of the world. And everything happened twice— both towers exploded, both fell, and there were attacks in two cities, here and in Washington."

"A sign?" Omar Yussef couldn't disguise the doubt in his voice.

"Call it a reminder, if you prefer. The same verse says: *We have made the Koran easy to remember; but will anyone take heed?* I took heed of that day. I brought the gang to an end. The boys of the PLO became active in the community, instead of running around at night doing unwholesome things. My part was to found this mosque."

"You built this yourself?" Omar Yussef said.

"I raised the money and led the work."

"By Allah, that's impressive."

"I told you there's no need to pretend that you're a believer. You have no bump on your forehead from prostrating yourself in prayer." Hantash lifted the edge of his stocking cap to show a dark notch like a rough knuckle at the center of his brow. He grinned slowly, so that the black hairs along his jaw seemed to rise one by one as his skin drew back from his mouth. "But I'm proud of this place. Our population is growing, and it needs more mosques."

Omar Yussef remembered the sheet printed with prayer times in Ala's apartment. "Where's the Alamut Mosque?"

"I haven't heard of it, *ustaz*."

"I think it must be nearby."

"That'd be a strange name for a mosque around here."

"Would it? Why?"

"Are you telling me you don't know, or are you pretending once again?" Hantash lifted a finger and faked a frown. "Alamut was the castle of the Assassins—a Shiite sect. Almost everyone in Little Palestine is a follower of Sunni Islam. I don't see why anyone would name a mosque here after a castle from someone else's tradition."

Is the Alamut Mosque just a joke by my little gang of Assassins? Omar Yussef wondered. *Or does it connect them to Marwan Hammiya, a Shiite with his roots in the Lebanese region where drugs are produced?* "You don't know any Shiites in this neighborhood?"

Hantash gave Omar Yussef a long look through narrowed eyes. "There's Marwan, who runs the café."

"Do you think I should ask him about the Alamut Mosque?"

"You should ask me some questions to which you don't already know the answers. That's what I think, *ustaz*."

Omar Yussef's spine rebelled against his cross-legged position and he shifted his knees with a grunt. "Let's get back to what you know about Nizar."

The skin below Hantash's eyes twitched. "Nizar lived a debauched life."

"Drinking and women?"

"I believe so."

"Where would he have gone for these wild times?"

"Maybe Manhattan. Some Arabic clubs there have belly dancers. But we're not far from Bensonhurst and Coney Island. You can get up to plenty of mischief in those places without having to leave Brooklyn."

"Is it easy for an Arab man to pick up a woman?"

Hantash ran his finger along the narrow line of his beard. "An American woman? No matter how easy it is, *ustaz*, it always ends in frustration."

"What do you mean?"

"An Arab can drink whisky with Americans and curse every other word as Americans do and even take their women to bed. But, to them, he's still a stinking Arab." The young man stared across the gray carpet, his heavy eyes sad and angry. "I don't think the wild times, as you put it, would've made Nizar happy."

Does this man know what was in Nizar's mind, or is he superimposing his own disappointments from the days before he turned to Islam? Omar Yussef thought. "That's all he was looking for, you think? Happiness?"

"If Allah has forgiven Nizar's debauchery, then he's in Paradise now with the Master of the Universe, so he found happiness anyway."

"Was Nizar involved in drugs?" Omar Yussef asked.

Hantash inclined his head in assent, slowly.

"How long was he dealing?"

"A few months."

"What did he sell?"

"Hashish."

"Who was his supplier?"

"Well, where does hashish come from these days?"

"Lebanon. The Bekaa Valley."

Hantash opened his hand and nodded.

Marwan again, Omar Yussef thought. He glanced at Khamis Zeydan. The police chief stroked the glove on his prosthetic hand.

Hantash pushed himself to his feet. "I have to leave, *ustaz*. I'm refereeing a basketball game at the community center. Where can I find you? I'll be in touch if I discover anything useful. Rashid is a good Muslim, and I want to help find him. Also, I like your son, though we never see him at the mosque."

"I'm at the Stuart Hotel in Manhattan."

Hantash flicked his fingers together as though he were counting money.

Omar Yussef gave a laugh that sounded as though he were choking. "We're not big-money men. My room is paid for by the UN. I'm the principal of their school in Dehaisha. My friend Abu Adel is security adviser to our president."

Khamis Zeydan whistled and raised his eyebrows. "My

friend gives away all my secrets," he said, standing and shaking his foot to get the blood flowing. "You've been very helpful, Brother Nahid."

At the cubbyholes in the hall, Omar Yussef fretted the tassels on his loafers. *Sergeant Abayat suggested that these former PLO gang people might deal out street justice to a drug dealer,* he thought. *Hantash knew Nizar was dealing drugs. He also knew that the Alamut Mosque was connected to the Assassins, so perhaps he'd be knowledgeable enough to have left the clue about the Veiled Man.* "If you were aware that a Palestinian was pushing drugs to people in this neighborhood," he called across the carpet to Hantash, "what would you do about it?"

The young man flicked out the lights in the mosque. In the darkness, his throaty voice was deep. "I'd turn him in to the police, *ustaz*. That's all."

Omar Yussef waited at the door for Khamis Zeydan to lace up his shoes. "Should we go to Marwan now?"

"It's getting late," Khamis Zeydan said. "Marwan might have customers—even a front has to have a few. He might not be free to talk. Go tomorrow, so you can catch him when the café is quiet."

At the top of the steps, the traffic lights dazzled on the wet pavement. Beyond the intersection at the end of the block, the warning blinkers flashed red on top of the Verrazano-Narrows Bridge. Cars rattled down the side street past the green light. Omar Yussef breathed the cold air. The men in the mosque prayed in the direction of Mecca, but the home of Islam in the Saudi desert seemed to be on another planet. He wondered how they even knew which way to turn. Did their prayers rise to the sky and bounce down to the holy city, like a call from a satellite phone?

Across the road, a man stirred in front of a thick retaining wall by the intersection. The traffic lights changed, and a car made a right turn, its headlights illuminating the man's face and his black coat. He was watching Omar Yussef. The car moved on, and the man disappeared. Omar Yussef headed toward the end of the block, but when he reached the corner there was no sign of the man. He stared into the darkness along the empty street.

"Just because you have a new coat doesn't mean we ought to hang around in the cold," Khamis Zeydan said. "The subway is in this direction. Hurry up."

Omar Yussef followed his friend reluctantly, looking back every few paces to search for the man who had been watching him. His pulse ran fast. Though he had seen it only for a moment, he had recognized the stern, bearded face.

It was Ismail. The fourth Assassin.

Chapter 15

T he snow drifted down over First Avenue. In the long
UN Conference Hall building, Omar Yussef wiped its
traces from his brow with a handkerchief. Delicate flakes
attached to the tall, picture window and slipped down the
pane as the heat from the hallway seeped through the glass.
A new snowflake settled, and he touched his finger to the
spot, wondering if the pattern of the ice crystal outside was as
unique as the fingerprint he left on his side of the window.

The brief glimpse the snowflakes gave of themselves
before they melted away reminded him of the flicker of light
that had illuminated Ismail's face. The sudden appearance of
the fourth member of The Assassins disturbed him. Was
Ismail's presence in New York connected to the murder in
the apartment where his three former friends lived?

A short Latino woman rolled her cleaning cart by him,
favoring her left hip as she hefted her heavy buttocks. She
halted outside the General Assembly Hall and polished the
window where a group of schoolchildren had been pressed
against it. Feeling guilty, Omar Yussef rubbed away his fingerprint with his handkerchief.

He followed the cleaner's progress down the hallway. Its

simple modernist design wasn't to his taste. He preferred the traditional vaulted ceilings and colorful tiles of the Middle East. But it was a good place from which to watch the snow come down, and he felt its delicate beauty touching his face still.

He checked his watch. It was almost 10 A.M. He would show himself at the conference this morning—just to keep his boss happy, since he had missed yesterday's opening session—then he would take the subway to Bay Ridge to talk to Marwan. He turned back to the window, but the magic of the snowflakes was sullied by his memory of the blood he had seen in Little Palestine.

A slim Russian blonde led a party of tourists toward the mural of Norman Rockwell's *Golden Rule*. "Do unto others as you would have them do unto you," Omar Yussef whispered. Behind the tour group, he stared at Rockwell's mosaic faces filling the wall. They were supposed to represent all the nations of the world. They looked back at him like the mélange of ethnicities that stared through the window of any crowded New York subway car. None of them, he thought, looked like him.

The Russian guide led the tourists past Omar Yussef. They broke around him as though he were a rock in a stream. When they were gone, only one man remained beneath the mural, leering at him.

"Morning of joy, Deputy Director-General Abdel Hadi," Omar Yussef said.

"Morning of light, Abu Ramiz." The schools inspector approached Omar Yussef and reached out to touch his quilted coat. "This isn't up to your usual fashionable standards."

"Perhaps I could borrow one of your polyester suits, instead."

"Or your son could lend you some prison fatigues."

Omar Yussef's head went back as though he had been jabbed on the nose.

"Your friend Khamis Zeydan was trying to get the president to intervene with the New York police last night. On behalf of your son. I just happened to be in the president's suite at the time." Smug at his proximity to power, Abdel Hadi's breath shivered sensuously, like a cat's purr. "Sadly, the president decided there was nothing he could do."

"There's no need for interventions. My son will soon be released."

"Perhaps your UN pals would do something for the boy. I'm sure it would interest them to learn that their keynote speaker is the father of a murder suspect."

Even if we were part of the same delegation, this man might undermine me. That's the way of Palestinian politics, Omar Yussef thought. *With me attending as a UN delegate, I'm truly fair game.* "My son isn't a suspect."

"How do they put it—he's helping the police with their inquiries? Is that it?"

Omar Yussef clicked his tongue.

"As he once helped the Israelis?" Abdel Hadi said.

"He did nothing of the sort. The Israelis arrested him along with hundreds of other youths from Bethlehem. It was a big intifada sweep. Almost every male below the age of thirty was taken in. There was nothing to it. You know that."

Abdel Hadi flattened a lick of black hair over his dark, bald scalp. He brushed the dandruff that adhered to his fingers onto the tail of his jacket and licked his lips with the tip of his yellowish tongue. "Your son is accused of murder—"

"Not accused of anything—"

"—yet you maintain that circumstances will soon enough reveal him to be harmless."

"Of course he is."

"Perhaps he's even been framed. Does that sound familiar?"

Omar Yussef clenched his fists in the deep pockets of his coat.

"My government work has led me to examine the archives of the old Jordanian administration. Mainly documents concerning education," Abdel Hadi said. "But I also came across a police report from 1965 regarding the arrest on a murder charge of a young Ba'ath Party activist from Bethlehem. He was expected to go on to great things, to be a leader of his generation, but he lost his nerve and ended up teaching in a backwater UN school."

Son of a whore, Omar Yussef thought. *I didn't think anyone knew about that old case.* "Maybe his generation was polluted by back-stabbers like you, so he turned his focus to the next generation—the one that'll shape a better future."

Abdel Hadi sneered at Omar Yussef with triumphal calm. "Your son may escape justice this time, just as you did forty years ago. But one day I shall use this information to protect our schoolchildren from your wicked ideas. Perhaps this week. Perhaps even today."

Omar Yussef tasted a splash of bile at the back of his tongue. "You should be in a profession more appropriate to your talents than education," he said. "Try the secret police."

Abdel Hadi dropped his hand as though waving away a compliment. "In a spirit of solidarity between Palestinian brothers, I hope for the best for your son." He gave a smile of compassion, as if he had felt some dull pain. Then he peeled away the expression like a price tag stamped over an earlier, outdated one, revealing a cheaper smirk beneath it.

The schools inspector pushed through the hazelwood doors of the Economic and Social Council. Omar Yussef held out his palm as the door swung back at him. It jarred his elbow, and he winced. Leaning a shoulder against the door, he entered the conference room.

An observers' gallery ten rows deep sloped down to the delegates' area. The chairman's table faced the hall, beneath a wall decorated with white concentric ovals on a dark wooden background, like a magnified section from an inlaid Syrian table. It rose to a ceiling that had been left incomplete to represent the UN's unfinished work in poor countries. Below the chairman, the recorders and clerks huddled, absorbed in their preparations with the businesslike energy of an orchestra in its pit. The delegates sat at long tables, and behind them were five rows of staff seats. From one of these rows, Magnus Wallander waved to Omar Yussef and gestured him toward a seat of ragged lime-green corduroy.

"What did I miss yesterday?" Omar Yussef asked when he reached his seat.

"The first day of the conference was what you Palestinians call *heki fadi*, empty talk," Wallander said. "It's only during the breaks that one can have interesting conversations and make some progress."

"Progress has no place in the Committee on Palestine."

The Swede slapped Omar Yussef's shoulder as the chairman brought the meeting to order. He was a thick-featured Egyptian diplomat in an expensive gray suit with the lazily watchful eyes of a bazaar trader. He rested his forefinger across his mouth even as he spoke into his microphone, as though he might later deny his words and challenge anyone to claim they had seen his lips move.

Omar Yussef blocked out the Egyptian's hard consonants and procedural ramblings. Focusing on his next steps to help Ala, he thought through his conversation with Hantash at the mosque. At first, it had been hard for him to accept that Nizar had been dealing drugs, but as he ran over his memories of the boy, he realized the revelation made sense. Nizar had always been intelligent, but not solely in an academic way. There had been something of the raffish con man about him. His sharpness had led him to understand that New York held no place for anyone who wasn't on the way up, on the make. So he had gone for fast, illegal money. Like the girl Rania, drugs were forbidden to Nizar, and Omar Yussef recalled the mischievous student who had always wanted what he wasn't allowed to have.

He came out of his reverie when he heard the chairman call on Abdel Hadi. He glanced at Wallander in surprise. The Swede fiddled sheepishly with the dial on the arm of his chair that controlled the choice of language for the simultaneous translation. "He *is* part of the Palestinian delegation, Abu Ramiz. I couldn't really stop him speaking," he said.

Abdel Hadi stammered through his introductory remarks.

Omar Yussef swore he could hear static from the man's cheap suit crackle over the microphone. Some of the delegates left the room. *A smoke break and a chat about the fun at the belly-dancing club last night, no doubt,* Omar Yussef thought. He almost felt pity for the stuttering functionary at the podium.

"Our new Palestinian Curriculum Plan at the Palestinian Authority's Ministry of Education is the result of five years of brainstorming, the collection of much data, reviewing of the data, and the exploration of experiences with curricula in other countries in the region," Abdel Hadi read from his notes.

With material like this, I'll soon be the only one in the room, Omar Yussef thought.

In a monotone, Abdel Hadi recited the details of the education plan he had designed. Omar Yussef had read the curriculum and hadn't been enthused. He was even less impressed now that he knew it had been Abdel Hadi's work.

"The pressure of the international community is constantly applied to the Palestinian curriculum, through the activism of sinister Jewish groups which accuse our schools of inciting children to hatred of Israel and Jews," Abdel Hadi said. "We ask, why is this pressure applied only to the Palestinian side, and why is an examination not made of what is taught in Israeli schools?"

Omar Yussef shook his head. *Take care of your own responsibilities,* he thought. *Let the Israelis teach what they like.*

Abdel Hadi's reading grew more fluent as his subject became harsher. "But it isn't only these shadowy Zionist groups that threaten our children. Within our schools, there are dangerous agents who pervert our children's minds with divisive propaganda." He cast his eyes over the delegates until they rested on Omar Yussef. "Later this week, you will hear from one such man. I will be present to rebut his accusations against the honor of the Palestinian people. I hope you will join me in rejecting his ideas."

Abdel Hadi descended from the podium to lackluster applause. Omar Yussef felt a loop of tension squeeze his skull. *At least I know now what I'll be talking about when I address this august body in three days' time*, he thought.

"In UN-speak, we would say we 'appreciate Mister Abdel Hadi's involvement,' but those comments were 'not productive,'" Wallander said.

Omar Yussef gave a bitter laugh that rolled in his throat. *I came six thousand miles to discuss our children's future*, he thought, *and this bastard Abdel Hadi brings the same petty quarrels and grudges that occupy him at home. I can't escape this stupidity. No Palestinian can.*

It was time he headed for Brooklyn. With a low curse for Abdel Hadi he rose and moved through a crowd of delegates who were eager to escape before the next speech. At first he carried his coat folded over his arm, but it puffed into the flow of oncoming diplomats, catching their arms in its hood and sleeves as they pushed past. He clutched it to his belly with both hands and made for the exit.

Beside the door, a group of men in dark suits chatted at a bench that bore a small Lebanese flag. When one of them turned, Omar Yussef recognized the same face he had seen fleetingly illuminated by headlights in Little Palestine the previous evening. *Ismail is with the Lebanese delegation*, he thought, sighing with relief. *He's here as a diplomat. May Allah be thanked, I was wrong even to suspect a connection to the murder.*

Edging sideways through the crowd, he clutched his coat tightly, but its volume still hampered his progress. Each time he looked up, he feared Ismail would be gone. The young man had aged badly—Omar Yussef would have said he was two decades older than his twenty-four years. His hair was thin and graying, and his olive skin had a sickly yellow undertone. But it was unmistakably Ismail.

When Omar Yussef was almost free of the crowd, he caught Ismail's eye. He detected a moment of panic in the face of his former pupil. Then Ismail's gaze narrowed. Omar Yussef raised his hand to wave, but the boy turned and went through the door.

Chapter 16

S hivering and hugging his coat to his midriff, Omar
Yussef slithered across the plaza outside the UN
building as the snowfall lightened. With a shake of his head
to free himself of the strange trance that had come over
him since he had left the conference hall, he remembered
to put the coat on. He was preoccupied with Ismail. Was
the boy so ashamed of his betrayal in the Israeli detention
camp that he would twice avoid his beloved former teacher?
Or could he have some other reason for his flight? *Maybe
I'm not so beloved after all,* Omar Yussef thought.

He meandered away from the conference, from the banal
chatter of the delegates and the overheated rooms that made
his head feel fuzzy. He tried to find innocent excuses for Ismail,
but with reluctance he acknowledged that the boy had acted
suspiciously. Omar Yussef's loafers slipped in the slush, and he
had to throw his arms up to regain his balance. He stood still,
breathing hard, sensing the aversion of the passing New
Yorkers to a stranger who couldn't walk on the snow. The UN
building disappeared into the low cloud. *Surely Ismail's here on
official business, to talk and talk and talk, nothing more than that.*

Omar Yussef made his way across First Avenue. The

involvement in this affair of The Assassins, his favorite pupils, bewildered him. It upset the contentment with which he was accustomed to recalling his years as a teacher. How many other pupils whom he had thought innocent had since grown into criminals, gunmen, wife-beaters? Could any of them now be killers? Ala had told him his roommates, two of Omar Yussef's dearest students, might have been planning to kill. Where had they learned even to consider such things? His classroom was a place of warmth and intellectual inquiry, but when his students emerged into the world, they became infected by its wickedness. It was a corruption that could no more be avoided than the flakes alighting quietly on his coat.

What good are my teachings? he thought. History was supposed to give his pupils insights into the damage violence had inflicted upon the Arab people through the centuries. He always hoped this knowledge would lead them to reject the ugliness of present Palestinian politics. In spite of himself, he returned to his suspicions about The Assassins and found he was angry that the learning he had passed on in his classroom seemed to be the basis for a conspiracy, perhaps even a murder.

He reached the sidewalk on the other side of the street and blew out a furious breath. Its tall buildings like the precipitous walls of a canyon, the avenue extended uptown and downtown, gaping into nothingness at each end as though it gave out onto the limits of the earth. Everything in New York seemed alien and outrageous to him. Before he took the subway to Brooklyn, he decided, he needed to reassure himself that there was a place where his relationships were uncomplicated and loving. He went back to the hotel and rode the elevator to his floor, assaulted by a raucous cartoon playing on a video screen above the door. In his room, he sat on the edge of the bed and dialed his wife.

"Omar, why didn't you call me?" Maryam said. "I left you a message yesterday."

Omar Yussef glanced at a flashing red light on the phone. *Now I know what that means*, he thought. "I didn't receive the message, my darling, but I'm so very happy to hear your voice."

"I've been worried."

He was about to ask how things were at home when Maryam spoke again, with an excited quaver: "But tell me, how's my dear son?"

Omar Yussef touched his fingers to his brow. *I'm an idiot*, he thought. *I didn't prepare a reply to this question. All I considered was my own loneliness. I shouldn't even have called her.* "Thanks be to Allah, he's well, my darling. I visited him in Brooklyn, and I expect to see him again soon."

"What's his news, may Allah bless him?"

"It's snowing here, Maryam. Sometimes very heavy snow. I'm up high in my hotel and looking down on the snow as it settles on the street."

Maryam giggled. "Looking *down* on the snow. You must be in a skyscraper. But I asked about Ala's news."

"Abu Adel is here, too, with the president."

"Don't let him take our Ala to a bar, and make sure Abu Adel eats correctly. He has to take care of his diabetes. What have you been eating, Omar?"

He sighed, relieved that he had diverted her from their son. "I had Lebanese food. It wasn't so bad."

"How did you find a Lebanese restaurant in New York?"

I went with the man who put our boy in jail, he thought. "An acquaintance of Ala's took me. How're the kids?"

"Miral and Dahoud are downstairs with Nadia. She's helping them with their homework."

He smiled fondly at the mention of his granddaughter and the two children he had adopted after the death of their parents during the intifada. When he returned to Bethlehem, he would give Nadia the NYPD cap. She loved detective stories, and she would be excited by the gift. He felt less foolish for buying it now. "I have a present for Nadia," he said.

"I should hope so, but don't forget to buy something for Miral and Dahoud, too, and for Ramiz's other two. I know she's your favorite, but you have to be fair."

"You're my favorite. Shall I find something to bring back for you, my darling?"

"Just a husband hungry for his wife's cooking after eating American fast food for a week. Did you give Ala the present I sent with you?"

Omar Yussef coughed. "Not yet. Later today, if Allah wills it. I'm sure I shall see him."

"If Allah wills it. Give him my love, and tell him I want to speak to him and to see him soon."

When Omar Yussef hung up, he let his wife's soothing voice linger in his head. But the comforting words faded, and he heard her speaking the name of their son like a guilty mantra, *Ala, Ala, Ala,* rebuking him for his deception. The message light on the phone seemed to blink out the boy's name, an alarming semaphore. He took off his spectacles and rubbed his eyes.

The phone trilled. Startled, Omar Yussef stared at it a moment. He picked up. "Maryam?"

"*Ustaz* Abu Ramiz? May merciful Allah bless you, O *ustaz*. This is Nahid Hantash. How're you?"

"Thanks be to Allah, O Nahid."

The PLO gang leader ran through a series of blessings and good wishes. *He's been a long time in America, where they always get right to the point,* Omar Yussef thought, *but when he speaks Arabic he's as formal and courtly as the* mukhtar *of a village back in Palestine.* "May Allah bring you peace," Omar Yussef said.

"Have you heard from Sergeant Hamza Abayat today?" Nahid asked.

Down to business, Omar Yussef thought. "No."

"He didn't call you?" Nahid chuckled. "I thought perhaps he wouldn't."

"What has happened? Is it something to do with my son?"

"It's connected to our discussion yesterday."

"Nahid, please. Spit it out."

"You could say the Café al-Quds is under new ownership. Marwan Hammiya is dead."

Chapter 17

T rees reached up from the road to hedge the elevated section of the subway, their bare silvery branches stark against the flat white sky, like a diagram of a bronchitic lung in a medical textbook. Through the trees, Omar Yussef stared out at the apartment buildings on the avenues and their rooftop water towers decorated with bulbous graffiti. The colorful characters seemed to puff out their chests, posturing like the writers who made them declarations of individuality. The houses on the side streets, their yellow planks layered like baklava, were shrunken and shunted close, parodies of spacious American suburbia. In the distance, the towers of the Verrazano-Narrows Bridge, stern and monstrous, rose over the low Brooklyn skyline.

Back underground, Omar Yussef checked his watch impatiently as he reached his station. He needed to get to Hamza, to tell him what Marwan had said when he stood in the street weeping—about the danger "they" posed. It had proved real enough for Marwan, and the poor man had warned that Ala might be next.

From the train, he rushed toward Fifth Avenue. Around the Café al-Quds, blue police barriers blocked the sidewalk.

He approached an officer who was slapping his hands against his ribs to keep warm while he stood guard.

"Is Sergeant Abayat here?" Omar Yussef asked. "I need to see him."

"Who're you, sir?" the officer said. Beneath his peaked police cap, he wore a close-fitting black felt headband designed to cover his ears. It came low over his brow and gave him the look of a medieval Crusader.

"My name is Sirhan. I'm involved in the case of this man who is now dead." He flicked his fingers toward the café. "May Allah have mercy upon him."

The officer muttered into the radio clipped to his collar. A voice crackled a response, and the policeman shoved the wooden barrier aside with his foot to let Omar Yussef pass.

Inside the café, he recognized the agitated crime-scene technicians he had seen at Ala's apartment. Hamza Abayat leaned against the bar with his back to the door. The female lieutenant emerged from under the bar and spotted Omar Yussef. The big Arab detective turned and frowned.

Omar Yussef made his way between the tables. The lights, which had been dimmed when he visited Marwan Hammiya the day before, were bright on the busy technicians. He remembered Khamis Zeydan's suspicion that the Café al-Quds was a front with few real clients. *Murder has turned it into a bustling café,* he thought.

"Hamza, why didn't you call me?" he said.

"Are you a detective on the case?" Hamza rolled his neck, and Omar Yussef heard a vertebra click as the big muscles moved. "I know that you like to play the sleuth back in Bethlehem, but what makes you think I'd need your help here?"

"I was in this café yesterday talking to Marwan. He even followed me along the street to plead with me. Maybe he told me something that might be useful to you."

"Take him into the kitchen," the lieutenant said, ducking behind the bar once more.

The lights glared off the stainless-steel counters in the kitchen. The floor was smeared with blood, like a butcher's shop on the day of the *Eid al-Adha*. Omar Yussef put his open hand flat against the doorpost and imagined he had left the bloody print with which he had seen Egyptians mark their entryways during that feast of sacrifice.

"Where's the body?" he asked, conscious that he spoke with a little extra force to compensate for the tremble in his stomach.

Hamza rubbed the back of his hand across his nose. "Gone. For autopsy."

"You're sure it's Marwan?"

"The daughter refused to identify the body. Says she's too traumatized. It's him. I'd seen him around."

"When did it happen?"

Hamza lifted his sleeve and glanced at his wristwatch. It was silver with a luminous blue dial, glowing even under the kitchen lights. In the dark, it would be very bright. "The middle of last night. About eight hours ago."

"You should've called me."

The detective blew out a breath of impatience and resignation.

Omar Yussef remembered Rania's testimony. "Did the girl confirm Ala's alibi?"

"She did."

"So you can release my boy?"

"It's done."

Omar Yussef felt relief flooding his chest, as though tension had constricted his breathing for days.

"But your son wasn't too pleased that Rania decided to speak up," Hamza said. "I think he preferred to play the wounded romantic hero."

Omar Yussef blamed himself for his son's stubbornness. It was an unfortunate trait the boy had inherited from him. "What did you find here?"

"What do you think? A dead man on the kitchen floor."

Omar Yussef averted his eyes from the bloody tiles. "How did he die?"

"He was stabbed repeatedly. With venom, I'd say. Someone wanted him dead, but they didn't do it efficiently with a single cut through the jugular."

"Do you have the knife?"

Hamza looked with curiosity at Omar Yussef. "The murder weapon? Yes. No prints on it. But I didn't say it was a knife."

"Is it a knife?"

"Sure, but how did you know?"

Omar Yussef let out a dismissive sigh. "Come on, you said he'd been stabbed. It's the same murderer, isn't it? The one who killed Nizar."

"We haven't established a definite connection between the two killings."

"Two murders within a few steps of each other in a couple of days. No connection?"

"Not a clear one. Nizar's killer didn't descend into the frenzy of the person who stabbed Marwan over and over again. And Marwan wasn't decapitated, as Nizar was."

"It's too much of a coincidence. What do you think this was—a random robbery that went wrong?"

"A robbery? No." Hamza let a nasty sarcasm into his voice. "If robbers had done this, they'd probably have taken the case full of hashish and the used twenty-dollar bills we found in that cupboard behind the tubs of hummus."

Hantash knew what he was talking about, Omar Yussef thought. *Marwan was involved in drugs, after all.* "Nizar was dealing drugs too. Nahid Hantash told me."

Hamza sucked his upper lip. "That's why I don't deny that there's a possible connection between the two deaths. If they worked together, maybe someone in their drug ring is tying up loose ends."

"Surely someone from the drug ring would've taken the hashish and the money after they killed him."

"Right." The skinny lieutenant came to the kitchen door. "And drug dealers usually don't kill with a bread knife. They like big, big handguns."

"A burglary gone wrong?" Hamza said.

"The techs don't think there's any sign of a break-in," she said. "It must be someone known to the victim, someone he'd allow to enter his kitchen with him."

"That could be a member of the drug ring, even if it doesn't add up that they didn't take the drugs and the money."

Hamza rubbed the black stubble of his close-cropped hair.

"They could've left that stuff behind to throw us off." The lieutenant removed her spectacles, breathed on them, and cleaned them with the end of her sweatshirt. "What'd you get from the girl?"

"The victim's daughter was sleeping upstairs in the family apartment at the time of the murder. She didn't hear anything."

"I guess it's possible she could've slept through it." The lieutenant replaced her spectacles. "Despite the repeated stab wounds, there's no sign that the victim fought back."

"The girl says she got out of bed in the middle of the night—bad dreams about headless boyfriends. She saw that her father's bedroom was empty. She came down here, found the body, and called nine-one-one."

The lieutenant tipped her chin. Her cell phone rang, and she went back into the café.

"Why wouldn't Marwan defend himself?" Omar Yussef said. "When he came after me on the street, he was terrified. I'm sure he'd have been prepared for an attack."

"Maybe he didn't like to hit anyone except his daughter," Hamza said. "Although she doesn't have any bruises today."

"What do you mean by that?"

Hamza rubbed his bottom lip with a coarse thumbnail. "You said Marwan came after you, to plead with you? About what?"

"He said it was safer for Ala to stay in jail. He thought my son would be in danger—and perhaps me too—because whoever killed Nizar might believe we knew something we shouldn't. He wouldn't tell me who they were, but he seemed to know who had murdered Nizar. Now Marwan's dead. That's why I think his killing is connected to Nizar's."

"Don't touch anything, *ustaz*," Hamza said. "Wait here."

The detective went up the stairs behind the kitchen. Marwan Hammiya's blood was swirled and smudged on the white floor tiles. For a second, Omar Yussef thought he heard the dead man screaming. *It's your imagination,* he told himself, *and in any case Rania heard nothing from upstairs. Marwan must've died quietly, despite the violence of the attack.*

The thought of death dizzied him. He turned from the bloody floor and braced his arm against the wall. His heavy breath rustled some bills in a bulldog clip pinned to a board beside him. His vision clouded, red like the blood on the tiles, and he staggered. His shoulder knocked the papers to the floor. They landed face down, so that the page at the back presented itself to him when he picked them up.

It was the prayer schedule of the Alamut Mosque. The same sheet he had seen affixed to the refrigerator in his son's apartment. The page bearing the name of a mosque that even Nahid Hantash hadn't heard of. Marwan had hidden it at the back of a pile of unremarkable invoices, turned to the wall so that even someone looking through the other papers would miss it.

Omar Yussef ripped the sheet away from the stack and lifted his spectacles to read the columns of prayer times for the month. He ran his gaze across from *Fajr* at 5:26 A.M. to *Isha* at 6:50 P.M. At first he could make out no special significance to it, but then he noticed that once a week the time of the *Maghrib* sunset prayers was off by an hour. "Five thirty-five, five thirty-seven, *six* forty, five forty-two," he read, rubbing his chin in puzzlement. *Something's wrong with this schedule*, he thought. *But the mistakes are too regular—one each week. It's no accident.*

Footsteps descended behind the kitchen. Omar Yussef stuffed the prayer schedule into his jacket pocket. Hamza entered, ducking his head beneath the low lintel. He stood to one side, and Omar Yussef saw his son in the doorway, his face gray and heavy with exhaustion. Ala stared at his father and some color came to his cheeks, as though he were angry to see him there.

"My boy, you're safe." Omar Yussef stepped forward. "Thanks be to Allah."

Ala pushed past his father. "I'm not safe, Dad. Was Nizar safe?" He pointed at the blood on the floor. "Was Marwan?"

"But they were involved in something bad. Drugs."

The young man turned his intense stare on Hamza. "You're a bastard, Abayat."

"Another satisfied customer." Hamza smiled with an indifference that puzzled Omar Yussef.

"A real bastard," Ala said. "You and your tribe of gunmen have ruined my hometown and now you're going to destroy what's left of my life here in Brooklyn."

Omar Yussef wanted only to get his boy away from the police. He knew Ala's temper and realized that he'd soon explode beyond all control. "My son, what're you talking about? Let's go."

"He brought me here to see what would happen when he

put me in a room with Rania," Ala said. "To see if she'd let slip some secret, and to see if I'm a part of all this." He gestured at the blood on the floor.

"Why?"

"He thinks we killed Marwan and Nizar, of course. Me and Rania."

Omar Yussef frowned at Hamza. "Where's Rania?"

Hamza's indifference seemed deeper still. "Upstairs."

"We sat up there in silence, Dad, which must've disappointed this bastard." Ala threw a hand out toward Hamza. "What did you think we'd say to each other? Two days ago I gave up the woman I loved, and at the same time her beloved was murdered. Now her father is dead. Did you think we'd put our heads together and figure out who to kill next, while you were eavesdropping?"

"It was worth a try." Hamza made his eyes hard and empty.

Ala slapped his hand down on a steel counter.

"But, my boy, it's over," Omar Yussef said. "Now you're free."

"Free? Dad, I'm ordered not to leave the city until the police finish their investigation." Ala's foot slid on the smeared floor and he grabbed at his father's shoulder to right himself.

"Don't fall over," Hamza said. "You'll get covered in blood."

"You'd like that, wouldn't you, you son of a whore," Ala said. "You'd be happy if this was my blood all over the tiles."

"I'm not taking bets on whose blood will be the next to spill," Hamza said. "But that isn't because I don't have a good guess. It's only because gambling is an 'abomination devised by Satan.'"

"Don't quote the Koran at me. You're not even really an Arab any more. You're an American. Infidel bastard."

The boy clutched Omar Yussef's arm, like a baby who fears slipping from his parent's embrace. His son's tension fed through his body. Marwan Hammiya had warned him to leave Ala in the safety of the jail. In this room where Marwan had died, Omar Yussef understood that his son would be in jeopardy until the killer of Nizar and Marwan was caught. He glanced at Hamza. The meaning of the cynical smile on the detective's lips came to him, and his eyes widened in outrage. "You're gambling, after all—with Ala's life. You're releasing him because you think he's next," he yelled at Hamza. "You're setting a trap for this murderer."

"A trap?"

Omar Yussef thrust his forefinger at his son and shouted, "My boy is the bait."

Chapter 18

Ala stepped out of the café and hurried between the low snowbanks on the sidewalk. Omar Yussef would have gone after him, but he was breathless even before he reached the door, and he knew he couldn't keep up. He returned to the kitchen and grabbed Hamza's thick arm. "You have to protect my son," he shouted.

"You think I should follow him?" Hamza settled back against the steel counter.

"I told you someone's been following me. They tried to run me down on Atlantic Avenue. Whoever they are, they think I know something I shouldn't about these murders. Now they'll try to kill my boy too." Rania had solved Ala's problem with the police; but without the protection of the jail, he would now be in greater danger. *Unless I can find the killer before he gets to us*, Omar Yussef thought.

"Your son won't go far." Hamza jerked his thumb at the back stairs. Slow feet descended. Rania came to the door. "You get what I mean, *ustaz?*" the detective said.

Rania was so pale that her veins showed blue through her skin, seeming to write across her face the fears she held within. She wore a long black coat cut tight around her upper body and a black *mendil* with a trim of gold sequins around her face. Her lips pouted and her big sullen eyes were edged with the slack purple skin of unhappiness and fatigue.

The detective reached into a large tin of olives, fished in the vinegar, and pulled out a handful. He fed one into his mouth. "Where're you going?" he asked.

"I'm going to work," she replied.

Omar Yussef sensed the girl's horror as she crossed the floor, skirting the smears of her father's blood. "Long life to you, my daughter," he said. "May Allah be merciful upon him, the deceased one."

Rania opened her mouth to speak the traditional response to these condolences, but her breath caught. "The Community Association will help me to arrange the funeral," she whispered. "It's best for me to go there as usual. I need to be with good people, Arab people." She turned away from Hamza with a sneer.

It seemed unnatural to Omar Yussef that her father's murder appeared to anger Rania, rather than sadden her. *Perhaps it's only her grief that makes her rage,* he thought, *or the detective's suspicion.*

She let Hamza see her curled lip again. "People with a heart," she said. Her voice stammered on a strangled sob.

Hamza chewed another olive.

Rania left the kitchen, her chin up and her glassy eyes straight ahead. If Omar Yussef couldn't keep pace with his son, he could at least follow this girl across the street. Perhaps she could tell him something that would help track the killer who now seemed a menace to Ala. Omar Yussef took a final look at the blood on the floor and went after her.

"I'll walk you to the Community Association," he said, rushing to reach the door before it closed behind her.

On the snowy sidewalk, Rania's back was very straight and she balanced easily beside Omar Yussef, who was tense and unsteady. "Your father will find forgiveness in Paradise, my daughter," he said.

"For what must he be forgiven?" Her voice was dismissive, clipped.

"Only you can know that."

Her neck twitched backward, and her eyes rolled like a thoroughbred in the moment of restraint before its rider lets it gallop.

"And only Allah knows your father's reward," Omar Yussef added, "whether Paradise or Hell."

"If it's Hell, then my father was paid in advance long ago." The girl crossed Fifth Avenue toward the Community Association, pulling her shoulders back. She stopped at the sidewalk to wait for Omar Yussef, something regretful in her face. "I'm certain he won't go to Hell," she said. "He'll receive the reward of the martyrs."

"If Allah wills it. But it'll be hard to convince people that your father is honored in the Gardens of Delight, once it's revealed that there were drugs in his kitchen," Omar Yussef said. "It'll damage your reputation too."

The girl folded her arms against the cold. "Do you mean even Ala wouldn't have me as a wife now?" she said, with a scornful smile. "Perhaps that will be *his* martyrdom."

"What about Nizar? What was *his* reward?"

Rania turned in the doorway of the Community Association and slapped her pale hand against her breastbone. "*I* was his reward," she sobbed.

She sucked in a breath to steady herself and entered the building. Omar Yussef kicked the snow off his loafers and followed.

Cheap couches fringed the reception room. Each seat was filled by an Arab waiting quietly for one of the counselors. They huddled in their heavy coats, the old men with their Astrakhan hats pulled low, silent and sleepy in the heat. A middle-aged woman turned a hostile glare on Omar Yussef. Her fat chins rubbed against her headscarf with each flexing of her jaw, chewing her gum. *She's already angry and defensive because she expects me to jump the queue,* he thought. *Even in America, where everyone's polite, we Arabs can bring the unfairness of the Middle East with us.*

"Peace be upon you," he said.

The two dozen people around the edge of the room murmured their response: "Upon you, peace."

He hurried across the gaudy floral carpet into the offices behind the reception counter. He found Rania in a small room papered with informational posters about the New York school system, basketball camp, and local businesses that offered satellite dishes with Middle Eastern stations. The desk was spread with pamphlets on health services and kindergartens. Her coat was draped over a filing cabinet, and she sat behind the desk in the same black smock and tight jeans he'd seen her wearing the day before. When she shuffled her mouse on its pad, the screen of her computer prickled into life.

Bitterness seemed to course through her movements and tremble beneath the tight set of her face. Omar Yussef wondered if it was more than the deaths of her father and her lover that ate at her, more than the loneliness of a girl with no family to console her. An unspoken anger underlay her grief, so that Omar Yussef found himself a little scared of her.

She clicked the mouse, and a photo expanded over the screen of the computer. Rania and Nizar were at a table in a restaurant which appeared to be part of a bigger public space. They were laughing for the camera with three smiling waitresses who wore white shirts and black ties. On the table, a short tube shot sparks from the center of a pink cake.

"Nizar made everyone love him, *ustaz*," Rania said. "This picture was taken on my birthday. He asked the waitresses to sing 'Happy Birthday.' He taught them the words in Arabic. They thought it was very funny." She murmured the refrain, "*Sana hilweh, ya jamil. Sana hilweh, ya jamil.*"

Now I know why she wanted to come to her office, Omar Yussef thought, as Rania clicked through more photos of Nizar on the computer. *But I've never heard the birthday song sound so broken-hearted.*

He tried to think of words to comfort her. He recalled the argument he had overheard between Rania and her father when he had returned to the café for his forgotten hat. The usual appeal to trust in Allah might not console a girl who had dreamed of Manhattan, he decided. "I've always had faith, my daughter," he said softly. "Not in Islam, I must admit, but in human qualities. Of course, my faith in love and humanity and intelligence is tested by life in the Middle East. There I see events in which these qualities are entirely lacking. But the times when they go missing only make me believe more strongly that they must exist."

Though Rania's wide eyes moistened, they made no appeal to Omar Yussef. He could read her only as clearly as he might have made out a goldfish at the bottom of a fountain, distorted and out of proportion.

"I had an opportunity," she said. "I seized it. Then it was destroyed. It's gone forever. Knowing that it was real does no good, because the joy was in having it. Thinking of it or dreaming about it only makes its absence harder to bear."

"Are you talking about Nizar?"

She slammed her hand down on the desk. "I'm talking about me." Something sensuous and strong reached out from her gaze. It seemed to Omar Yussef that it touched his cheek and stopped his breath.

"'We created the *houris* and made them virgins, living companions for those on the right side,'" he murmured. He grunted, only then realizing that he had spoken the words of the Koran aloud as he watched Rania's face.

"That's what Nizar used to call me—his *houri*," she said. "But they're supposed to be 'perfect companions,' so I'm no *houri*, and Little Palestine is no Paradise."

"You must allow yourself to mourn without being too hard on yourself."

"I disappointed my father, and Ala too. I even disappointed Nizar. I'm a faithless woman, *ustaz*."

"Faith in human qualities is like faith in Allah—"

"I don't mean faithless in that way."

"Faithless in love? Disappointment is a part of love. You will overcome—"

"I disappointed them." She shook her head, and she hammered her palm onto the desk again. "But I didn't disappoint *myself*. I went to Manhattan, and there I did things that are forbidden. I did them for myself. I didn't want to wait until Paradise to be happy. I loved the things I did that were supposed to be barred to me, and I loved the man I did them with, though he also was forbidden to me. That's what infuriates me. I live here among people who'd condemn me for the only things in my life that've been worthwhile."

Omar Yussef shuddered. He saw in Rania's dark eyes confusion, copulation, prohibited things he had renounced, and things not even known to him because they were so blameworthy. It was as if he found in one of her eyes the restrained life of a conservative Arab girl and in the other the world that pawed at her as she passed along the streets of Brooklyn—the advertisements displaying half-naked bodies, the crude language, and the disrespect. He wondered which eye had the better vision.

He watched her sob, her fingers knitted together before her eyes, her face lowered to the papers on the desk. He recognized the guilt in her then, visible on her pale flesh like a bruise. He knew he had to push her now, before the tears washed away the signs.

"What's the Masjid al-Alamut?" he said.

She shrugged without looking up.

"The Alamut Mosque?" he repeated. "You've never heard of it? Your father didn't pray there?"

Rania blew her nose on a tissue. "He didn't pray, *ustaz*." She dabbed at her eyes. No makeup had run, and Omar Yussef realized that the shining ebony of her long lashes was natural.

"What was Nizar like as a boy, *ustaz*?" Her voice was suddenly clear and free from bitterness, like a child's.

"I thought you said joy was a present happiness, not a future Paradise or a memory of a good time."

She smiled through her tears, and Omar Yussef felt the touch of her gaze against his cheek again.

"Nizar was a bit of an operator, I remember," he said, "but never malicious. He was one of those devilish types who surprises you by how caring he can be."

"Was he religious, as a boy?"

"Not so much." Omar Yussef was unsure if her curiosity was a diversion or a true desire to track the intimate traces of a lost love. "Did your father kill Nizar to protect your good name?"

"You think my father worried so much about my reputation? Just because he lost his temper about me being with a man, when you were at our café?" She shook her head. "He was all talk."

"It's true that drug dealers aren't usually so concerned with the family image."

Rania flinched, and her tears stopped. "My father wasn't a bad man." The girl blew her nose into another tissue. As she tossed it into the wastepaper basket, the end of her nose was briefly red. Omar Yussef watched its pallor return. If someone were to attack her with a knife as they had assaulted her father, this spot on her nose confirmed that she would bleed, perhaps until her veins emptied. He thought she had cried out all her capacity for pain, and with it had gone the healing that scabs over a wound.

"He was in jail in Lebanon, wasn't he?" he said.

She ran her tongue over her lips, pale pink like a fingernail.

"Could his killer have been someone from his past?"

"He was forced into the drug business during the civil war," she said.

"Forced?"

"By Islamic Jihad people. They came to the Bekaa to train with the Iranians, the Revolutionary Guards, and they recruited local people like Dad to do their dirty work. He had no choice. They didn't ask him nicely, if you see what I mean. When the government wanted to jail some drug producers, Islamic Jihad sacrificed my father, because they knew he wasn't one of them."

"What do you mean?"

"He didn't believe in Islamic revolution. He didn't love the Iranian mullahs or want Hizballah to take over Lebanon, and he didn't care at all about the Palestinian cause. He just loved me and my mother."

"Then he was freed in the government amnesty."

"Amnesty." Rania laughed scornfully. "We left Lebanon right away, so that he could forget how he'd been forced to live. We came to the U.S."

"But someone back home would've known he lied on his

U.S. immigration forms about his drug conviction," Omar Yussef said. "If he'd told the truth, the Americans would've never allowed him to become a citizen. They wouldn't even have given him a visa as a tourist. Isn't that right?"

Rania fingered a plastic paperweight in the shape of the Dome of the Rock. The dome was painted in a garish egg-yolk yellow. "Someone from Islamic Jihad found him here. I don't know who it was. My father called him 'the little bastard.' Excuse my language, *ustaz*."

"That's all right. I'm not a fan of the Jihad. This man forced your father to sell drugs here in Brooklyn?"

Rania's chin dropped to her chest.

"Can you forgive him?" Omar Yussef asked.

She was briefly confused. "For selling drugs?" she said.

"This is the day that you'll bury your father. Make your peace with what he did."

"I can forgive him for the drugs, *ustaz*. That was the fault of the son of a whore from Islamic Jihad. But I can't forgive him for letting Nizar work with him."

"Is that why Nizar died? Because of his connection to the drugs?"

Rania shook her head, and tears brought a higher sheen to her black lashes. She waved Omar Yussef out of the room. He shut the door behind him.

Chapter 19

As Omar Yussef went out through the waiting room, the woman chewing her gum looked him up and down with disdain. *Calm yourself, dear lady,* he thought. *This was one queue I'd rather not have jumped.* He stepped outside, fumbling with the zipper of his parka. A boy of about seven years nipped through the glass door as it closed behind him and pulled at the coat.

Omar Yussef came slowly down onto his haunches to face the boy. He smiled. "What is it, clever boy?"

The boy gave a cry and lifted a knife. Reflexively Omar Yussef threw himself against the wall, sliding onto his backside. The boy giggled and waved the knife. It was an elaborate Omani dagger with a curved eight-inch blade.

In his shock, it took Omar Yussef a few seconds even to be angry with the crowing child. "Where's your mother?" he said.

"It's for you, *ustaz*," the boy said.

"What is?"

"The knife." The boy dropped the dagger. Omar Yussef gasped as it landed flat on its side in his lap. The hilt was carved into an hourglass shape from a mottled olive-green length of rhino horn.

"This is also for you." From his pocket, the boy took the dagger's scabbard, embroidered with silver and gold thread. "Isn't it nice?"

The boy's appreciation for a traditional art soothed Omar Yussef. "Very." He took the scabbard and went to sheath the dagger, but he found a paper rolled inside. He pulled it out. Before he could read it, the boy giggled and ran off. Omar Yussef slithered to his feet. The boy was already around the corner and gone.

Omar Yussef unrolled the paper and read: "'If I had wished you dead, this dagger would've been in your soft breast.' Come and see me. Playland, near the Boardwalk, Coney Island, 10 P.M."

He brushed the slush from the back of his coat. The swift pulsing of his heartbeat filled his head. He rustled the paper in his hand and ran through the message once more—he knew what it meant.

Rashid was inviting him to meet.

He crossed the avenue and headed for the police barricade outside the Café al-Quds. He held the knife in his right hand, the scabbard and note in the other.

Your soft breast.

You remembered your lessons, Rashid, he thought. In the twelfth century, the leader of the Assassins had bribed an enemy's servant to deliver a note while his master slept. The man awoke to find the very words Omar Yussef had read nailed to the floor beside his bed with a dagger. Fleetingly, Omar Yussef considered that Ismail might have sent him the message after he had glimpsed him on the street and at the UN. But this was the block of Fifth Avenue where Rashid had lived, and Rashid had always been more interested in the historical Assassins than Ismail had been. It had to be Rashid.

If Rashid was indeed the killer, then meeting him was a terrible risk. *But this message is a signal to me that he wants to talk*, Omar Yussef thought. *If he had wanted me dead. . . .* He fingered the dagger.

"What happened here?" A man in a brown bomber jacket, a Mets cap, and thin, gaudy pants with a burst of flame drawn around the ankles passed Omar Yussef and approached the policeman guarding the barrier around the café.

"Guy got killed," the policeman said.

"Murdered?"

"That's right."

"You catch the terrorist?"

"Say again."

"Catch the terrorist?"

"It's not terrorism, sir."

"It's an Arab café, buddy. You think there's no terrorist link?"

The policeman wandered slowly to the other side of the area enclosed by the blue barrier.

"This is how it starts," the man continued. "They carry out an attack here, and no one cares because, hey, it's only Brooklyn. Next thing you know they'll blow up the Statue of Liberty or the Empire State Building, and then you assholes will have to pay attention."

Omar Yussef reached the barrier. "My dear sir, it's not a terrorist attack. The dead man is an Arab," he said.

"They're killing each other, eh, buddy? Less of them for us to deal with." The man turned a fat face on Omar Yussef. The unshaven flesh around his neck rolled over the upturned collar of his bomber jacket. He glanced down and noticed the dagger in Omar Yussef's grip.

"Shit, man," he said. He held his hands above his head and backed away. "Oh shit, man."

Omar Yussef thrust the dagger into the scabbard and buried it in his pocket.

"Officer, hey officer," the man called.

The policeman turned at the shrill note in his voice. "Will you quit it?" he said. "It's not a terrorist case."

"This guy over here—Jesus, oh Jesus."

Omar Yussef ducked onto the side street. He walked, fast. He could've explained, but he would surely have sounded ridiculous trying to make the policeman understand that a seven-year-old boy had given him the dagger. He was an Arab and, despite himself, he was overcome by images of blindfolded men shuffling with their hands and ankles cuffed under the guard of American soldiers. He searched within himself for some calm, but he found only a hunted, terrified foreigner. He feared that if he tried to take the knife to Hamza, he would be arrested before he could speak to the detective. He looked at his watch. It was almost five in the evening.

In a few hours, he would go to Rashid. Alone.

Chapter 20

W hen the D train came to the end of the line at the Coney Island station, Omar Yussef dropped down the steel steps, crossed the cold concourse beneath the elevated rails, and followed the lights to Surf Avenue. He watched a police cruiser roll slowly by, like a heavy eater drifting back to a buffet, sated and gloomy. The wind volleyed piercing pins of ice off the Atlantic. He gazed up at the bright night sky. A jagged cloud streaked across the full moon, and he thought of the passage Nahid Hantash had quoted from the Koran.

"The hour of Doom is drawing near, and the moon is cleft in two," he murmured.

He looked around at the shuttered amusement arcades and the sad façades of empty hotels. The spindly superstructure of a Ferris wheel was silhouetted above the storefronts like a gigantic machine of torture. *The moon doesn't have to split apart,* he thought, *for it to seem like the world is ending in this place.*

Omar Yussef went along the avenue to a side street beside a rollercoaster. A long sign descending from the tallest part of the ride told him it was the Cyclone. His eyes strained at the rickety mess of wooden struts and whitewashed girders under the tracks, and he rattled the chain on the high corrugated-iron gate. He stared through a chain-link fence across the street at the rides within. Even a coating of snow couldn't dress the dodgems, pirate ships, and shrimp stands in an aura that might defy their wintry cheapness. Every ride came with a laughable name promising an experience beyond its mere mechanics. He saw that the big Ferris wheel was *The Wonder Wheel*, as though it turned by some miracle and rose higher than anyone had ever before soared.

He skirted the fence until it brought him up a wooden ramp to the Boardwalk. The wind cut across his face, and a few seagulls hovered black against the moon. The birds were silent, and Omar Yussef wondered if they slept on the wing. The slate sea rolled beyond the strand with a sound like the strangled respirations of a disturbed sleeper. The shuttered pizza stands on the Boardwalk, painted gaudily with signs for Italian sausage and cold beer, seemed to Omar Yussef to be unsanitary places from which to serve food. As he looked along the wide, solitary promenade, he had an impression less of a place to spend leisure time than of a lonely depressive's recurrent nightmare.

Omar Yussef saw no sign of Playland on the Boardwalk, so he cut back toward the avenue. He gravitated to the green neon lights of a corner restaurant advertising its "famous" hot dogs. Checking his watch, he saw that he was fifteen minutes early for his ten o'clock assignation. Since he had fled the policeman outside the Café al-Quds he had eaten nothing, and he was suddenly aware of his hunger. He wondered how a hot dog tasted.

The restaurant was brightly lit, staffed by people in

identical striped shirts and green hats. At the tables, clutches of people buried pale rolls lengthwise in their mouths. The bread dripped a livid red sauce onto their hands. Through the window, the scattered shows of bonhomie made Omar Yussef feel isolated. Were he to enter the restaurant, he feared the diners would fall silent, recognizing the loneliness he broadcast like a leper with his bell. He experienced a flash of hate, and he understood how it might happen to him—the resentment that made Arab immigrants like Nahid Hantash, seething in his mosque, despise American society. He recalled the token-booth clerk who had cheated him and felt the man's insults lingering, a little clot of stress that could suddenly lodge in his brain and destroy him. The diners disturbed him because they were in a place where they belonged with people they liked, and he was outside the window in the cold, alone, far from home.

He went unsteadily along the sidewalk, crunching through a thin, unshoveled layer of snow as the wind turned its surface to ice. The buildings here seemed permanently abandoned rather than merely shuttered for the season. Before a wide façade with red doors that looked like a disused fire station, he stamped his feet against the cold and decided to enter the restaurant after all, but only to ask where he might find Playland. As he turned, he looked up and noticed the sign above the red doors in freestanding art deco–style lettering: *Playland.*

In the time it took him to read the sign, Omar Yussef sensed the fear that must have lurked within him since he had received the note from the boy with the dagger. It came upon him in a gust of adrenaline that chilled his heart like the wind off the breakers. A man awaited him in this building who had been a nervous, intelligent boy when Omar Yussef had known him in Bethlehem. Now, perhaps, he was a killer. All Omar Yussef's doubts about Rashid's ability to have slaughtered Nizar were erased by the flood of tension he felt. He glanced along the avenue, hoping the patrol car would come to save him.

As he hesitated, one of the red doors swung open and slammed against the wall in the wind. It creaked on its rusty hinges and Omar Yussef's jaw trembled. Inside his coat pocket, he gripped the Omani dagger in a sweating fist and slid slowly toward the door.

From within, a chilly damp escaped fast on the air, like a breath that had been trapped in a corpse long dead. It surrounded Omar Yussef and drew him inside, shivering. The windows at the back of the building were shattered. Their empty mullions split the moonlight into square shafts glimmering in the pools of still, stinking water on the floor and illuminating the cracked plaster on the pillars across the big hall.

Omar Yussef rubbed his mustache. His breath trailed wispily into the cold.

In the darkness, someone whistled the refrain of the old Lebanese song Omar Yussef had heard on the stereo when he first went to the Café al-Quds.

Take me, take me, take me home.

The tune echoed through the silent building. Omar Yussef scanned the strips of moonlight for Rashid.

The whistler trilled the first verse of the song.

The breeze blew at us from where the river split.

The sound seemed to come from the far end of the building. Omar Yussef made for the row of smashed windows there.

"Rashid," he whispered. "Is that you?"

His feet sloshed through a puddle. He cursed low as the freezing water filled his loafers.

The refrain came again, closer this time: *Take me, take me, take me home.* Omar Yussef turned. A foot scraped against the concrete floor. A man in a black cashmere overcoat stepped from behind a pillar. He lifted his head, pushed up the brim of his gray cap, and shook his long hair from his collar.

"Greetings, *ustaz*," he said.

Omar Yussef reached out with the terror and compulsion of somebody who has seen the ghost of a loved one. "Nizar? Is it you, Nizar? You're alive."

He saw a flash of white teeth as Nizar smiled, and the moonlight caught the young man's high cheekbones. Omar Yussef stepped forward, but a sudden gunshot roared from across the empty hall. Nizar's eyes shifted toward the shadows where the shot echoed. He ducked behind the pillar.

Omar Yussef flattened himself against the wall as another shot came. He heard Nizar's feet on the concrete, running, splashing through a puddle. A door opened along the back wall and Nizar went through it. The moonlight flickered as the door swung in the wind.

A great weight seeped into Omar Yussef's limbs. His old body surely couldn't keep up with Nizar or elude whoever had fired the shots. He felt stupid for putting himself in this danger. *Did you think that simply because you were invited to*

Playland, this would be a game? he thought. He clenched his fists and pounded them against his thighs.

He bent low as he made for the exit. His soaking socks squelched and his loafers slipped. Another shot splintered wood from the doorframe. Running footsteps sounded in the building. He went through the door and pulled it shut.

The empty lot in the rear of Playland was a thicket of brown winter scrub. Omar Yussef plunged into the stiff, fawn bushes. Plastic Fanta bottles and bucket-sized Coke cups littered the ground like the seed pods of a virulent weed, hidden by the new snow, tripping him. He cut toward the fence and tumbled into a ditch.

Scrambling to his feet, he went along the depression, slipping on the snow that drifted deeper there. He halted to listen for Nizar's footsteps ahead of him or the gunman's chasing him. He heard only his own wheezing. A shot sounded. The snow kicked up a few yards behind him. He scampered along the ditch and dragged himself up a slope toward a six-foot fence.

It truly was Nizar, he thought. *He's alive. But someone wants him dead.*

He shook the fence until he found a loose section and edged through. His coat caught on the ragged chain-link. He twisted to free himself. Another shot, and he dropped on his hip beyond the fence. Pain burned red-hot in the small of his back, so intense that he was sure he had taken a bullet.

He bellowed as he shambled toward the beach. Rubbing his back, he discovered there was no bullet wound, only a wringing sensation that gripped his spine deep beneath the meager muscles.

If Nizar is alive, whose body did I find in the apartment? he wondered. *Rashid is still missing. Could it have been his?*

Between his irregular, limping footfalls on the concrete, he heard the gunman crashing through the undergrowth parallel to him. Cheap signs covered the fence, painted with fat letters advertising clam bars and knishes, candy apples and shish kebab, screening Omar Yussef from the shooter. He touched an ad for a seafood restaurant with his fingertips and whispered his thanks.

Omar Yussef turned on to the Boardwalk and hobbled past the shutters of a fried-chicken stand. He came to a waist-high wall at a gap between the food booths, and collapsed against it. The wall was painted in blue characters on an orange background: *Shoot the Freak—Paint Ball. Live human targets.* Behind the low wall, there was a drop of ten feet to a derelict lot spread with empty oil drums, dried-out branches, and sections sheared off a car's body. Omar Yussef frowned. This was a game? He imagined a summer's day, the Boardwalk crowded, people eating ice cream and cotton candy, coughing up a dollar to shoot pellets filled with paint at men paid to dodge behind the concrete blocks and packing crates. It seemed to him like something from ancient times of human sacrifice and mortal entertainments.

Footsteps mounted the ramp to the Boardwalk. A man came to the corner of the fried-chicken stand, the moon behind him. He lifted his gun.

It's not a game and I'm not going to be the freak, Omar Yussef thought. He jumped the low wall and fell into the dark lot.

His ankle twisted when he landed. It hurt badly, but he

had to move. He hobbled toward a car hood propped against two oil drums and dropped behind it.

The shooter halted by the wall and was still.

Is he going to come down here? Omar Yussef rubbed his ankle and fought to calm his breathing. He peered through the air ports on the car hood and saw the gunman silhouetted against the moon over the Boardwalk. The man lifted his arm and Omar Yussef ducked.

A shot smacked into a tree trunk a few yards from him. He recoiled, pressed his back against the car hood, and hoped that the oil drums would hide him if the gunman descended to search at close quarters. In his pocket, he ran his fingertips over the scabbard of the Omani dagger. Should the gunman come near enough, would he be able to use it?

Another shot hit a crate of bottles, and a third connected with metal somewhere very close. Omar Yussef figured he might escape if he could reach the shadow of the fried-chicken stand and work along to the rear of the lot. But he wasn't sure he could walk well enough on his twisted ankle. He might end up flat on his back, immobile in the moonlight, an easy target.

He was about to make a break, when flickering red and blue lights illuminated the side wall of the fried-chicken stand and he heard the low hum of a police patrol car's engine.

The muffled voice of a policeman burst from a loud-speaker: "Put down the gun, and put your hands in the air."

There was a crunch of undergrowth and a grunt in front of Omar Yussef. *The gunman has jumped. He's in here with me,* he thought.

The winter undergrowth crackled as the gunman jogged through the lot. The footfalls were slow enough that Omar Yussef knew the man was still looking for him. Then he heard the warning voice of a policeman at the wall. The gunman went into a run.

Omar Yussef wriggled as tightly as he could against the empty oil drum. The gunman ran low and fast through the shadowy edge of the lot. He wore a stocking cap and a quilted black jacket. He went around the back of the fried-chicken stand toward a parking lot filled with yellow school buses.

Peering through the air duct on the hood, Omar Yussef saw one of the policemen disappear along the Boardwalk to try to head off the fleeing gunman. His partner flicked a flashlight across the debris below the *Shoot the Freak* sign.

Omar Yussef rolled out from behind the oil drum and called to the policeman. "Don't shoot. I'm not armed. It's me he was after."

The policeman held a gun in his right hand. Omar Yussef squinted against the light in the man's left. He crawled toward the cop, shielding his eyes from the glare. He kneeled in the snow, put his hands on top of his head, and tasted vomit on the back of his tongue.

Chapter 21

Sergeant Abayat pushed two eight-inch-long boxes toward Omar Yussef on a green plastic tray. "Famous hot dogs in traditional sauce," he said. "Eat them, and you'll really be American."

Though he was ravenous, Omar Yussef restrained himself out of politeness. He reached for one of the hot dogs, lifting it from the box with care, so that the sauerkraut wouldn't fall to the table, and ate. He rarely consumed food that hadn't been prepared by his wife, because he preferred the most traditional and time-consuming Arab recipes. Still, he had to acknowledge that the faint savor of smoked meat from the spongy hot dog and the spiciness of the sauce were pleasing. *Or perhaps I'm even more hungry than I realize,* he thought.

"It's very good, O Hamza." He swallowed a bite. "Many thanks."

"We must thank Allah. To your doubled health, *ustaz.*" The detective checked the luminous blue dial of his watch. "We'll give the technical team another few minutes to scope out the scene, then I'll take you to show me around, to describe what happened."

Omar Yussef wiped his fingers on a paper napkin and took

the Omani dagger from his pocket. He gave it to Hamza with the message that had been hidden within. Hamza slipped the knife out of the scabbard to examine the blade and laid it on the tray. He read the message. "If you had only brought this to me right away, we might have captured the man who tried to shoot you."

"And Nizar."

"I'm a good detective, but even I couldn't trap a phantom."

"I was going to show you the dagger, but I was side-tracked." Omar Yussef finished the hot dog and took a swig of lemonade. "Why don't you believe that I saw Nizar tonight? Are you really so sure of the identification of the headless body?"

Hamza fingered the slip of paper that had come with the dagger. Omar Yussef recognized in his face the kind of stubborn stiffness that came over his pupils when they refused to admit an error in the classroom.

"I saw Nizar right here, down the street from this restaurant," he said. "Then I was chased by a man who tried to kill me. He wanted to kill Nizar, too, I'm sure."

"To kill him again," Hamza said.

Omar Yussef ate the second hot dog, glaring over his glasses at Hamza.

"Those dogs are kosher." The detective's smile was hesitant, as if he wanted to make up to Omar Yussef for his suspicion and hostility. "That's almost as good as *halal*."

"I don't care about our dietary laws. I care about these murders in Little Palestine." Omar Yussef reached into his pocket for the prayer schedule he had taken from the bulletin board in the café. His thumb smeared sauce on the corner as he handed it to Hamza. "I found this in Marwan's place," he said.

Hamza's look was reproachful. "You took it from the crime scene?"

Omar Yussef wiped his mustache with a napkin. "I thought I might need to know what time I should pray."

"Screw your mother, *ustaz*. I bet you haven't prayed since you were a child young enough to believe in *djinns*."

"According to you, I still believe in *djinns*. I saw one tonight."

Hamza cast his eyes across the top of the sheet of paper. "The Alamut Mosque."

"A schedule from the same mosque was on the refrigerator in Ala's apartment, where I found the headless body. Isn't it worth finding out more about this mosque?"

"Do you think I'm an idiot, *ustaz*? I already tried. It doesn't exist. I even asked your son about it during our interview. He said he hadn't heard of it."

"Someone just prints up a prayer schedule for the fun of it? I'm sure these prayer times refer to something else. It must be a code or a signal. Look, once a week the time for the *Maghrib* prayer is wrong by an hour, but always on a different day."

Hamza stood, pocketing the paper. "If we find Nizar's head, we'll ask it the secret of the Alamut Mosque."

"The message that came with the dagger referred to an incident in the history of the Assassins." Omar Yussef rose, wincing at the pain in his ankle. "Allusions such as this are everywhere in this case. 'Alamut' is another one. It was the Castle of the Assassins. I think this mosque—or at least its listing of prayer times—is connected somehow to the murders."

Hamza headed for the door. Omar Yussef noticed the knife still on the green tray. He picked it up and called after Hamza, but the detective was already outside. He slipped it into his pocket and took his tray to the trash can by the exit before he went out.

The full moon lit the empty lot behind Playland a chalky blue. A cloud cut across it, and Omar Yussef remembered the prophecy of the end of time from the Koran. He lifted a finger to the sky. "When the Day of Judgment arrives with the splitting of the moon," he said, "the Mahdi will come as our Messiah, according to the ancient sect of Assassins. He will deliver Allah's judgment on humankind."

"You think he'll come to Brooklyn first?"

"The veil on the corpse in Ala's apartment is a sign that the killer thinks of himself as the Mahdi, because the Veiled Man is the Mahdi's enemy." Omar Yussef's mouth tingled from the spicy sauce on the hot dogs. He ran his tongue over his teeth.

"What's the Mahdi supposed to look like? I seem to remember he'll have gaps in his teeth, right?" the detective said.

Omar Yussef clenched his jaw as the pain in his ankle bit hard. "That's right. It's written that he'll be very handsome, with long hair and a beautiful face—"

"Like Nizar."

"—and he'll die and come back from the dead."

"As you claim Nizar just did?"

"Correct."

Hamza pointed upward. "Well, that cloud just moved away, and the moon is full once more. So your Mahdi is out of luck."

"That depends on how deluded he is." Omar Yussef gave a laugh that came out like a hacking cough. "I caution you, if the world is about to end, it'd be best not to be surprised by it."

"I'm a policeman in New York City. Nothing could surprise me."

"The end of civilization and all humankind?"

"Least of all that."

Hamza led Omar Yussef into the Shoot the Freak gallery. Floodlights at both ends of the area illuminated the oil drums, the branches, the blocks of concrete. Omar Yussef whispered his thanks for the darkness that had made it possible for him to evade the gunman.

A forensics officer in a blue raincoat slouched toward Hamza. He handed two transparent plastic bags to the detective. Inside each was a bronze-colored lump of metal the size and shape of a piece of well-chewed gum.

"One of them was embedded in that dried tree trunk there by the wall," the technician said. "The other one was in the base of the oil drum over by the hood of the Mustang."

The hood of the car, Omar Yussef thought. *He shot that close to me.*

"They're still very slightly malleable, suggesting they were discharged recently. I mean, they certainly haven't been sitting here a month since some bunch of gang-bangers had a shootout. So I'd guess they're from the gun of our perpetrator. Of course, it could just be that someone had a real rough game of paintball, eh, Sergeant?"

Hamza handed the bags back to the technician and swallowed hard. He spoke quietly to Omar Yussef, but didn't look at him. "Where did you say you saw Nizar?"

At the entrance to Playland, Hamza took a flashlight from his pocket. As he pulled the door open, its hinges squealed and echoed through the hall.

"I went in this direction," Omar Yussef said, leading Hamza by the hand across the puddled floor. "This was where I first heard him whistle. When I got to this spot, I saw him."

"And the shots came from behind you?"

"From over there, I think. Near where I entered."

Hamza paced slowly toward the door from which Nizar had made his escape. He peered closely at the shattered doorframe where the third bullet had hit, then went outside.

Without the flashlight, Omar Yussef felt suddenly blind and alone. He struck his shoulder on the crumbling plaster of a pillar. Edging around it, he caught his knee on an old metal garbage can. He cursed and paused. He thought he had heard something move inside the garbage can when he jogged it. He lifted his foot and gave the can a gentle kick. The sound was repeated, a solid, dull connection, not the hollow crackle of trash.

"Hamza, over here," he called.

When the detective directed his flashlight into the garbage can, he recoiled and braced himself against the pillar.

"What is it?" Omar Yussef said.

Hamza puffed out his cheeks and blinked hard.

I thought nothing could surprise a New York City detective, Omar Yussef said to himself. He took the flashlight from Hamza and shone it inside the garbage can. He gasped and turned his eyes away, as though they might somehow erase the few seconds during which they had focused on this awful sight.

In the bottom of the garbage can, staring up with eyes that seemed to register all the hopeless dereliction of the building where it lay, was the head of Omar Yussef's former pupil, Rashid.

Chapter 22

Aman reeled out of an all-night Korean bodega on Fifth Avenue, sliding on a patch of ice with a Miller in his hand. He took a few comically fast paces on the spot, brought himself upright, and rolled his shoulders back under his red mackinaw to restore his dignity. He sucked a long belt of beer and hurled the can back into the store.

"Fuck you, you fucking gook bastard," he yelled.

Omar Yussef halted on the frozen sidewalk a few yards from the man, on the edge of the light cast by the storefront. The loud obscenity in the quiet street shocked him. He checked his watch and saw that it was two in the morning. In his hometown, nobody would be out at this time for fear of Israeli undercover squads. Certainly no one would wander drunk in the night. Those who overindulged in alcohol, as Omar Yussef had once done, closed themselves away with their shame and did their cursing in low voices aimed at themselves.

The Korean storekeeper emerged between the plastic sheets that protected his fruit and vegetables from the freezing weather. He held the open beer can between tense fingers. "You pay for beer," he shouted, "or you fuck off."

The drunk belched and wiped his heavy beard. "No money for you, gook bastard. No tickee, no laundry."

"Fuck you, go away." The Korean went back into his shop. The drunk bent double, breathless, chuckling quietly and repeating his joke.

As Omar Yussef approached the Café al-Quds, he heard the drunk vomit. The Korean came out with a bucket of water to sluice down the plastic sheets on the storefront.

Omar Yussef rang the bell outside the café and waited. He tried to turn his mind from the scene he had just witnessed and the memories it revived of his own ugly, hateful drinking. Murder seemed less distasteful. *Did Nizar leave the severed head in the trash can?* he wondered. *Couldn't it have been the gunman who dropped the head at Playland? Maybe he slaughtered Rashid and now wants to kill Nizar too. Was he the same man I saw at the apartment? The one who's been tailing me?*

A light came on in the staircase behind the kitchen and then another low bulb behind the bar. Rania weaved between the tables and slid back the bolts. When she opened the door, she stared at Omar Yussef with a brittle glimmer in her eyes, but confrontation in her jaw.

"Greetings, my daughter," he said.

She stepped aside. "You're in your own home and with your own family," she murmured.

He limped through the door and unzipped his thick coat.

"It's very late, *ustaz*," she said.

"But you're awake."

"When I sleep, Nizar comes to me and I feel his loss too greatly."

"Do you feel the loss of your father too?"

Rania clasped her fingers in a fist and led Omar Yussef through the kitchen. Her father's blood had been scrubbed from the floor tiles, but Omar Yussef smelled something dark in the air, as though the dead man's final breath lingered. He winced with regret for his critical tone at the door.

He followed her up the narrow stairs into a living room lit only by a single fluorescent strip in the galley kitchen behind the sofa.

She poured ground coffee and water into a small tin pot and set it to boil on a gas burner.

"No sugar," he said, and waited in silence. He savored the cardamom scent of the coffee as she stirred it with a spoon.

Rania brought a tray with his coffee and a glass of water to the low Syrian table in the living room. He ran his fingers over the mother-of-pearl in the tabletop as he waited for the grounds to settle in his cup.

She sat with a straight back on a cheap folding chair and put her hands in her lap. Her eyes were preoccupied and desolate.

Omar Yussef tasted the bitter coffee. "May Allah bless your hands," he said. "It's very good."

"Blessings upon you."

He put the cup on its saucer and returned it to the tray. "Nizar is alive," he said.

Her long lips parted, and her head dropped forward. She adjusted her *mendil* along her hairline and returned her hands to her lap. Omar Yussef saw a little vein pulsing on her neck as though it were trying to creep around the edge of her headscarf.

"He's alive," she said, with a bitter note of triumph. "Where is he?"

"I don't know. He disappeared again."

"If you expected to find him here, he won't come."

"Why not? Surely he'd want to be with you?"

"The police would be waiting."

"Why should he be worried about the police? Is it a crime in New York *not* to have your head chopped off?"

She nibbled at the quick of her thumbnail and watched Omar Yussef so intensely that he felt as though it were him she was biting.

He finished his coffee and wiped his mustache with his handkerchief. "Rania, why did Nizar reveal himself to me? Now that the police know he's alive, they'll suspect him not only of killing Rashid, but also of the murder of your father."

She twitched her head toward Omar Yussef. "That couldn't be."

"Murders around here are usually drug-related, so surely the police will assume that the closest man to your father in the drug trade was also the one who killed him."

Omar Yussef saw a flash of desperation on Rania's face. "That's crazy, *ustaz*," she said. "Where did you see him?"

"At Coney Island."

Rania's eyes were wet. "He took me to Coney Island in the summer. We rode the Wonder Wheel and the Cyclone."

"It's all closed now."

"Only for the winter."

"In Brooklyn, that appears to be a long, hard season." Omar

Yussef gazed around the room. On a cheap wicker bookshelf, he noticed a photo of a woman with a deeply lined face and a wide mouth smiling tiredly between Marwan and Rania. *The departed mother,* he thought. "Nizar faked his death, but he decided to reveal himself after your father died. What was it about the murder of your father that changed Nizar's mind?"

The girl looked as near to death as the woman in the photograph. She shook her head.

"I think that whatever Nizar's doing now, it's somehow because he wants to be with you," Omar Yussef said.

"What makes you say that?" Her voice was a whisper.

"His life in Brooklyn seems to have been full of indecision. He was sure of his religion; then he went wild. He was close to Rashid; then they argued. He drove a taxi and worked honestly; then he dealt drugs to make money. The only thing he didn't doubt was his relationship with you."

Rania seemed to search Omar Yussef's face for sympathy. "You're just like Ala, *ustaz.* Honest and good." She glanced at the quilted coat, splayed open across the sofa behind him, and the NYPD stocking cap on his head. "Although he dresses rather better than you do."

Omar Yussef pulled off the cap.

"I see that you have his sensitivity too," she said.

The seductiveness had returned to her dark eyes. *The eyes of the houri,* Omar Yussef thought, as he pushed his hair, rumpled by the cap, into place.

"Ala was too Palestinian for me," she said. "He was unwilling to venture out of our culture. He wouldn't enter into American life as Nizar did. No matter how often I said I wanted to break out, Ala thought he knew what was good for me. He's a typical Arab man."

"You think I'm like that too?" Omar Yussef lifted his chin.

"Of course you are. No matter how liberal your ideas may be, *ustaz*, I can smell the Middle East all over you."

"You're mistaken. You assume I'm a Middle Eastern man like your father."

"My father wasn't like that at all. He hated the Middle East. He wanted to leave it behind, but it followed him here and dragged him down. You, *ustaz*, can't wait to leave this city and get back home, can you? Admit it. You want to return to your little town where everyone knows you and respects you."

Omar Yussef covered his mouth with his hand. He liked to think of himself as a cosmopolitan, educated man, but each day in New York made him long for his family, for the traditions and routines of Bethlehem. The girl had judged him correctly.

"But *you* cover your head like a Muslim believer," Omar Yussef said.

"You see, you can't imagine that a woman might retain some of our traditions and reject others. You assume that if I bend the rules a little bit, I'll soon be a whore. You think it's easy to wear this headscarf in Brooklyn? Once I leave these couple of blocks in Little Palestine, people laugh and curse at me. 'Look at the ninja,' they shout. But *I* decide who I am. I follow our traditions of dress and modesty, but I don't want to live as though this was the Bekaa instead of Brooklyn."

"I understand."

"You didn't understand my father, and you don't understand me." Her voice quivered with the force of so much emotion finally uncovered. She spoke with the pace of one who mustn't cease talking for fear that her words would be stopped by sobbing. "You're a refugee. Everyone in the Arab world at least pays lip service to your human rights and says they respect your cause. My father and I had to flee Lebanon, but no one calls us refugees and no one respects us. We had to slink away from Lebanon like criminals." Rania reached out a finger toward the photo on the wicker shelf. "My mother died while my father was in prison. He was convinced no decent man would marry me, because he had been jailed for the shameful act of dealing narcotics, which is against the laws of Islam. We left my mother's grave behind and came to America. My father thought we could start again. He opened a new business and tried to find me a suitable husband."

"May Allah have mercy upon your mother," Omar Yussef murmured.

"May you have a long life." Rania picked at the hem of her black smock. "Maybe hatred and violence are just part of being an Arab. Maybe you can't escape them. Maybe the mistake is to try. Anyway, they've got me."

"You're still young, my daughter. Don't give up hope for a better life."

"I deluded myself, visiting the Broadway theaters with Nizar, going to movies, to expensive Italian restaurants. All the time, the Middle East was in me like the cancer that killed my mother." Rania rubbed a tear from her eye and stared at the moisture on the back of her hand. "I dreamed that Nizar had returned. But he came to you, not to me." She spoke petulantly, like a thwarted child. Her shoulders dropped, as though the anger had seeped out of her and left only an inanimate sadness. "For me, it will be as though that body in his apartment really was Nizar's corpse."

"I can't believe that you'd rather think of him as a corpse than a living man," Omar Yussef said. "You told me you wanted to experience happiness now, not in the hereafter."

"His memory will always be with me."

"Do you believe he killed his friend?"

"That wouldn't make him the worst man I ever met. I'm from Lebanon."

Omar Yussef left her in the glow of the kitchen light. He went through the café and pulled the door shut behind him. He took a few painful steps on his swollen ankle, pushed through the entrance next to the boutique, and mounted the stairs to Ala's apartment. The handwritten sign with the words *The Castle of the Assassins* written across it had been removed, but the tape that had affixed it to the door remained, like the frame of a painting cut away by thieves.

His son's face was gray and tired when he opened the door. He barely spoke as he showed Omar Yussef to the single bed. The door to the next room, where the corpse had lain, was closed. Omar Yussef wondered if the police had finished their work in there.

"My son," he said, "I saw Nizar tonight. He's alive."

Ala sat on the edge of the bed. He rubbed his palm against the cheap blanket and tried to speak, but he managed only a stuttering gasp.

"I saw him at Coney Island."

"Saw him?" Ala croaked.

Omar Yussef turned away from his boy. "I also saw Rashid's head. It was *his* body we found in this apartment, not Nizar's. I'm sorry to be so blunt, my son."

Omar Yussef heard his son whisper the name of his dead roommate. The sound seemed like a cold wave in the air, chilling Omar Yussef's throat and lungs, and he wondered if that was the way a final breath might feel.

Ala stared at his father, as though it were he, not Nizar, who had come back from the dead. "I don't understand," he said.

"Go and rest. We'll talk about it in the morning."

The boy shuffled out of the bedroom and flopped onto the couch.

After Omar Yussef had turned out the light, he heard the sibilant whimpers of his son in the other room, shivering through a nightmare.

Chapter 23

In the dull dawn, Ala's hand dangled off the sofa and a trace of saliva glistened on his jaw. Omar Yussef lifted the boy's wrist, laid it on his chest, and went to the kitchen. The coffeepot was wedged beneath a tangle of dirty dishes and pans. He grappled with it, but the crockery shifted noisily as he brought the pot out of the sink.

Ala sat up on the couch and rubbed his face. "Let me do that, Dad," he mumbled. He took the coffeepot from his father and rinsed it.

Omar Yussef leaned against the windowsill. He watched the rain erase the snow on the sidewalk and thought about the man who had returned from the dead the night before.

Ala measured ground coffee into the battered pot and ran some water. He put it on the heat. The smell of burning gas was comforting and homely.

"I dreamed about severed heads," Ala said. "Not just Nizar's or Rashid's. Everyone's head, cut off."

The coffeepot ticked gently against the stovetop as Ala swirled the thick liquid. "The meaning of the severed head, the Veiled Man—it's so strange and mystical," he said, his voice raw and dry. He smiled at his father with a twitchy concentration that made Omar Yussef worry for his sanity. "Somehow it's most appropriate for death to come that way."

"What do you mean?"

"Death is spiritual. But murder is usually so ordinary. It should take something more mystical than a bullet to kill a man. We're created through a miracle, formed in the image of Allah from the clot of blood that he used to make human-kind, according to the holy Koran. Then the end comes—a plain little chunk of lead, red hot, flying through the air, shattering your body, breaking your skin and bone, all in a second."

"What's more mystical than a piece of metal that can fly?" Omar Yussef rasped out a grating laugh. "It's no wonder reli-gious extremists love bullets so much. They're Allah's great-est miracle."

Ala took a small cup from the cupboard, wiped it with his forefinger, and poured Omar Yussef's coffee. He added a long stream of sugar to the coffee that was left in the pot and heated it some more.

Omar Yussef left his cup in the kitchen and went to the bedroom. He lifted his coat from the bed, took the package Maryam had given him from the pocket, and brought it to his son. "I've been carrying this around. It's time you had it," he said. "Your mother spoils you."

Ala held the gift as though it were his mother's hand, his eyes tearing up and his lips quivering.

"Open it, quickly," Omar Yussef said.

Inside, Ala found the Mont Blanc pen in its plush black box. "It's marvelous," he said. "It's like the one you have, Dad."

"Now you can write proper letters to your mother, instead of sending her e-mails through Nadia."

Heavy footsteps came up the stairs. The pen held Ala's attention, but Omar Yussef turned toward the door as the bell rang. At the entrance, he noticed a brown smudge on the matchstick model of the Dome of the Rock. He remembered that it was blood from the corpse in the bedroom and that he had smeared it there as he tried to repair the model. His hand shook as he opened the door to find Sergeant Abayat shaking the rain off his parka.

"Greetings, *ustaz*. Morning of joy."

"Morning of light, O Hamza," Omar Yussef said gloomily. The detective brought murder firmly back into the room, and Omar Yussef knew that Ala's comforting thoughts of his mother would be crowded out. "Come in."

Hamza lowered himself onto the couch and slapped his thighs. "I've just been in the gym doing squats. My quads are dead."

Ala stepped out of the kitchen, the pen balanced like an offering on his fingertips.

"Are you going to write a confession for me?" Hamza asked.

Ala shoved the pen into his pocket.

"It's you who must confess, Hamza," Omar Yussef said. "You failed to identify the body I found in this apartment as Rashid's. Even though it had no head, surely you could've checked the fingerprints."

Hamza let his shoulders slump. "It was a mistake. We should've matched his prints against his visa application, but we would've had to call in the INS. Those guys treat anything involving an Arab like a big terror scare, and to tell you the truth, they aren't respectful to me, because I'm a local cop."

"Your performance is about what I'd expect from an Arab detective," Ala said. Omar Yussef saw the dangerous intensity on his son's face and gestured toward him with a calming motion of his hand.

"I thought you said I was no longer an Arab. Infidels can mess up, too, I suppose." Hamza looked hard at Ala. "The identification was a mistake, and it cost us a couple of days. But now Nizar appears to want to make himself known to us anyway."

"You think Nizar will come here?" Omar Yussef asked.

"Remember what you said yesterday—your boy's the bait. Any kid fishing for sprats off a jetty in Gaza could tell you it's no good baiting your hook if you're not going to keep your hands on the rod."

"Does that mean you have this apartment under surveillance?"

The policeman rolled the big muscles in his back. "Did Nizar sound friendly when he spoke to you at Coney Island? Or do you think he was intending to kill you?"

Omar Yussef remembered the fear that had been upon him like the cold air inside Playland. Beneath his initial shock at seeing Nizar, he realized that he had been comforted by the presence of his old pupil in the empty amusement arcade. "I'm quite certain Nizar wanted to talk. He gave me a friendly greeting before the shooting started. I'm sure he wouldn't have harmed me."

"You think so? Rashid was his best friend, and that proved to be no protection. Maybe you'll hear from him again. You or Ala—the Old Man of the Mountain and the third Assassin."

Omar Yussef ignored the detective's mocking smile. The mention of the childhood gang drew his thoughts to the fourth Assassin. Had Ismail followed him to Coney Island? Though he was confused by the boy's behavior, Omar Yussef couldn't believe that Ismail would have fired the shots at Playland. He narrowed his focus to the one member of The Assassins he was sure he had seen alive there. "If Nizar appears again, I'm convinced he'll try to contact Rania."

Hamza pursed his lips. "Why? To ask forgiveness, perhaps? You see, I think we'll discover that Nizar killed Rania's father, as well as Rashid."

"Over drugs?"

Hamza scratched his groin. "No better reason for murdering someone—apart from being married to them."

"You're a real romantic."

"I've already given my wife her Valentine's Day present this morning, so I'm free to say what I really feel about love."

Ala brought a coffee cup to Hamza.

"May Allah bless your hands," the detective said.

"Blessings." Ala choked on the word. He stepped into the kitchen and stared into the coffeepot, all his rage seeming to collapse into hopelessness. Omar Yussef watched him with pity as he listened to the heavy breath through Hamza's mouth. Ala wiped the back of his hand across his eyes. He poured the thick coffee dregs into the sink.

After Hamza left, Omar Yussef stayed all day with Ala.

The tears he had seen the boy shed in the kitchen convinced him that his son was in shock. He also considered that Hamza could be right—if he waited here, Nizar might come to him. He found a backgammon board in the bedroom and forced Ala to play until the boy had won many games in a row and Omar Yussef, in spite of himself, became annoyed at losing.

"Sorry, Dad," Ala said. "I haven't had much to do lately, so I've become very good at *sheysh-beysh*." He went into the kitchen.

Omar Yussef watched him soaping the plates in the sink. "Did the police finish in the bedroom?"

His son scrubbed hard at the smears of *hummus* and fava bean *foule* that had dried on the plates. "I guess so. They took away the body and left the room in a mess."

Omar Yussef was shocked. "So, inside that room—"

"You'd better be glad it's not summer, or we'd have a lot of flies, Dad."

Omar Yussef gasped at his son's callousness. "How're you going to live in this apartment with your friend's blood all over the bedroom?"

Ala reached into a dirty coffee cup and rubbed hard at the grounds. "I'm not staying. I'm going home to Bethlehem, Dad. The woman I loved betrayed me. My friends are dead or destined for jail. New York is too harsh for me. I'm going back to the Middle East." He snorted a bitter laugh. "At least with the Israeli occupation, you know where you stand."

Omar Yussef eased his son aside and knelt to open the cupboard beneath the sink. He pulled out a bucket, a pair of rubber gloves, and a bottle of floor cleaner. In the bathroom he filled the bucket with warm water and hauled it to the bedroom.

He pushed the door open and held his breath against the humid, coppery stink in the room. Lunging for the window, he shoved the frame until the old wood squeaked a few inches away from the sill, admitting clean, chilly air. The blood on the cold floor hadn't decomposed yet, and Omar Yussef was glad he didn't have to smell that. He remembered the places in Bethlehem where people had been killed in a gunfight or smashed by a tank shell and their blood had remained plastered on the wall or pooled black and sticky in a corner. Even outdoors, the sharp fermented scent of rotten blood was repulsive. In this room, it would have been unbearable.

He went onto his knees and scrubbed hard at the blood— in part to keep himself warm, as the cold air swept through the gap he had forced in the window.

Omar Yussef wrung the cloth. Rashid's blood spattered into the bucket. In Bethlehem, his nightmares were racked by violent death, stalking his pupils as they walked home from class down streets where the Martyrs Brigades and the Israeli army met. *Even in those distressing dreams, I never imagined that it would be one of my little Assassins who'd become a victim*, he thought.

He sat on the second bed and stared at the empty space across the room where the corpse had lain. So many difficult nights Nizar must have passed there, unable to sleep, wrestling with his religious beliefs and his desire for Rania.

Peeling off the rubber gloves, Omar Yussef ran his finger

along the bookshelf at the foot of the bed. He pulled out the Koran, bound in imitation brown leather, and let it fall open. The spine dropped and the pages settled at the thirtieth sura, *al-Rum*. Omar Yussef read two sentences that had been underscored with a fingernail on the delicate paper: "He created for you spouses from among yourselves, that you might live in peace with them, and planted love and kindness in your hearts. Surely there are signs in this for thinking men." He closed the book.

When he left the bedroom, the sudden warmth of the living room made him dizzy. He put his hand to his eyes, and the Koran slipped to the floor. The pages fluttered open to the same verse. Ala came out of the kitchen as Omar Yussef bent to retrieve the book.

"Isn't that Nizar's Koran?" Ala asked.

"Do you think I carry a copy around in my back pocket? Of course it's Nizar's." Omar Yussef laughed with a rough choking sound. "He seems to have a penchant for *al-Rum*."

Ala smiled wistfully. Omar Yussef was relieved that his son could still visit at least the furthest edges of pleasure. "That's his favorite verse," the boy said. "He liked the lines about spouses for us to live in peace with."

"Rania?"

Ala's smile took on a brittle edge. "When he was religious, Nizar used to talk about achieving martyrdom. He seemed to think he'd be able to have endless sex with the *houris* in Paradise if he was killed fighting for Islam."

"Come on, that's how village boys think. Nizar was too clever for that."

"I think he was trying to convince himself of something—of the rightness of religion, perhaps—so he boiled it down to that simplistic concept."

"Did he change those views when he stopped praying?"

"When he met Rania. They fell in love, Dad. That's why he liked that verse so much."

The sheikhs cite that passage as evidence the houris *aren't heavenly beauties at all. They're our earthly wives, polished up by Allah in Paradise*, Omar Yussef thought. *Which would've made it even more important for Nizar to have Rania now.*

"He stopped talking about martyrdom then too," Ala said. "He didn't need the seventy-two virgins up in Paradise. All he wanted was the girl next door on Fifth Avenue."

"And you, my son? What reward do you expect to receive here or in Paradise?"

"I want to taste Mamma's hummus and see my nephews and nieces," Ala said. "I'm not speculating about Paradise, but I know it's not here in Brooklyn."

Chapter 24

As Omar Yussef stood by the window, the pallid twilight put him in mind of the charcoal skin of a heavy smoker. He wondered if that was why the sky lacked breath to shift the flat clouds. Ala snored on the sofa, overcome by his sleepless nights in the cell at the Detention Facility. His asthma gave each exhalation a coda of wheezing high notes like the cries of a frightened dog.

Omar Yussef blinked as the streetlamps flickered into a purple glow. A bell rattled on the door of a shop below, and he glanced down. A woman hunted in her handbag for her keys, a placard resting against her leg. She wore a black head-scarf edged around with gold. As she locked the café, Rania looked up. Omar Yussef stepped behind the curtain. He noticed that she was smiling.

End the criminal Israeli siege of Gaza, her placard read. Omar Yussef was surprised that she cared enough about politics to be on her way to a demonstration. He had thought she detested the Middle East. With the placard under her arm, she cut left onto Bay Ridge Avenue. *She's going to the subway*, he thought. At the corner, a red ribbon, pinned at head height, stood out bright against the trunk of a bare gray tree. Omar Yussef stared at the tight bow. *Hamza said it was Valentine's Day today*, he recalled. *Is Rania on her way to a pro-Palestinian demonstration, or is she meeting her lover?*

He limped down the stairs on his aching ankle, struggling into his coat. He turned the corner, heading toward the subway station, and hurried to catch up with Rania. Under the antiseptic light of the Manhattan-bound platform, he pulled his stocking cap low over his brow and affected the slouching, fatigued immobility of the other passengers. On the R train, he ran the zipper on the front of his coat up past his mustache and pretended to doze in his seat. Rania sat a few places over from him, the printed side of the placard pressed to her legs, as though she were embarrassed by its slogan. A lock of black hair fell from under her headscarf and lay across her brow. She rolled it around her forefinger and half-smiled. She was the only person on the train who didn't appear to be at least partially asleep.

Rania left the train at Pacific Street. Omar Yussef hobbled behind her through the underground passages toward the Atlantic Avenue station. He caught up with her just as she stepped aboard a 4 train. He was perspiring in his coat, but he wasn't the only one in the crowded subway bundled as though he were still out in the cold, so he kept his hood up. Rania paid him no attention.

They left the 4 train at Grand Central. Rania went through the early evening commuters to a side exit onto Lexington Avenue. She rushed to the corner of 42nd Street and ducked under a blue police sawhorse to join a group of two dozen people waving placards similar to hers. Omar Yussef was disappointed—perhaps she simply intended to join the protest.

A few of the demonstrators wore red-and-white *keffiyas* around their necks or on their heads. About half of them seemed to Omar Yussef to be Arabs. A couple of converts to Islam wore white skullcaps low on their brows. The rest were white men and women with hair shaved short, the raddled sallow skin of extreme vegetarians, and eyes gleaming with outrage. A press photographer knelt to get a low shot of the demonstrators, and a television reporter in a tan trench coat bellowed into his microphone.

Rania went quickly to the center of the demonstration, brandishing her placard and crying her willingness to sacrifice for Palestine. The photographer snapped her repeatedly, because she was the most vociferous of the women wearing a picturesque headscarf. The television man raised his voice to be heard above the insults Rania brought down on Israel. He clearly enjoyed being in the midst of the mayhem, like a grandfather joining in when the children bawl and scream.

Within minutes, the television crew was packing up. The reporter shoved his hands into the pockets of his trench coat with a shiver. The photographer clicked through his images to check that he had one good enough to transmit on the wire. Rania handed her placard to the man beside her and edged back through the crowd of demonstrators. Omar Yussef strained to see where she had gone. With the journalists no longer attentive to them, the demonstrators turned their slogans on the commuters, who avoided the protest with the same harsh disapproval Omar Yussef had noticed on the faces of subway passengers when a beggar entered their car. It was as though a mere whiff of something bad might let in the full stink of the city. He felt sorry for the demonstrators, so animated and passionate, and so ignored. The commuters were the only people he had ever seen who looked as unhappy as the refugees sweating in the Palestinian camps back home.

A woman wearing the same black coat as Rania came around from the back of the crowd, shaking her long hair free of her collar. She turned her face from the demonstration like any other commuter. Her skin was pale against the shining blackness of her hair, and her eyes were big and full of anticipation. Rania had taken off her headscarf. Omar Yussef was surprised to discover that this breach of Muslim propriety shocked him, even though his own wife wore her hair uncovered. As he wove through the crowd behind her, she checked her reflection in the window of the Grand Hyatt Hotel, squeezing and lifting her hair with both hands to give it body, and he smiled because he knew that his suspicion about Valentine's Day had been correct.

He followed her through the swinging wooden doors into the main station concourse and almost lost her when he gazed up at the famous ceiling. He traced the looping gold lines linking the stars across the concave emerald roof and saw that, indeed, they were misplaced, as he had once read, because the Frenchman who painted them had made a mistake and set them out backward. Hurrying to catch up, he reached the foot of the steps to the mezzanine restaurant just as Rania skipped to the top.

When he had climbed to the hostess's lecturn, he was breathing heavily. The restaurant was open to the elaborate ceiling of the concourse and to the drifting shafts of orange light through the tall windows. Omar Yussef recalled the photo on Rania's computer and her sad rendition of the birthday tune, as he watched the girl arrive at her table. A man stood, jumped into a few laughing steps of *dabka*, and hugged her, stroking her hair with his hand.

It was a long embrace, as the hostess waited with a frozen smile to leave their menus, and it was still unfinished when Omar Yussef pulled an extra chair up to their table and dropped into it.

"Happy Valentine's Day." Omar Yussef extended a finger toward the hostess and said, "Nizar, don't you want to hear the specials?"

They broke their clinch. Nizar came to Omar Yussef and gave him five kisses on his cheeks. He was as cheerful as an emir watching his hawk bring down its prey in the desert. "*Ustaz*, I'll have the crab cakes. In fact, we'll all have them. I know the menu very well. Rania and I eat here whenever we're in Manhattan. We like to look down on the entrances to the platforms and imagine we're going on a journey."

"To where?"

"Who cares? Poughkeepsie, New Canaan, Wassaic." Nizar read off the names from the Departures board in the concourse. "They all sound a little exotic to my foreign ear, even if they're really just boring commuter towns. One place you don't see up on that list is Bay Ridge, Brooklyn. I'm never going back there." He poured a glass of ice water for Omar

Yussef. "Drink it, *ustaz*. You look like you got a little over-heated keeping up with my darling Rania."

"Welcome, *ustaz*," the girl said. She seemed not to share Nizar's pleasure at Omar Yussef's intrusion upon their romantic dinner.

"She set a good pace." Omar Yussef swigged from the glass. "She was obviously eager to reach you, and my ankle hurts from our last meeting at Coney Island."

Nizar showed the gap between his front teeth.

"Who fired at us in Playland?" Omar Yussef asked.

Nizar stroked Rania's hand against his prominent cheek-bones and giggled. "Coney Island is a dangerous place at night, *ustaz*. But I supplied you with an Omani dagger for self-defense. If someone gave you trouble, you could've carved them up." He made two swift motions of the wrist like a swordsman pressing home a coup. "You had no reason to be scared."

"Neither did you. You're immortal. You're the Mahdi, after all."

"You liked that stuff? The Veiled Man? The dagger that could've been planted 'in your soft breast'? I knew you'd appreciate it. But don't worry—I'm not insane enough to think I'm actually the Mahdi, even if I do have the looks for it."

Rania reached out and touched her fingertip to the boy's front teeth with a playful smile. "Your appearance is just as it was written in the prophecies."

He bit down on her finger and snarled, but when he let go he swallowed hard, as though he had tasted a bitterness on her hand. *There's something between them that they're pretending isn't there, for the sake of their celebratory dinner*, Omar Yussef thought. *Is it murder?*

Omar Yussef put his palms flat on the glass table and glared at the liver spots, the wrinkled knuckles, the long black hairs on his fingers. He had loved these four boys, his Assassins. His innocence had been tarnished long ago, but he felt its final traces obliterated by the words he had to speak: "You killed Rashid."

"I had to do it." Nizar stopped while the waitress uncorked a half-bottle of champagne and poured two flutes. Omar Yussef put his hand over the top of his own glass and shook his head.

"To you, my life, my heart, my love," Nizar said to Rania, and they drank. "I had to get rid of Rashid, *ustaz*. He was an assassin. Not the kind of Assassin we pretended to be in your classroom, but a real one." He cut his hand through the air once more as though handling an épée.

"This is very romantic talk for Valentine's Day." Omar Yussef sneered at the champagne in its ice bucket. "How do you know he was an assassin?"

Nizar mugged like a guilty schoolboy.

The Israeli jail, Omar Yussef thought. *As Ala suspected, they joined Islamic Jihad.* "You were recruited in prison," he said. "You came here to kill someone?"

"Rashid was supposed to do the killing. Despite his nervous nature, he showed himself to be a determined little fellow in training. That's why they picked him. I was ordered to provide him with backup."

"Why did you murder him?"

Nizar drained his champagne and watched Rania fill his glass. "I lost interest in sacrificing myself. I found my dark-eyed *houri* right here." He touched her hand.

"Allah is most great," she murmured, with a sardonic smile.

He slapped her hand playfully and clicked his tongue. "The streets of Brooklyn at first disgusted me with their commercialism and immorality. But then I walked the same avenues with Rania. She sprinkled the streets with magic. I couldn't hate the place any longer, because some part of it was hers, and she was all beauty."

Omar Yussef said, "Rashid didn't like that, I suppose?"

"It displeased him quite spectacularly."

"You could simply have taken one of these trains. Gone away with Rania and disappeared in America."

"And sent my letter of resignation to the men who recruited me? *Ustaz*, they would kill my brothers and make my mother's life hell back in Bethlehem if I sabotaged their operation. I had to make them believe I was dead."

"So you murdered Rashid, dressed him in your clothes, and left your identity cards on him."

"Rashid threatened me, my family, and Rania." Nizar watched the bubbles streaming to the surface of his glass. "I realized it wasn't the Americans or the Israelis I hated; it was us, the Arabs. I despised the mess we've made of our struggle, the way we fight each other. My father died at the hands of another Palestinian. After a lifetime of struggle for our freedom, it wasn't the enemy, the Israelis, who killed him. He was murdered by one of his comrades."

"Killing your friend doesn't exactly stop that cycle."

"Hear me out, *ustaz*," Nizar said. "I can't blame the Israelis for wanting Palestine. It's a beautiful land. Neither can I fault the Americans for living like pigs—what else would you expect from infidels? But we Palestinians are destroying ourselves, and it makes me sick. So I abandoned our cause."

"Very fine reasons. But you decapitated your friend and carried off his head. Now you're sitting here for a Valentine's Day celebration?" Omar Yussef said. "Are you mad?"

"I was prepared to do anything to be free of Islamic Jihad. I wanted them to think *Rashid* was psychotic—too crazy to carry out his mission. That way, they'd call everything off, and I'd be in the clear."

Omar Yussef thought bitterly of the civil war among the Palestinians at the end of the intifada. In Bethlehem, people had tortured each other, because they belonged to one faction or another—people who had grown up together in the same village or refugee camp. *Our politics is so extreme*, he thought, *it drives us to do disgusting things that are against our true nature. Nizar was following our political traditions.*

"After you slaughtered Rashid, why didn't you stay under-cover?" he asked.

Nizar touched the end of his finger to the condensation on his champagne flute. "Slaughtered him? It gave me no pleasure. It made me—" He closed his eyes.

Omar Yussef continued: "Why did you reveal yourself to me at Coney Island?"

A waiter swung his hips between the tables to bring the crab cakes. Omar Yussef watched Nizar gather himself, take

211

a bite, and wipe his mouth with his napkin. He was chewing as he replied: "I killed Rania's father."

The girl bowed her head, pushing a crab cake across her plate with her fork.

Omar Yussef let out a small wheeze of shock. "Because of the drug business?" he said.

"The drug proceeds were intended to finance the assassination. An operation like that costs money, whether it's for equipment or bribing people to give you access to secure locations. When I got rid of Rashid, I had to tidy up that last loose end."

"I still don't see why you came back from the dead."

"I feared the police would suspect Rania of killing her father. He often beat her. I thought they might accuse her of murdering him to prevent further abuse."

Rania covered her face with her hands.

"I didn't want to give myself up to the police, but I thought that if I confessed to you about Marwan's murder, you'd tell the cops and they might leave Rania alone," Nizar said.

"Don't believe him, *ustaz*," Rania said. "I don't know why he'd tell you this, but it isn't true."

You just don't want it to be true, Omar Yussef thought. *I'm starting to think I'd believe this boy capable of any horror.*

Nizar's lips stretched in a tight grin. "It's true, all the same. I intended to tell you at Coney Island."

"That was the flaw in your plan—that the police might suspect Rania. Why didn't you think of that before you killed her father?"

"I made a mistake. Like I said, I was only pretending to be the Mahdi. I'm not really divine."

"Now Islamic Jihad will be on your trail again."

"It was me or Rania. I had to sacrifice myself for her sake." Nizar pulled at a shred of crab between his front teeth. "I only wanted to talk to you, *ustaz*. I didn't expect the gunfire. I really don't know who shot at us."

"Maybe it was the true Mahdi?" Omar Yussef sneered.

Nizar extracted the crab and rubbed it into his napkin.

"The Prophet Muhammad came to bestow mercy," Omar Yussef said, "but the Mahdi is a bringer of vengeance."

"You think the shooting at Coney Island was supposed to be vengeance for killing Rashid?" Nizar's eyes became disturbed and small. "Forget about the Mahdi stuff. It was just my joke."

"Who was Rashid intending to assassinate?"

"Our president." Nizar announced the title with jocular pomposity, like the identity of a lottery winner. "Rashid intended to kill him this week when he speaks at your UN conference. Islamic Jihad wants him dead because he's been arresting our boys back in Palestine. The secret police SWAT teams making the arrests were trained by the CIA. Killing him in the U.S. was supposed to deliver a message to Washington to keep out of Palestinian affairs."

Omar Yussef sipped his water and grimaced as it chilled his gums.

"I knew that if Rashid went ahead with the hit, it'd bring down the full force of the police and the Feds right on my head," Nizar said. "I'd either go to jail for life or be on the run forever. I'd never be with Rania."

"May Allah forbid it," Rania said.

Nizar's good humor dissolved into morose despair. He emptied his glass and brought it down fast, chipping the stem against his plate. "Nothing's more important to me than her. Nothing."

Rania took Nizar's hand. His long fingers quivered with adrenaline as she kissed them.

"My boy, you have to give yourself up," Omar Yussef said.

Nizar squeezed Rania's fingers and shook his head.

"Whatever one might say about your methods, you prevented the assassination of the Palestinian president," Omar Yussef said. "Perhaps you can give the police other leads, too, about the drug ring. About Islamic Jihad's activities in America. If you help them, they might forget what you've done. What's more important to them—two dead Arabs in Brooklyn, or an entire terrorist network?"

Nizar crooked his lip sarcastically. "They'll give me a new identity with a season ticket to commute from this station to my beautiful wife and delightful American family in Pleasantville?"

"Where? Stop kidding me. This is serious."

"It's a real place. Can you believe it?" Nizar jerked his chin toward the Departures board. "It's on the Harlem Line."

"At the very least let me talk to Abu Adel. Maybe he can secure you a deal."

"Who?" Nizar's face became stony.

"Brigadier Khamis Zeydan. He's the president's security adviser in the consultations with the Americans and at the UN."

Nizar stared distantly into his champagne.

"He's a friend of mine. If you tell him everything, I'm sure he'd be willing to help do a deal with the Americans so that you wouldn't be prosecuted for what you've done."

"A deal?" Nizar glanced at Rania.

"We can go to my hotel now and I'll get in touch with him," Omar Yussef said.

Nizar tapped his thumbnail against the edge of his plate. It sounded loud until Omar Yussef realized he was hearing the bell of a departing train beyond the main concourse. Nizar held Rania's eyes in his somber gaze. "Where's your hotel, *ustaz*?" he said. "Let's see about that ticket to Pleasantville."

Chapter 25

Nizar lit one of Khamis Zeydan's cigarettes and exhaled toward the open window of the hotel room, while Omar Yussef shivered. The police chief watched the young man with the hard confidence of an experienced interrogator. Nizar took that stare, rolled it around in the black depths of his eyes, and let it drift back toward Khamis Zeydan like the smoke on his breath. Omar Yussef wondered if it was only the freezing air that made him shudder.

He shoved the window until it was almost closed. "This room is getting as cold as your blood," he said.

The two men shifted their jaws slowly and kept their stares firm.

"I don't believe a word of this," Khamis Zeydan whispered.

Nizar blew smoke out of his nostrils.

"It's three in the morning," Omar Yussef said. "He's explained his story to you three, no, four times already."

"The president's speech is tomorrow at nine A.M. That gives us thirty hours." Khamis Zeydan rolled his thumb slowly across the wheel of his lighter, watching it spark. "Plenty of time to confirm the truth before I have to panic."

"I brought Nizar here so you could help him get

immunity." Omar Yussef slapped his thigh. "You've heard his story. You know he killed Rashid to prevent the assassination of the president. We have to talk to Sergeant Abayat to get Police Department protection for Nizar."

"You mean Islamic Jihad will be sitting around now thinking, 'Well, Nizar's end of things was a bust. Let's just forget about assassinating the president.'" Khamis Zeydan opened his eyes wide like a simpleton. "No, I want to hear the backup plan."

"How could Nizar know? He's not the assassin. The assassin is dead."

"By your ancestors, will you shut up and let me talk to him?"

"You weren't talking to him. You were having a staring contest."

Nizar's laugh was warm and smoky. He stubbed out his cigarette. "Is this some kind of comical third-degree? You two old fellows bitch at each other until I get worried one of you'll die of a heart attack—then I confess to everything, just to calm you down?" He sniggered and lit another smoke.

Omar Yussef scratched his mustache in embarrassment. Khamis Zeydan stared at his prosthetic hand.

"Let me attempt to convince you another way, Abu Adel," Nizar said.

"Try me." Khamis Zeydan poured himself a whisky.

Nizar stroked his long hair. "In Palestine, everyone knows what it means to be from Bethlehem. Here, I tell people where I'm from, and they look at me with incomprehension. I explain that I come from the town where Jesus was born, and that's about all the detail they can handle. Even then they sometimes get confused, because I'm an Arab, and Jesus wasn't an Arab, was he?"

The boy stared beyond the two older men, as though he were tallying the lighted windows in the UN building at the end of the street.

"At first, I responded to this ignorance by turning my back on Americans," he said. "I became more religious than I had ever been before. I couldn't have been more of an Arab if I'd gone on the Hajj to Mecca, shaved my head, and thrown seven pebbles at the Pillar of Aqaba. But I couldn't keep that up." He clapped his hands and gestured like a magician who has conjured an object into thin air. "You know the oath from *surat al-Waqi'ah*? 'I swear by the shelter of the stars that this is a glorious Koran.' Well, I could never see the stars in Brooklyn. At night, the sky was illuminated with the orange glow of the city, blotting out the heavens."

Omar Yussef thought of the clouds and rain, sleet, and snow that had obscured the sky most of the time since he had arrived in New York. "So this city blotted out Allah's creation and left you an unbeliever?" he said.

"In truth, I left religion because I'm a bad man." Nizar's eyes seemed to turn in on themselves, closing around his memories, smothering his emotions. "After I had been in the U.S. for a while, I had sex with an American woman. It made me hate myself, because I had betrayed what I thought I believed in."

"That doesn't make you bad, my son," Omar Yussef said. "It just means you were living outside our culture. At home, sex is possible only with your wife, but here everything is permitted. You did something natural."

"I didn't do it with pleasure, *ustaz*. I screwed her like a frightened rabbit. I was scared of the fact that she welcomed sex, that she wanted to do it. She cooperated because she saw how bad I was—that's what I thought. She had recognized my wicked character, and so she allowed me to do these disgusting things to her."

Khamis Zeydan whistled and slugged some whisky.

Nizar slapped a fist into the palm of his hand. "That's why women are forbidden to us, except in marriage. Because in sex a man sees how weak he is, unless the woman is his possession, his wife. Give me some of that whisky."

Omar Yussef passed a glass from the minibar and Khamis Zeydan slopped out another large Scotch. Nizar drank it and wiped his mouth with his hand.

"I remember everything about that woman's disgusting body, *ustaz*. The dimples in the flesh of her legs and the stretches in the skin around her breasts. The cold trace of sweat between her buttocks. Her paleness. As soon as I had finished, I made my excuses to leave. She lay in bed, staring at me with impatience and contempt while I dressed." He drained the rest of the whisky. "I tried to be American. I drank Scotch, I ate all the pork they put in front of me, and I fucked a woman whose name I barely knew. But I may as well have trotted down Broadway on a camel. I wasn't a good Muslim. Still, it was evident that I was no American."

"Could you see no compromise between the two ways of life?" Omar Yussef said.

Nizar closed his eyes. "I found it in Rania. I thought I could marry her, experience bliss on earth here in America, and then she would come with me to Paradise after our deaths."

"Why didn't you do just that?" Khamis Zeydan's voice was low and suspicious.

"Because of Islamic Jihad. They forced me into the drug trade with Rania's father. It made me an unacceptable son-in-law for Marwan."

"But it was his drug ring."

"He was in jail on drug charges while his own wife died of cancer. He didn't want Rania ever to experience the same abandonment."

"So you killed Rania's father, because he objected to your marriage," Khamis Zeydan said. "What did Rania think of that?"

The young man hesitated. He grinned weakly and averted his eyes.

Khamis Zeydan tapped the cap of the whisky bottle against his prosthesis. "What's the fallback plan? What do you do in a case like this where the preparations for the murder have fallen through?"

"We wait for instructions."

"How do you receive them?"

Nizar wagged his finger at Khamis Zeydan. "Brigadier, you're a clever fellow."

"No stalling."

"The command places an ad in a local newspaper."

"Haven't you heard of e-mail?"

Nizar's smile was condescending. "And I've heard it can

be traced too. This is simpler. It can't be connected to us. It'd be meaningless to the police."

"Which newspaper?" Omar Yussef asked.

"The *Metro Muslim*. It's a weekly."

"What day does it come out?"

"It would've been distributed early yesterday evening about the time you spoiled my date. The command has had time to place a message since Rashid's death, so I expect there'll be new instructions in the current edition of the paper."

Khamis Zeydan turned to Omar Yussef. "Where can we get a copy?"

"At this time of night," Nizar said, "you won't be able to find one."

"We've only got a day to figure everything out before the president's speech," Khamis Zeydan said. "We can't just wait for the stores to open."

"Now you're in a hurry?" Omar Yussef remembered the stacks of newspapers by Hamza's desk in the precinct house and reached for the phone. "Let me call Sergeant Abayat. I have his cell-phone number."

Nizar pushed the handset back into its cradle. "Not yet, *ustaz*. I want to know if the Honored *Pasha* is going to protect me from the American police."

Khamis Zeydan glared at Nizar. He reached for the whisky. "I'll make sure you're protected," he said. "Let's drink to it."

Nizar took his hand off the phone, and Omar Yussef dialed.

"Greetings, O Hamza," he said, when Abayat picked up the phone. "Thanks be to Allah, everything is fine, yes. I need you to come to my hotel room right away. There's someone here you'll want to see. . . . Nizar, that's who. Please bring the latest copy of the *Metro Muslim* also. The edition that came out this past evening. Do you have it?" He put his hand over the receiver and turned to Khamis Zeydan. "He has one in his office. Then come quickly with it, Hamza. It's urgent." He hung up.

Khamis Zeydan's eyes were moist and gleaming as he took another drink, wild with excitement born of danger. The tiny broken veins high on his cheeks flushed.

"We're halfway to stopping this," the police chief said, pouring another drink for Nizar. "Changing a plan at the last minute is tough, even if the police aren't on to you. And to carry out a hit in New York City is no easy task."

"Really?" Nizar murmured over the lip of his tumbler, his eyes still, intense and probing. "Surely for you PLO people, New York presented no special problems."

"In Europe, we had some freedom of movement. We made deals with the national intelligence services." Khamis Zeydan emptied his glass and grinned. "In West Germany, we were allowed to operate freely, so long as we didn't attack German targets. But the Americans were always too close to Israel to give us any such leeway. I can tell you, the only operation I carried out in New York—it stretched even me to my limits."

Nizar drank slowly.

Chapter 26

Nizar leafed through to the classifieds at the back of the *Metro Muslim*. Hamza stood over him, his lips peeled back from his teeth and his tired eyes dry and hostile.

"I don't like this," the detective said. "I ought to take him in now."

Nizar kept his eyes on the newspaper. "How far had you progressed in your crack investigation of the headless corpse? You'd never have found me. You didn't even match fingerprints on the dead body."

Hamza turned a glance of hurt and betrayal on Omar Yussef.

"If I hadn't come forward, you'd still be hunting for poor old Rashid," Nizar said.

"May Allah be merciful upon him," Hamza said, "and may you beg the pardon of Allah for what you've done."

Nizar murmured, "'He whose hand is in the water isn't the same as he whose hand is in the fire.'"

That's true, Omar Yussef thought. *You can't condemn someone's behavior until you've experienced their situation.* He took Hamza's hand and held it close to his chest like a man imploring a lover. "I know you see Nizar as a murderer, but you have to work with him now to save the president."

Hamza frowned at Khamis Zeydan. "How severe is the danger to the president?"

The police chief rolled his tongue behind his mustache. "I wouldn't let my dear old auntie sit next to him at dinner in case of a ricochet."

"You're canceling his speech?"

Khamis Zeydan bit at the ends of his mustache. "Not just yet. But I'm thinking about it."

Omar Yussef remembered the Jerusalem girl he had met on the subway during his first day in New York. He recalled wishing that Palestinians back home could live as she did, driven neither by politics and ideology, nor by murder and greed. If the president died here, Omar Yussef's granddaughter would never experience the security that girl knew. The children at Omar Yussef's poor little school for refugees would be engulfed once more in civil war and the viciousness of thugs and killers.

"O Hamza, you need to be a little less of a New York cop and a little more of a Palestinian," he said. "You're from Bethlehem. You have a duty to the Palestinian people, as well as to New York. Bend the rules. If you don't, the president may be killed here in New York. The Palestinians will have a dead leader and perhaps a civil war."

Hamza cursed quietly.

"It's here," Nizar said, his voice exuberant and uneasy.

Khamis Zeydan drained his glass and leaned over the young man's shoulder.

Nizar's fingers rustled the margins of the *Metro Muslim*, an expression of bewilderment on his face. He looked like a newspaper subscriber whose breakfast had been upset by an unexpected obituary for a friend. His hopeless gaze brought Omar Yussef to his feet. "What is it?" he said.

He came to Nizar's side and scanned the page of ads. *Feidy's Halal Butcher and Grocery. Muhammad Hammad, Esq., Attorney at Law. Experienced Muslim Babysitter Available.* "Which one is it?"

Nizar's finger hovered until it came down on an ad at the bottom of the page.

Omar Yussef read aloud: "The Hassan-i Sabbagh School. Recruiting for teachers. Qualifications: Good Islamic character. Sound knowledge of Islam. Legal U.S. status with valid Social Security number. Proficiency in English. One year experience preferable. Apply: Alamut Mosque." An address in Bay Ridge followed.

"That address—it's your apartment." Hamza shoved Nizar's shoulder. "The place you shared with Rashid and Ala."

"What the hell does that tell us?" Khamis Zeydan slapped the page.

"It tells us our friend Nizar isn't misleading us," Omar Yussef said.

"How do you know?"

"Hassan-i Sabbagh was the Old Man of the Mountain," Omar Yussef said, "the greatest, most feared leader of the medieval Assassins. We've come across references to them at every turn, and here they are again."

"The Alamut Mosque too," Hamza mumbled.

"A mosque which doesn't exist at an address that matches Nizar's," Omar Yussef said. "What's the message, Nizar? Is it in code?"

Nizar seemed to have drifted into a dream. It took him a moment to come back. He shook his head, and his long black hair slipped over his eyes. "You missed the logo," he said, his raw voice catching in his throat.

Above the text, a small graphic showed a man in traditional Arab dress walking with an axe held above his head. Behind him came a horse bearing a turbaned rider, dignified and upright.

"Do I have to remind you of the lessons you gave us, *ustaz*?" Nizar said.

"What does he mean?" Khamis Zeydan asked.

Omar Yussef rubbed the white stubble on his chin. "When the leader of the Assassins rode out of his castle, he was always preceded by a man bearing an axe who would shout, 'Turn out of the way of him who bears in his hands the death of kings.'"

Khamis Zeydan dragged Nizar's face toward him with the back of his hand. "Well?" he said.

Nizar murmured, "There's another assassin here to kill the president."

"You know that from the logo?"

"The man who called out about the death of kings—that's the signal. Another hit man is in town. Maybe he's been here all along, as a backup. If the graphic showed just the man on his horse, it would mean we were to proceed as planned. But this is different."

Omar Yussef stroked his mustache. "Islamic Jihad is using references to the Assassins to send secret messages."

"That's right," Nizar said. "All our messages were based around the Assassins."

"When you killed Rashid, you left a veil where his head

ought to have been—another element from the Assassins' religious lore. What message were *you* sending to them?"

Nizar grimaced. "I wanted them to think that the operation had been betrayed—the Veiled Man was a traitor. I expected them to call it all off."

Omar Yussef remembered the man in black who had fled Ala's apartment. *Because I was there, he never entered the bedroom,* he thought. *He didn't see the reference to the Veiled Man. If he was from Islamic Jihad, then the group didn't get Nizar's signal, so they went ahead with the plan.*

"Another hit man is in place." Khamis Zeydan grabbed Nizar's collar. "How do we find him?"

"I don't know," Nizar said.

"If this was the backup plan, you must know what to do."

"I was supposed to wait. When I saw this ad, I'd know that the new assassin would come to me. He'd find me and let me know what he needed from me."

"So this newspaper message is useless to us," Hamza said.

"Not quite. We know that the danger to the president didn't end with the death of Rashid, his intended killer." Omar Yussef looked at Khamis Zeydan. "We have to call off the speech. The president can't appear in public."

Khamis Zeydan's leg rocked nervously. "You care so much about his life? I thought you despised politicians."

"I care about the civil war that would start between our worthless political factions if the president were attacked. I care about the family and friends who'd be caught up in it. So do you. You have to keep him out of harm's way."

The police chief muttered his assent.

"Speaking of harm's way, I'm taking this bastard with me." Hamza put his big hand on Nizar's shoulder.

"You promised not to arrest him," Omar Yussef said.

"Do you see any handcuffs? If he's to get immunity, I have to discuss it with the lieutenant, and from her it'll go higher. I'll take him to the station."

"So you'll try?"

"That's the best this son of a whore'll get."

Nizar's shoulders fell and his chin dropped to his chest, as though he were already in chains.

"When this is all finished and the president is safe, you'll be free," Omar Yussef said.

Nizar's eyebrows twitched. He spoke as though he were listening to his own words being played back to him. "What will I do then?"

"Return to Palestine. That's Ala's plan."

"Ala's going home?"

"When I've finished with my speech at the conference, he'll fly back with me. You could join us."

Nizar ran his tongue over his lips. "Rania can't go there."

She's Lebanese, Omar Yussef thought. *The Israelis wouldn't let someone from an enemy state live in Bethlehem.*

He reached for Nizar's hand. "My boy, tell me one thing more. What happened to Ismail?"

Nizar registered a reluctant flicker of distaste, like a parched man who finds a fly in his water. "He left Palestine after we were released from the Israeli jail."

Omar Yussef scratched his neck and wished he could find

time to shave. "I'm sure I saw him the other day at the UN conference, with the Lebanese delegation."

Nizar straightened, his features sharp and nervous.

To be an Assassin is no longer a game, a schoolroom entertainment, Omar Yussef thought. *Nizar turned out to be a murderer. What might Ismail be capable of?*

Chapter 27

T he bodyguard ran his hands down Omar Yussef's slack torso and bony legs. He looked hard at the schoolteacher with brown eyes that had all the warmth of a mud brick and twitched his neck to signal that he could enter the president's suite. Inside, the Palestinian delegation loitered about the long conference table and lounged in the armchairs by the window, watching the cherry-red taillights of the cars on the 59th Street Bridge disappear into the snow. Cigarette smoke choked the room.

From the sofa, the former schools inspector, Haitham Abdel Hadi, rose to fill his coffee cup from a silver thermos on the sideboard. He wore a cheap suit the vibrant burgundy of a baboon's bottom. He turned a nasty yellow smile on Omar Yussef.

"You look tired, Abu Ramiz," he said. "Have you been out on the town?" He rattled his cup in its saucer and covered his eyes, miming a hangover. The men in the armchairs—the justice minister and the chief peace negotiator—laughed. Abdel Hadi turned to them. "Our friend Abu Ramiz here is an old soak. He claims to have cleaned up."

"That's right," Omar Yussef said. "No matter how worthless

something may appear, I always believe in the possibility of reform—for individuals, as well as for corrupt governments."

The ministers stroked their neckties over their fat bellies and glanced nervously at the surly chief of secret police, who was smoking a cigarette at the conference table. Colonel Yazid Khatib's head was bald and bony, and at the moment it was lowered slightly, as though he were preparing to batter forward with it. His eyes were still and menacing beneath surprisingly pretty, long lashes. They had the attentive, restrained malevolence of a Canaan watchdog prowling an olive grove.

Khatib must be in the U.S. to meet his CIA contacts, Omar Yussef thought, *the ones who train his goons in torture and assassination—the SWAT teams making the arrests that prompted Islamic Jihad to try to kill the president.* Suddenly it was obvious to him that the president's speech would be so much hot air. The real business on this visit would be carried out by Khatib. It would be dirty and do no good for the Palestinian people.

Khamis Zeydan took Omar Yussef's elbow, drew him away from the other men, and whispered, "Stay quiet and show respect. Imagine you're a student in your classroom. Whatever you do, don't lose your temper."

Omar Yussef threw off his friend's hand. "I'm in control," he said.

"Screw your mother. You don't even recognize when you're losing it," Khamis Zeydan hissed.

"Let's go."

They went through a door off the lounge. The president sat on the edge of an armchair, reading a slim file and drinking tea from a white porcelain cup. A young aide with thinning black hair greeted Khamis Zeydan with a few muttered words and offered a clammy handshake to Omar Yussef.

Buttoning the jacket of his brown business suit as he came to his feet, the president shook hands and wished each man a quiet welcome. "Greetings," he murmured to Omar Yussef, leading him to the dark red couch.

Omar Yussef had feared that he would be swept into the brisk, unforgivingly businesslike atmosphere that chiefs usually cultivated. But in his gold-rimmed spectacles and sober suit, the president seemed more like a bank manager than a politician. He unbuttoned his suit and settled into his armchair. The jacket rode up around his shoulders as he rested his chin on his fingers. His eyebrows were black, his short mustache gray. His cheeks were a pale olive color that suggested weak health, and the skin of his neck was loose over the white collar of his shirt.

"Greetings," he repeated.

"Double greetings," Omar Yussef whispered in response.

Khamis Zeydan lit a Rothmans. "Abu Raji, forgive me for speaking bluntly—"

"On which occasion? I don't remember a time when you prevaricated." The president laughed, and his aide slapped his hand on the file that rested over his knees.

"There's a significant threat to your life, we believe," Khamis Zeydan said.

The smile faded from the president's face. His fingers slipped over his mouth and played in his mustache.

"We've broken an Islamic Jihad cell here in New York. Their hit man is still out there."

"I'm sure he'll try to strike during your speech at the UN,"

Omar Yussef said. "The cell uses the motif of the medieval Assassins in its communications. The Assassins used to carry out their operations in public. They attacked sultans and caliphs when they were in procession or praying at a mosque. I believe these modern Assassins will do the same thing, and the UN is the most public stage in the world."

"I'm a leader. There's always someone who wants to shed my blood," the president said.

"Because you have other people's blood on your hands." Omar Yussef held up his palm. "Even if it was only left there by the hands you agreed to shake."

The president cleared his throat. "We haven't been introduced, brother—"

"Abu Ramiz. He's part of the UN delegation." Khamis Zeydan laid his good hand on Omar Yussef's knee. The strong pressure from his fingers was a command for restraint. "I told you about his son, who's being held by the American police."

"Greetings, Abu Ramiz," the president said. "Remember, you shook my hand, too."

"I've been covered in blood since I arrived in New York."

Khamis Zeydan grimaced at his friend, then leaned across the glass coffee table. "Abu Raji, I've interrogated a member of the Jihad cell. I, too, believe they'll try to get you at the UN. We have only a day to track down the assassin before your speech. It's not enough time. You have to postpone."

The president shrugged beneath the bunched shoulders of his suit. "How would it look if I just went home? What would people say?" He shook his head slowly. The loose skin of his neck rolled around the knot of his tie.

"What would they say if you didn't come back at all?" Omar Yussef said. "More to the point, whom would they shoot? Whom would they arrest or lynch? What buildings would they burn to the ground?"

"It's a risk I must take."

"The risk is someone else's in the end. Our society will be destroyed because of your pride."

The president fingered the buttonhole in his lapel. "I remind you it's my life we're talking about."

"Many lives are at stake. There'll be a civil war if you're killed. That's what Islamic Jihad wants. Do you think they care so much about you personally?"

Khamis Zeydan grabbed Omar Yussef's hand again, but the schoolteacher pushed him away. "Let go of me," he said.

"Are you sure you aren't more concerned for your little crew of Assassins than for the president?" Khamis Zeydan muttered into Omar Yussef's ear. "You're too emotional. Stop it."

"These terrorists want to show that I don't represent the Middle East, because I came to New York to work with the Americans," the president said. "They want to destroy our coordination with Washington. Look, I told the American president I'd make a statement about the peace process at the UN. I can't let him down—"

"But that's not why you're—"

The president raised his voice above Omar Yussef's objection. "—no matter what the risks are."

May Allah save me from the self-importance of politicians, Omar Yussef thought. "It isn't your talks with the U.S. that make you a target," he said. "It's the ties of your secret police chief to the CIA—the training his special forces receive in interrogation and killing."

"Colonel Khatib? His work is vital. We can't police Palestine just by handing out parking tickets, you know."

"The people want a decent police force, and Khatib gives them gangsters and the gun."

The aide tapped his wristwatch with his forefinger.

The president turned his teacup carefully, aligning the hotel logos on the saucer and on the rim of the cup. "It's my job to speak at the UN tomorrow, and that's what I intend to do." He raised his eyes to Khamis Zeydan. "Abu Adel, I expect you to help protect me and share this information about Islamic Jihad with Colonel Khatib. As for you, *ustaz* Abu Ramiz, you have a speech to make at this conference, too, I gather. Perhaps it's you they really want to assassinate?" The president laughed heartily and held out his hand to his aide for a big, loud slap. "Would that start a civil war?"

"I imagine not," Omar Yussef said. "But that isn't because no one would wish to avenge me. The difference between me and you is that no one would celebrate my death."

The president's laughter halted, and he fiddled with his glasses. He rose and shook hands with his two visitors.

They left the room. When Khamis Zeydan had closed the door behind them, he bared his teeth and grabbed Omar Yussef near the top of his arm. "Didn't I tell you to keep calm?"

"He was determined to speak at the UN. It made no difference what I said," Omar Yussef whispered.

Khamis Zeydan glared around the lounge. The ministers and their aides dropped their eyes, but the chief of secret police stared back, his expression sullen and blank.

Chapter 28

Abdel Hadi rattled his coffee cup again in imitation of a shaky drunk and sniggered. Omar Yussef stared at him and muttered, "May Allah curse your father, you son of a whore." Khamis Zeydan shoved his friend toward the exit of the president's suite.

The door came open sharply, and Hamza Abayat staggered through it, bracing himself against the dining table. Colonel Khatib pulled his heavy body straight in his chair and slipped his hand inside his shapeless black leather jacket.

Hamza surveyed the room with wide unfocused eyes. One of the president's bodyguards followed him through the door and shoved the police I.D. he'd been examining into Hamza's pocket. A cut over the detective's eyebrow dribbled blood across his temple.

"Hamza, what happened?" Omar Yussef said.

"Nizar knocked me out." Breathless, Hamza winced as he touched his swollen brow.

Khamis Zeydan laid his hand on Hamza's back. "Where is he?"

"Gone, *pasha*," Hamza said. "He jumped me at the elevator. I think he knocked me out cold with a flowerpot—it was on the floor when I came to. I went to the lobby, but I couldn't find him."

Omar Yussef dabbed the cut on Hamza's forehead with his handkerchief. A blue bruise swelled around it, lengthening the split in the skin.

"I got one of the police officers detailed to the hotel during the conference to wait in your room, Abu Ramiz," Hamza slurred, "in case Nizar returns." He stumbled to the phone on the sideboard and dialed the 68th Precinct.

"What's this fugitive supposed to have done?" Colonel Khatib spoke from behind hands cupped to light a new cigarette.

Khamis Zeydan watched the secret police chief with blank reserve and spoke slowly. "He was helping us track someone down."

"Allah is the only one whose help can be relied upon." Colonel Khatib took a tissue from a box on the table and blew his nose. He tossed the wet pink ball toward a burgundy leather wastebasket beside Khamis Zeydan.

The tissue landed at Khamis Zeydan's feet. He kicked it away and glared at Khatib.

"We can't afford sloppiness." Khatib made his eyes burn at Khamis Zeydan. "You're only an *adviser* on security. I'm the real protection. If there's a danger to the president, I want to hear about it."

Omar Yussef pointed a finger toward Khatib. "If any harm comes to the president from these assassins, it'll be because of you. You're a thug and you're corrupt."

"What assassins?" Khatib said, his voice low and rumbling.

"In America, a man like you would be in jail," Omar Yussef said. "In the Arab world, you're the recipient of hundreds of thousands of dollars in American aid. Ordinary Arabs hate America for supporting our rulers when they do things that would carry a life sentence in the U.S. The president is hated because of your torture squads and your thugs."

Colonel Khatib slammed his hands on the table and pushed his chair back to rise. Khamis Zeydan grabbed the man's heavy shoulder. "Did you finish your call, Hamza?" he said.

The detective nodded.

"Then let's take Abu Ramiz to his room."

Colonel Khatib subsided into his chair and resumed his sullen smoking.

Omar Yussef hurried along the corridor to keep pace with Khamis Zeydan, wincing with each step on his injured ankle. "Do you think Nizar escaped because he didn't trust Hamza to get him immunity?"

"Could be."

They came to Omar Yussef's room. He pulled the key card from his pocket. "Maybe he escaped because he still intends to take part in the assassination," he said. "The medieval Assassins employed the doctrine of *taqiyya*. It allowed them to deny their faith if that helped them carry out their missions. When he told us about losing his belief in Islam and rejecting the ideology of Islamic Jihad, perhaps he was just engaging in *taqiyya*."

"An interesting theoretical question. You can write an academic paper on it for *The Journal of Things You Remembered*

Too Late to Be of Use." Khamis Zeydan pushed open Omar Yussef's door.

A uniformed police officer turned toward them, reading the *Metro Muslim.* "The guy didn't come back, Sergeant," he said to Hamza.

Hamza slumped into a chair by the minibar, his face pale and tired. Khamis Zeydan took his hand. "We're leaving. You and I have work to do."

The detective and the uniformed man went into the corridor. Omar Yussef made to follow them, but Khamis Zeydan blocked his way.

"Not you. Your little display of moral outrage with Colonel Khatib is about all I can take from you," Khamis Zeydan said.

"Someone needs to tell that bastard the truth."

"The important thing to remember is that he's a bastard, and bastards have their uses. I need him today to ensure that the president is safe. After the speech tomorrow morning, I'll have time to debate human rights and justice in Palestine with you. Until then, I'm all business, and I want you to go across the avenue to the UN conference as if everything was normal."

Omar Yussef slapped his palm to his thigh in irritation.

Khamis Zeydan laid a hand on his chest. "My dear old friend, you have my cell-phone number. If you see anything unusual at the conference, call me. There's nothing you can do to help the security operation now. Your job is finished, and I want you out from under my feet."

He gave Omar Yussef three kisses on his cheeks and closed the door behind him.

Omar Yussef sat on the edge of the bed. He took his diary from his suitcase, found Ala's phone number, and dialed. "Ala, my son, greetings. It's Dad."

"Double greetings, Dad." The boy's voice was quiet and somber.

"I'm at the hotel." He had intended to tell his son what he had learned from Nizar, but Ala sounded so burdened that he only warned him: "Nizar is on the loose. He was in custody, but he escaped. Bolt your door, and don't open it to him."

"If I opened the door, he'd find nothing here anyway. I'm packing. I already booked a ticket on your flight."

"But he's a killer. He confessed to murdering Rashid, and Rania's father."

"Like I said, he'll find nothing here. Good luck with your speech, Dad." Ala hung up.

The emptiness in his son's voice shocked Omar Yussef. He realized how deep was the void that had been left within Ala when he had lost Rania. *Don't look for a woman who lights you on fire*, he thought. *She may just as easily douse your flames, and then she has only consumed you.*

Outside his window, the blue glass of the UN building glimmered in the dull morning light. Omar Yussef slouched to the bathroom, showered, shaved, and fussed with the tendrils of white hair that he combed across his bald scalp. The mirror steamed up. It wouldn't stay clear even after he rubbed cold water across its surface. He felt as though he had been hit in the head as hard as Hamza: no matter where he looked, his vision was obscured.

Chapter 29

The morning session at the conference was an emotional parade of pledges to finance schools and clinics in the refugee camps of Palestine, which convinced few among the UN staff that the money would ever be forthcoming. From his seat beside Magnus Wallander in the observers' section, Omar Yussef stared across the hall of the Economic and Social Council toward the Lebanese delegation. Ismail's place remained empty until shortly before the lunch break, when the boy entered through the double doors. He joined his colleagues at their long desk, whispered a few words to the man beside him, who covered a snigger with his hands, then set to taking notes on the speeches.

Omar Yussef tapped Magnus Wallander on the arm. "Back soon," he whispered.

He padded across the thin green carpet in the gallery at the back of the conference hall and waited in an empty seat a few rows behind the Lebanese delegates. When the Egyptian chairman wearily mumbled that the proceedings would recommence after a two-hour break for lunch and slapped down his gavel, Omar Yussef stepped toward the boy who had once been his pupil.

He found Ismail in conversation with the tall Iranian representative whose round collar and trim beard he remembered from the opening reception. They spoke in a language Omar Yussef didn't understand, and he realized that Ismail must have learned Farsi. *You don't just pick that up in Lebanon,* he thought. *He's been with Iranians, maybe the Revolutionary Guards that Rania said were stationed in the Bekaa Valley.* Ismail's companion gave him an affectionate stroke on the cheek and slipped away.

"Greetings, O Ismail," Omar Yussef said.

In their dark, pouched sockets, Ismail's chestnut-brown eyes were wan and surrendering. He looked like the note-taking civil servant he was supposed to be. When he smiled, it was with the feeble helplessness of one admitting a silly mistake. "Double greetings, dear *ustaz* Abu Ramiz."

"We have to talk."

"Wasn't this morning's conference enough talk for you?"

"That would be my sentiment if it weren't for the fact that the alternative to talk may be disaster." Omar Yussef held Ismail's arm as the room cleared. He felt a strong bicep beneath the well-cut fabric of the boy's dark blue chalk-stripe suit.

"Nizar has confessed everything," he said.

Ismail twitched his head, confused.

Omar Yussef recalled the deal the Israelis had forced on the boy, selling out a sheikh to earn freedom for his friends. He wanted Ismail to feel forgiveness, to extract him from the destructive embrace into which he had fallen. "I know you feel you betrayed the other Assassins in the Israeli jail—"

Ismail put a finger over his old teacher's lips and watched the last delegates heading for the door.

"They told me you were ashamed, and clearly you remain so," Omar Yussef whispered. He took the boy's finger from over his mouth and held it in his hand. "But they've forgiven you. You don't have to live in exile to make up for what happened in the jail."

"Ala may have forgiven me, *ustaz*, but Nizar never will." Ismail's voice was dour and rough.

"And Rashid? Will he forgive you?"

"In Paradise, when I join him as a martyr."

"So you know he's dead. But how will you be martyred? By a severe paper cut at one of these conference sessions?"

"They say 'the sword brings more accurate news than books,'" Ismail said.

"You're an intelligent boy. Don't take that path."

Ismail pulled his hand away. "Who said I had done so?" He turned and Omar Yussef saw pity and regret on his face. "Will you walk with me a little while, *ustaz*? It'd be good to hear the news from Bethlehem."

"Then why not return to your hometown?"

Ismail pressed his notepad to his chest. "How do you think the Israelis would welcome a member of the Lebanese UN delegation? I can never come closer to Bethlehem than holding your hand now as we walk."

In the public gallery, the school groups left gray blotches on the carpet where snow melted from their shoes. Omar Yussef led Ismail to the tall windows.

"There's an assassin here in New York," Omar Yussef said.

243

"The police know he's going to try to kill the president during his speech tomorrow. For that assassin, whoever he is, it
would be a suicidal mission."

"So?"

"Consider this a warning."

"*Ustaz*, do I look like a trained killer?"

"I've met men with blood on their hands. I've even shaken
those hands in some cases. But I still don't know how to
recognize them by their faces. I always imagine they must
give themselves away with some trace of horror and disgust,
but they can just as easily look amiable and kind."

Ismail watched another group of schoolchildren ramble
along the gallery. "What do you see in the faces of these
American students visiting the UN today? They're just as
guilty of murder as the American soldiers shooting tank shells
at crowds of Iraqi civilians."

Omar Yussef's fingers felt cold in the boy's grip. "When I
was young, I, too, blamed America for all the problems of the
Arab people. But as I matured, I saw that our biggest trouble
is our determination to accuse others—to play the victim."

"This is an unholy place." Ismail threw his arm toward the
yellow taxis jamming the avenue and the buildings vanishing
into the descending snow. "Who among the believers would
lament if it were destroyed today?"

"Perhaps the believers who live in Little Palestine."

"What's that?"

"Bay Ridge, Brooklyn. You were there. I saw you when I
came out of the basement mosque."

"Little Palestine?" Ismail grinned. "As if Palestine itself
wasn't already little enough."

Omar Yussef felt separated from Ismail by the angry cynicism of the zealot. He struggled to find a language the boy might comprehend. "You think Allah is known only in the places where everyone already submits to his will? Allah is here. Allah lives in New York."

"That's blasphemous. Allah lives in Mecca."

Omar Yussef laughed. "I'm surprised at you. You think like a peasant. Allah exists where he's needed."

"But you're not even a believer, *ustaz*."

"I believe that Allah is a mystery. Do you really think he sits on top of the Kaba in Mecca? Doesn't he feel compassion for the people of New York, even though they're physically far away from him?"

They came to the empty General Assembly and passed into the visitors' area at the back. A map of the world, spreading out from the North Pole, shone in gold leaf above the dais.

As he stared down the long aisles toward the futuristic podium, Ismail seemed transformed to Omar Yussef. Gone was the delicate, wounded clerk, and in his place stood a killer, ready to put his faith in truths so simple that nothing could be easier than to die for them, because they made of death something facile too. He had ceased to be one of Omar Yussef's little group of Assassins. He had become simply an assassin.

"If you carry out your plan, then this is where Allah dies," Omar Yussef said. "Wherever he has lived—Mecca, New York—he dies here."

Ismail glanced along the back row of desks in the Assembly Hall, each marked with the name of its national delegation. "My plan?"

245

"It's suicidal."

"How could it be done in such a closely guarded place?"

"I'm not an assassin. I can't give you details. Who knows what components could've been sneaked in here? Perhaps you used money from Nizar's drug sales to bribe a cleaner, who smuggled in a rifle, piece by piece. It could be hidden in this very room."

"You're not as purely academic as you pretend to be." Ismail stroked his beard and smirked. "Maybe I'll recruit you for the Iranian Revolutionary Guards, *ustaz*."

"I don't like the retirement plan. I'm not interested in Paradise."

"If you aren't careful, someone might try to retire you very soon." Ismail strolled behind the empty desks of the delegations.

"As you already did. You shot at me in Coney Island. Or were you trying to hit Nizar, because he backed out on your operation?"

"*Ustaz*, I'm a diplomat."

"Let's say you *did* try to kill me and that I forgave you. How would you feel about that? Because I do forgive you, my boy."

The corners of Ismail's mouth twitched into a fragile sneer. Omar Yussef grabbed his shoulder. "I forgive you, do you hear me?" he said. Ismail blinked and looked away.

"In the days of the Assassins, *ustaz*, their suicidal attacks were reviled. It was seen as unnatural to die that way." Ismail scanned the names of the small, unimportant countries arranged in rotating alphabetical order at the delegates' desks. "Today, suicide attacks are accepted by everyone in the

Muslim world. We have no other weapon against the power of the West. You're out of step. Your thinking belongs to another time, another world."

"Ismail, I won't believe that my world and yours are as separate as you suggest," Omar Yussef said.

They reached the final desk in the back row. Ismail raised his chin and pointed to the single word PALESTINE, its white letters pinned to a black plastic rectangle ten inches long.

"You see our place in your world? Right at the back and on the edge." Ismail turned a circle with his arms wide. "Everyone is more important than us. There are one hundred and ninety-two member states with desks closer to the front than us. Who can we see from here? Oh, look, there's Kiribati. And Kyrgyzstan. Over there, Vanuatu, and Zambia. Superpowers on the world stage, indeed. But here at the back, we find Palestine, with only observer status—not even a full member. Poor little Palestine."

"So when we *are* accorded the right to speak, you think we should refuse it?" Omar Yussef said. "We should kill the president at the podium of the UN while he's trying to remind the world that this desk at the back of the hall exists?"

"They know we exist. They just don't know the power we're prepared to wield."

"The power to die?" Omar Yussef shook his head and sat in one of the visitors' seats. "This desk at the back is the place in the world Palestine has found for itself. Perhaps it's all we deserve. What about *your* world? There was a time when I knew you better than you knew yourself. As I listen to you now, I believe I still do."

Ismail dropped his head and knitted his fingers tightly.

"O Ismail, I'm sorry to see what's happened to you. I don't blame you, my boy. You suffered so much in the jail during the intifada, then being away from your family and alone in Lebanon."

"Don't feel sorry for me. I found my belief in Islam, *ustaz*. My love for Allah."

"You only love Allah this way because you haven't loved anyone here on earth," Omar Yussef said. He reached out a hand for Ismail. The boy sat beside his old schoolteacher, his eyes narrow and bitter.

"What happened in the jail made me scared and angry with everyone and everything. Except you, *ustaz*." Ismail stroked the back of Omar Yussef's thin hand.

"Angry enough to listen to some bloodthirsty imam? To be convinced that murder is a part of politics?"

"I didn't kill Rashid."

"That's not what I meant. The president?"

"You're the only one I'm not angry with, *ustaz*." He gave Omar Yussef's fingers a final squeeze and rose. "I have to go to my colleagues now."

"I'll see you later?"

Ismail shook his head and blinked hard to stop his tears. "Give my love to Umm Ramiz when you get back to Bethlehem. And to my friend Ala."

"Ismail, wait."

"May Allah grant you grace, *ustaz*."

Ismail went quickly through a group of tourists who were settling into the ragged corduroy of the public seats to hear their guide describe the General Assembly Hall.

Omar Yussef squinted toward the podium where the president would speak the next morning. He tried to picture Ismail's tired eyes and the premature gray in his beard, but all that came to mind was the happy boy who had been the least gifted and most exuberant of his Assassins.

The P in PALESTINE was slightly askew on the desk in front of him. He clicked his tongue, leaned across the pine barrier, and reached for the black plastic mounting to correct it. The guide who was lecturing the tourists called to him and warned him not to touch. He waved his hand to calm her. He couldn't reach the plaque anyway.

Chapter 30

C olonel Khatib slouched through the entrance of the
General Assembly. He caught the eye of Khamis
Zeydan, who was standing in the doorway, and grinned with
a sardonic malice. From his seat a few rows away in the
public gallery, Omar Yussef detected some kind of under-
standing between the two policemen in the grim, curt nod
with which Khamis Zeydan responded. Khatib lumbered
down the steps and settled into a seat directly behind the
president in the back row of the Assembly. He gathered his
black leather jacket over his paunch, rubbed his square, bald
head, and surveyed the chamber with a surly detachment.

Khamis Zeydan followed Khatib down the steps, his pale
blue eyes glaring around the Assembly. He came to the barrier between the public gallery and the delegate area in front
of Omar Yussef, leaned over, and whispered: "Your boy Ismail
is here, right?"

Omar Yussef's eyes tracked along the ranks of desks, as he
quietly recited the English alphabet to be sure he wouldn't
pass over the Lebanese delegation. Ismail was in his seat,
sharing a joke with his boss. "I see him," Omar Yussef said.

Khamis Zeydan followed Omar Yussef's gaze. "The

president's due to speak in a few minutes, and that boy's sitting there laughing like a baby playing with a rattling gourd. Maybe you're wrong about him."

I've never wanted so much to be mistaken, Omar Yussef thought, biting the knuckle of his forefinger.

Khamis Zeydan took up a vantage point beside Colonel Khatib and leaned forward, whispering to the president. Omar Yussef's throat was dry; but when he fingered the UN identity card in his pocket, it became slippery with sweat. He extended his neck to check that Ismail was still in his seat.

The door of the public gallery came open with a sudden burst of shouting. Shoving past a white-shirted guard, four young Americans ran down the short aisle. One of them, wearing a blue sweatshirt with the Israeli flag across the chest, unfurled a banner: *President of the Murderers*, it read. The others called out insults and charged at the Palestinian delegation. The president dropped low in his chair, the shoulder pads of his suit nuzzling his ears.

"Terrorist Jew-killer," one of the protesters shouted. "Worse than Hitler."

Khamis Zeydan and Colonel Khatib came to their feet, grappling with the protesters. Khatib took a slim girl in her early twenties and slammed her to the floor. Her heckling became a wail of shock and pain. Khamis Zeydan slapped the youth who held one end of the banner and shoved him so that he tumbled over the girl. The president's bodyguard wrestled with the other two demonstrators as a pair of UN security guards hurried down the steps to help.

Omar Yussef looked away from the melee toward the

Lebanese delegation. Just then, Ismail rose and, with a smile, whispered to his boss. He went down the aisle and headed for an exit near the front of the hall.

Behind the turquoise marble of his desk on the podium, the chairman glanced nervously toward the fracas as he gabbled through the day's agenda. The president would be the second speaker, after the Jordanian foreign minister's introductory remarks. Omar Yussef stared at the exit Ismail had used. Above it, tired green lights flickered in the translators' galleries. He turned toward Khamis Zeydan, but the police chief was on the floor, pinning one of the protesters.

Omar Yussef checked his watch. The president was scheduled to speak in less than ten minutes. He hurried out of the hall. To his left, a security guard barred the entrance to the delegates' area. Omar Yussef wiped the sweat from his UN I.D., flashed it at the guard, and entered a long corridor, which sloped down along the side of the General Assembly. At the far end of the passage, he saw Ismail dodge around a corner.

The corridor was silent as Omar Yussef limped over the thin carpet. The pain in his ankle lanced through his shin. What would he tell Ismail when he caught up with him? That the president's speech would be nothing but empty rhetoric? That it would be foolish to sacrifice oneself only to prevent this man making promises he could never keep? Omar Yussef had tried the previous day to dissuade Ismail. He could think of no new arguments with which to reason against a boy determined to kill for his god—and he was certain that Ismail had risen from his desk to commit murder.

At the bottom of the corridor, it split into a staircase and a gallery that curved behind the stage of the General Assembly Hall. Omar Yussef assumed that, if Ismail wanted to shoot the president, he would position himself as close to the stage as possible. Omar Yussef went into the gallery. His loafers tapped on the bare, whitewashed floor, echoing in the empty quiet. On the other side of the wall, the world was gathered, but Omar Yussef felt profoundly alone.

As the gallery rounded the back of the hall, Omar Yussef realized that it had no outlet onto the stage. He came to a few small windows with a view of the plaza behind the UN building. The bare trees cowered in the wind, and rain splattered from a massive tubular steel sculpture like blood spitting from a body under the volley of a machine gun.

Omar Yussef doubled back. Applause rattled through the wall from the Assembly, and he knew the president was making his way to the stage. He clicked his tongue: the detour through the gallery had wasted time. With a hissing intake of breath and a grimace at the agony in his ankle, he mounted the stairs.

Two flights up, he was sweating with pain and exertion. Beside a heavy door marked TRANSLATION, a red light flashed in a black pad mounted on the wall. Omar Yussef swiped his UN I.D. across the pad and jerked the door handle. It didn't move. He was flushed with adrenaline. He felt sure that Ismail must be behind this door.

He had to find another way in. He was about to continue to the floor above, when the entrance opened and a middle-aged Asian woman emerged. She smiled at Omar Yussef and held the door for him. *Premature aging has its advantages*, he thought.

He entered another curving gallery, but this time there were doors along the left-hand side. He opened the first one and saw a low-lit booth with two seats. Its window fronted onto the General Assembly Hall. Before each seat, a microphone on a long black neck reached out of a desk. An olive-skinned woman, enunciating clear, loud French, turned quickly to Omar Yussef, then looked away. Below the window, the president was at the podium, organizing his papers. Omar Yussef spoke no French, but he heard the woman use the words "Mesdames et Messieurs." *The speech is starting*, he thought.

He went along the corridor, pushing open the doors. Beyond them, translators with Arab features transformed the president's words into Russian, Spanish, Chinese.

The last door stuck when Omar Yussef turned the handle. He shoved with his shoulder, groaning as he pushed hard off his injured ankle. He took a breath. Inside the room, he heard a familiar voice. With another effort, he forced the door back a few inches and edged around it.

He stepped on something soft that resisted his weight. Looking down, he saw a young Arab man in a white shirt and blue necktie, his wrists tied to his ankles behind his back. He shifted his stance, and the man rolled beneath him. Omar Yussef came down on his elbows as the door slammed behind him.

Ismail sat in the translator's seat. He held a pistol in his left hand, training it on Omar Yussef.

"Keep still, *ustaz*," he muttered, his hand cupped over the head of the long black microphone.

"Ismail, don't be foolish."

The man on the floor beside Omar Yussef nudged him with a twitch of his neck and whimpered in a frantic falsetto. "By Allah, don't say a word. Can't you see he's got a gun?"

Ismail read into the microphone from an English text on the desk before him. "We, the Palestinian leadership, have shamefully abused our people. We have allowed corruption to reign in Occupied Palestine. We have murdered our heroic Islamic fighters, even as they struggled toward martyrdom against the Zionist Occupation Forces."

The boy glanced at Omar Yussef and smiled as he read on. From the discarded headphones on the desk, Omar Yussef heard the familiar uninspiring drone of the president's voice.

Ismail's doing his own mistranslation of the president's speech, Omar Yussef thought. *This fellow tied up on the floor must be the real English translator.*

"Worst of all, we have involved ourselves in a scandalous sham called the 'peace process,'" Ismail continued, "which surrenders the Islamic land of Palestine and our people's birthright to the Zionist Occupation, in return for the vague promise of a slave state."

Omar Yussef gripped the corner of the desk and pulled himself up slowly. He looked down at the Assembly Hall. The president seemed small at the podium. Khamis Zeydan was at the side of the stage, scanning the room. Most of the delegates lounged in their seats, but there was more motion on the floor than Omar Yussef would have expected. *Those are the ones listening in English*, he thought. *This speech isn't what they bargained for.*

The Israeli delegate came to his feet, shouting. The Americans rose and hesitated, before walking out.

The president paused, adjusting his spectacles and peering after the Americans. Ismail halted his deviant translation, covering the microphone again. "This'll make some headlines, don't you think?"

"Put the gun down, Ismail. Stop this."

"The speech isn't over yet, *ustaz*."

The president stumbled through another paragraph. Ismail used the opportunity to plug Islamic Jihad's backers in Beirut and Tehran. By then the hall was chaotic. Confused and angry, delegates stared toward the translators' gallery. Khamis Zeydan mounted the dais and ushered the president toward a door beside the stage. As he left, the president dropped his speech. The pages spread across the floor. His sweating young aide gathered as many as he could before following his boss.

Ismail turned his pistol toward the ceiling and whistled across the barrel, as though blowing away gun smoke after a fine shot.

Omar Yussef watched the president disappear, shielded by the body of his friend, the police chief. "You're not going to shoot him?"

"You sound disappointed, *ustaz*." Ismail lifted the translator into the spare seat and ruffled his hair. "Thanks for behaving yourself, pal."

The translator kept his pleading eyes on the gun in Ismail's hand. His mouth was open and he made feeble moaning noises.

"Nizar warned us about an Islamic Jihad assassin," Omar

Yussef said. "Where is he? When's he going to hit the president?"

"Nizar was right. But I'm the one."

"Then what was this all about?"

Ismail watched the delegates gather in excited groups on the floor below. "I was never the best student in your class, *ustaz*. Still, I always listened to you. Nizar was your favorite, yet can you say the same of him?"

Omar Yussef flexed his injured ankle, balancing with his hand against the window. "You chose not to kill?"

Ismail flicked the safety catch on the gun and caught his bottom lip in his teeth. "I wanted to do something to make you proud of me."

Omar Yussef felt tears coming. *Perhaps my teachings weren't as useless as I feared*, he thought. But he was still a teacher, and he suppressed his emotions with a rough clearing of the throat. "You think I'm proud of what you said into that microphone?"

Ismail's eyes glistened. "Proud that I decided not to murder the president. Proud that I made my protest peacefully instead."

"You weren't so peaceful when you tried to run me down with that Jeep."

Ismail licked his lips. "*Ustaz*, I placed my faith in people who took advantage of my weaknesses. They made me into a machine. Even so, I felt awful when I was tailing you, threatening you. Once you spoke to me, it was as though I had become human again."

Omar Yussef caressed the side of Ismail's neck and laid his hand on the boy's chest.

"I saw you in Ala's apartment—just a glimpse," Ismail said. "You looked dreadful. There was blood all around you. I wanted to console you, but I knew I had to get away. You must've heard me, because you came to the door. I thought you might identify me to the police, so I'm sorry to say that, in my fear, I tried to put you out of the way."

"I see."

"When you said you would forgive me, I felt all the hatred in me collapse. All I could think of was the memory of my school days and the faith you placed in me back then. I failed you, and I tried to destroy you as though that would erase my failure. But when you spoke to me, I thought that perhaps I could give myself another chance."

"But what a risk you've taken."

"I'm prepared to pay the price for all this." Ismail examined Omar Yussef's face, as though seeing a dear friend for the last time. "Just as I was ready to pay with my life if I had assassinated the president."

"I'm glad that you chose this way instead. But I'm afraid you'll go to jail here in America for what you've done."

"I'll manage."

"Once you're released, Islamic Jihad will try to track you down," Omar Yussef said. "I've forgiven you, but I doubt they will. They expected you to kill the president, not to play a joke on him."

"It's true. They'll come after me."

"Could you disappear like Nizar did?"

"The Jihad always catches up with you. They'll find Nizar in the end, too, just as I tracked down Marwan Hammiya for them."

"It was you who forced Marwan back into drugs?"

"I blackmailed him into running a drug operation for us. I connected him with Nizar and Rashid. I ran the whole thing. Unfortunately I didn't pay attention to Nizar's—distractions."

Omar Yussef heard a hammering on a door down the corridor. "The girl?"

"I only found out about her after Nizar committed the murder."

"Which murder? He killed Rashid *and* Rania's father."

Ismail shook his head. "I was waiting for Nizar outside the café the night Rania's father died. I thought he might need money and try to get some from Marwan. But he didn't go to the café."

"Then who killed Marwan?" Omar Yussef said. "Did you do it, Ismail? Had he double-crossed Islamic Jihad somehow?"

The boy let his head dip from side to side in good-humored supplication. "Not guilty, *ustaz.*"

Heavy boots beat along the gallery. The door opened, and Colonel Khatib stepped inside. He lifted a Colt Python, massive even in his big hand, and trained it on Omar Yussef. "I knew you were a stupid bastard, schoolteacher," he said, "but not this stupid."

Omar Yussef stared into the broad barrel of the gun. It seemed to dilate like the angry nostrils of the man who held it. His mouth was dry. He felt a sudden cramp in his bowels.

"It's me you want." Ismail laid his pistol on the desk and lifted his hands.

"You're the fucking translator?" Colonel Khatib's voice was hoarse, as though he had spent the previous night yelling in a crowded bar.

"No, *I'm* the translator." Khatib swept his big revolver toward the young man bound in the chair. The man became shrill. "No, really, I'm only the translator."

"He wasn't doing the translation for the president's speech," Omar Yussef said.

Khatib spoke through his bared teeth. "Who did that?"

"That was me." Ismail held himself straight. "I'm thinking of making translation my new career."

"Translation? You bastard," Khatib said.

Omar Yussef went toward Ismail. "When Nizar showed me the ad in the newspaper, I remembered the Assassins' phrase about 'he who bears in his hands the death of kings.' I couldn't stand to think that the happy boy I once knew had become that man. I'm glad you changed your mind."

Ismail took Omar Yussef's hand and rubbed the bones along his wrist affectionately. Omar Yussef smiled and squeezed back, but the boy went pale as he looked over his old teacher's shoulder. He whispered the declaration of faith: "There is no god but Allah and Muhammad is the Messenger of Allah."

Omar Yussef followed Ismail's eyes and saw Colonel Khatib stepping forward with his Colt raised. The blast was tremendous. Ismail's hand wrenched out of Omar Yussef's grip as his body lurched back onto the desk, shot through the chest, slamming against the window of the booth. A few delegates in the hall looked up at the smear of blood on the glass. Ismail pitched to the floor, spraying his papers under his body.

"*Allahu akbar.*" Colonel Khatib sneered at the corpse. "Translate that, you son of a whore."

"Allah is most great," Omar Yussef murmured. He went to his knees and took Ismail's lifeless hand. Trembling, he averted his eyes from the boy's wounded torso. His breath caught in his throat. *Is any speech, any political declaration, worth this death, O Ismail?* he thought.

"He'd surrendered," he said to Khatib. "Why did you shoot him?"

Khatib shoved the big Colt into his shoulder holster. "Unlike your friend the Bethlehem police chief, I don't take chances."

Blood seeped into the pages from which Ismail had read, strewn across the carpet. Omar Yussef looked down at them. The paper was soaked, and the words were all illegible.

Chapter 31

K hamis Zeydan bent to stroke Omar Yussef's hand and spoke with unaccustomed gentleness. "You don't have to make this speech if you don't feel up to it," he said. "Isn't that right, Magnus?"

Omar Yussef's boss nodded with such fervor that his chair creaked. "Stay here in your hotel room and rest," he said. "You've had a dreadful shock. It's only been a few hours since that poor fellow was shot right in front of you."

The schoolteacher lay on his bed, propped against the pillows, his shirt open to his navel. The sweats had stopped since he had taken some aspirin, but he couldn't get enough water down to cut the dryness in his mouth. He tried to talk, but only croaked and choked. He drank another sip from the glass on the nightstand. "I'm determined," he said, with a cough.

Khamis Zeydan settled on the edge of the bed. "Our president's already on his way home. His flight left JFK an hour ago. I have no more responsibilities here. I can stay and look after you."

"I'd prefer a prettier nurse."

"I have a duty to your wife, who is also my friend, to protect you from such temptations. Even so, I'm not offering to give you a sponge bath."

The mention of his wife made Omar Yussef think of his family and of his son, who was alone in Brooklyn. "Go to Ala," he said to Khamis Zeydan. "He's leaving with me tomorrow. Help him pack his things. He likes you—try to cheer him up."

Khamis Zeydan patted Omar Yussef's wrist. "If Allah wills it, your son'll be on the plane with you."

"Go now. Magnus can take me over to the conference, after I tidy myself up."

Khamis Zeydan went to the door. "Come to Ala's place after you give your speech. I'll see you there."

When the police chief was gone, Omar Yussef dressed and allowed Magnus to help him on with his coat. At the entrance to the hotel, he pulled the hood over his feverish head and bent into the wind.

They crossed the plaza at the side of the UN building. The East River was choppy and charcoal all the way across to the opposite bank. A barge glided past a derelict smokestack and an old-fashioned Pepsi-Cola sign on the roof of a red brick factory on the Queens shore. The air was cold on Omar Yussef's clammy face, and he smiled. For the first time since he had come to New York, he felt comforted by the freezing weather. He took Magnus's hand as they went toward the low door in the green marble façade.

In the Economic and Social Council, a Moroccan delegate completed his speech with some hopeful clichés. The Egyptian chairman let his bored stare drift over to Magnus Wallander, who gave him a thumbs-up. He called Omar Yussef to the podium.

"Do you have your speech ready?" the Swede said.

Omar Yussef grinned and coughed hard.

He shuffled up the steps to the stage and squinted over the heads of the UN staff in the pit below him. Abdel Hadi leered from the row of Palestinian delegates, his yellow teeth glowing in the low light of his desk lamp. The envoy from Libya picked his nose, and the leader of the Mauritanian delegation was asleep in his colorful robes. Omar Yussef had addressed more attentive groups of twelve-year-olds in his classroom on the last day of a semester.

"We've heard this week the political statements of all the Arab countries on the subject of the Palestinians. As a resident of the Dehaisha Refugee Camp, I've been asked to tell you about the reality of Palestinian life." Omar Yussef's voice sounded thin in his head, but when he heard it through the amplifiers after a moment's delay it seemed stronger. He laid his hands flat on the podium so that they wouldn't be seen to shake. "Let me begin by saying that whatever you already know—the suicide bombs; the battles with the Israeli soldiers; the names of the factions, Hamas, PLO, PFLP, DFLP—these are nothing but background. The real story is the smell of cardamom in the sacks outside a spice shop in the casbah. It's the laughter of little schoolgirls in their blue-and-white-striped smocks going home after a day at an overcrowded school. It's the noise of the lathe in a single room in Bethlehem where men are making olive-wood beads for tourist rosaries. It's the life that remains when politics is sluiced away like the filth a stray dog leaves in the street. Let me flush away the rhetoric of the last three days and show you the Palestine I know."

Abdel Hadi shook his head with disdain. The Syrian

delegate rose and, taking a cigarette from his pocket, beckoned for his Lebanese counterpart to follow him to the back of the room. Magnus Wallander smiled his encouragement.

Omar Yussef surveyed the hall. He realized that he wanted very badly to prick the complacency of the diplomats lounging before him. "You wonder how these people, whose lives you think are so full of victimhood and despair, get up in the morning. Perhaps people are killed beside them, or homes are destroyed, or relatives are held without charge for months. But they *do* rise in the morning, and they work and eat and laugh, and then they sleep. You don't know how they go on, because you don't know what's in their heads. You only know the political clichés, the stereotypes. They don't spend their days longing for an independent state—they know their politics is too corrupt and divided for that to be achieved. They aren't all determined to sacrifice their children for this struggle, either. It may be hard for you to understand, but what ordinary Palestinians want and what they battle for every day is precisely what's denied to most of your citizens in the Arab countries: freedom and economic prosperity."

The Libyan delegate removed his finger from his nose and flicked it angrily. The Syrian strode down from the rear of the hall, dropping his cigarette. The Lebanese stepped the butt into the carpet as he followed. The Americans glanced toward the translation gallery, fearful that this was another hoax.

"How can you, the Arab countries, dictate a solution for the Palestinians, when you suffer from many of the same problems? In fact, you, the governing class, thrive on the lack of democracy, the inequality of wealth. Take away the Israeli occupation, and the Palestinians would be closer to freedom and a functioning economy than most of your peoples."

"Shame, shame on you," the Syrian called out.

One of the Egyptian delegates stood and yelled, "Collaborator." His colleague hauled him back into his seat with a simpering glance at the Americans.

Omar Yussef hammered the podium. "It is not only the Israelis—it is *you* who drive Palestinians into violence and poverty. You, who take no responsibility for the lives of your Arab brothers." He lifted his hand to point at the American delegation and spoke in English. "And you, gentlemen of the United States, when you send your money to these corrupt Arab governments, pause to ask yourselves: Would I be willing to live there as a citizen? Would I live in a mud shack raising beets in the Jordan Valley for no reward? Or sit in the heat to sell a few orange sodas for ten cents on a desert highway in Syria? This week I've seen how people battle against the difficulties of life in New York. They fight to attain goals that may be of doubtful worth—the prosperity that brings a bigger house, a shinier car, or more luxuries at home. But at least they have aims and the possibility of achieving them. We Arabs are aimless. We wander like our forefathers in the desert, seeking water, waiting for some fanatic to come and enslave us."

Omar Yussef paused. Colors danced in front of his eyes. He heard the blast of Colonel Khatib's revolver over and over. Then he realized that it was his pulse sounding in his head. He gripped the podium. When he reached for the water glass, the Egyptian chairman dropped his gavel and, with relief, declared the day's proceedings at an end. The chairman nudged his aide, who immediately came to Omar Yussef with a congratulatory handshake and bore him away from the microphone toward the steps.

"Fabulous, Abu Ramiz." Magnus Wallander took Omar Yussef's hand in both of his as he descended from the stage.

"You're the only one who seems to think so. I don't feel so good. I'm a little dizzy."

"I'll get you some more water." Magnus hurried to the back of the room.

Abdel Hadi approached with a facetious sneer. "I thought you were about to blow yourself up, *ustaz*," he said. "That was a suicide speech."

"Today there has been no need for suicide." Omar Yussef heard Khatib's gun in his head again. "It has been a day for executioners."

"You mean that animal who tried to shoot the president."

"He wasn't going to shoot him."

"He was a suicide attacker. He knew he'd die, but he wanted to take the president with him."

Anger drew Omar Yussef up straight. "He was killed in cold blood."

"Nonsense. Khatib shot him as he was taking aim at the president. A suicidal attack by an animal, not a human being."

"No animal would seek its own death. An animal doesn't expect to elevate itself by dying. It's our civilization that leads down the disgusting course to the suicidal assassin. Our search for meanings higher than mere existence, life after death. It's the ultimate achievement of our dreadful civilization."

Magnus returned with a glass of water.

Abdel Hadi wagged a finger at Omar Yussef. "For a school-teacher, *ustaz*, you seem to find it hard to learn a lesson."

"I'm a Palestinian. If I learned from my errors, I might run out of mistakes to make, and then I'd have to change nationality." Omar Yussef drank some water. "What's the lesson?"

"Suicide is the entire basis of our politics."

"You're forgetting murder."

"Either way, we always seem to find new ways to destroy each other."

"Not such new ways," Omar Yussef said. He recalled the classes in medieval history that had inspired Nizar to decapitate his old friend.

"The assassination of the president by another Palestinian here would've been a first, would it not?" Abdel Hadi said. "Many Palestinians were killed by rival factions during the seventies and eighties in Europe and the Arab world, but never, I believe, in New York."

Omar Yussef thought of Nizar's father. "There was one. A writer named Fayez Jado."

"Who told you about that? Was it your old friend the police chief of Bethlehem?"

Omar Yussef's head cleared, and his eyes snapped to Abdel Hadi's face.

"I see the former PLO hit man has been reminiscing," Abdel Hadi said. "If only he was as good at doing his job today."

Omar Yussef's thoughts came in a rush. *Nizar's father was the only Palestinian official assassinated in New York during the eighties. What did Khamis Zeydan say? It was difficult to organize a hit in New York, but he managed it anyhow. It was him. When he was a PLO assassin, he killed Nizar's father, and Nizar knows it. That's why he agreed to come with me after I found him at Grand Central—to see the man who shot his father. Now he'll try to murder him. What if Nizar goes back to Ala's place as Hamza thought he would? He'll find my friend there, and he'll kill him.*

Omar Yussef jogged to the chair where he had left his coat. Water spilled over his wrist. He drank the remainder quickly, put the glass on the chair, and picked up his coat. He hurried to the exit.

He stumbled along First Avenue, searching the steady traffic for a vacant taxi. He needed to get to Khamis Zeydan to warn him. There was no time to take the subway. A cab pulled over, and Omar Yussef dived inside. The driver, a Sikh in a black turban, leaned toward the divider for instructions. "Brooklyn, Bay Ridge," Omar Yussef said.

The cab raced down the FDR Drive to the Manhattan Bridge. Omar Yussef blinked into the dark as the driver dodged between the brake lights from lane to lane.

They came off the bridge in Brooklyn and turned onto the Interstate that followed the shoreline. Across the bay, the Statue of Liberty bent her head under the dark clouds moving in from New Jersey. *It'll rain soon*, Omar Yussef thought. *That's all right. Finally I've started to like this cold weather. It reminds me that my body is warm and alive.*

As he reached Bay Ridge, the rain was coming down hard and thick, like blood from a sheep gutted for the 'Eid. It was six o'clock. The day, which had never been bright, was dark and gone.

Chapter 32

O   mar Yussef hurried to the shelter of the doorway that
    led up to his son's apartment. Raindrops slashed onto
the deserted sidewalk and drummed on the awning of the
Café al-Quds. The skyscrapers and the avenues like canyons
and the bridges of the great city of New York were reduced
in his mind to this one street in Brooklyn where the Arabs
lived. He scanned the darkness, looking for Nizar. It was as if
the whole metropolis flooded down like the rain onto this
block, a teeming, distracting chaos of noise and smells,
flashing lights and video screens. He tried to close the city
out of his head and imagined that he was leaving it behind
him, watching it recede from the window of an airliner. He
backed through the entrance, as though to ensure that
neither Nizar nor New York stalked him up the stairs.

Ala opened the door at his knock and kissed him three
times on the cheeks. The boy had been weeping, and his
mustache was slick. Rania stood in the kitchen doorway, her
arms folded and her big mouth a pouting crescent.

Omar Yussef stared at her with surprise and disapproval.
She dropped her eyes to the floor.

Ala took his father's hand. "I asked Rania to come so we

could say good-bye. Abu Adel is in the bedroom." He gestured toward the room where Omar Yussef had discovered the body.

"Since the local police don't seem to have been too sharp, I'm looking for evidence they may have missed. Maybe something about the Islamic Jihad cell," Khamis Zeydan shouted. He grunted, and Omar Yussef heard a sliding sound, as though the police chief had gone under the bed.

Omar Yussef blew out a long, shaky breath. He realized that he had been worried he might find Khamis Zeydan murdered. He glanced out of the window. The blue glow of a wristwatch briefly illuminated the interior of a car in front of the Community Association. *Hamza, on surveillance stakeout*, he thought.

A lone man walked quickly along the opposite sidewalk, his head covered by the hood of his coat, his shoulders hunched. He crossed the street and went under the awning of the café.

The model of the Dome of the Rock sat on the low table by the door. Omar Yussef touched his fingertip to the brown bloodstain on the yellow dome. "You aren't packing this to take with you, Ala?" he asked.

"I don't think I'll bother. Where I'm going, you know, we have something similar." Ala smiled, and Omar Yussef wagged his finger at him, nodding.

The door swung open behind Omar Yussef. As he turned toward it, Nizar stepped into the room, dripping rainwater onto the floorboards. He pushed back the hood of his coat. Around his face his long black hair was wet, clinging to his skin. He shook his head and sprayed water over Omar Yussef.

"You're here, Rania, my darling," Nizar said. "I've been looking all over for you. This place was my last hope of finding you."

"Ala came to me," Rania said, poking her hair behind her ear and straightening the embroidered edge of her black headscarf.

Nizar glared at Ala. "What did you want with her?"

"To say good-bye and to be sure she wasn't alone," Ala mumbled. "I've been worried about her since her father—"

"She'll never be alone. She'll be with me." Nizar's teeth were set, and his lips rolled back.

Omar Yussef glanced toward the bedroom, nervously. "Take Rania and go, Nizar," he said. "Make a break for it now."

Khamis Zeydan emerged from the bedroom. "Nizar, what did you run off for?" he said.

Surprise registered on Nizar's face, but it was replaced instantly by a dark satisfaction. He reached for his coat pocket.

"Wait," Omar Yussef called.

Nizar drew out a pistol. Khamis Zeydan's eyes widened, and he pulled his own gun from his shoulder holster. They held their weapons on each other, arms tensed and breathing shallow. Nizar's tongue flicked against the gap between his front teeth. "This is what the Americans call a Mexican standoff," he said.

"It'll be a Palestinian standoff when you both kill each other," Omar Yussef said. He fingered the Omani dagger in his pocket. *Take your hands off it*, he thought. *You'll never use it.* "Nizar, you can't win. Let us help you. Abu Adel can still get you immunity."

"Help from the man who killed my father? No, thanks, *ustaz*." Nizar sneered. "I would've killed the bastard at the hotel if I could've done it and got away."

Khamis Zeydan stepped toward Nizar. "Drop the gun."

"That's close enough." Nizar's handsome face flushed with panic, and his finger tightened on the trigger. The sweat lay in beads on his face.

Stop sitting in your car checking your watch, Hamza, Omar Yussef thought. *Get in here.*

Rania reached for the young man's arm. "My darling, forget all this. Take me away from here, please."

Inside his pocket, Omar Yussef wiped the perspiration from his palm. He grasped the dagger. If he distracted the boy, Khamis Zeydan could overpower him, and the danger would be over.

He tossed the dagger. The stones in its scabbard flashed garnet and green, as it twisted through the air. He shouted, "Nizar."

The dagger struck Nizar on his gun hand. His arm jolted to the left. The pistol discharged, and Rania spun back against the wall.

The reverberations of the shot died away. The room was silent but for Nizar's horrified moan and Rania's desperate breaths. He went down on his knees, lifting her torso with his free arm and stroking her head with the hand that held his gun. He pushed her headscarf back and kissed her black hair.

The door of the apartment slammed back against the wall.

Hamza burst through and took up a firing position. "Put down your weapon," he shouted. "Let her go."

Waving his hands at the detective, Omar Yussef stepped toward the two young people on the floor. "Hamza, it was my fault," he called. His voice trembled and faltered.

Nizar stroked the girl's long hair with the wrist of his gun hand.

Hamza fired and Nizar recoiled. He clutched at Rania, but her body slipped lifeless from his arms. Nizar let his gun hand rest on the floor and sobbed.

"Hamza, no." Omar Yussef reached Nizar. "The shooting you heard was a mistake."

"I thought she was a hostage." The detective dropped his hands.

"Get an ambulance."

Hamza went to the phone and dialed.

Omar Yussef pushed Nizar's pistol away and held the young man's head against his shoulder.

"Rania's gone, my boy," Omar Yussef said. "I'm so terribly sorry. When I threw the knife, I didn't mean—"

Ala stared at the dead girl. "So soon after her father," he murmured.

Omar Yussef remembered that Ismail had watched the café the night of Marwan's murder and been sure Nizar couldn't have killed him. "Rania murdered her father, didn't she?" he said to Nizar. "It wasn't you. She killed him because he had beaten her so often."

Nizar gave a weak shake of his head. "Not for the beatings. The body in the bedroom—she thought her father had killed me to prevent us marrying. She murdered him to avenge my death."

Omar Yussef had thought Rania's anger incongruous in a bereaved daughter, when she sat in her office with him the day of her father's murder. But now he saw that it had been her rage toward the man she'd killed, simmering even after his death.

"That's why you claimed his killing?" Omar Yussef said. *Nizar was already a murderer, after all—he had killed Rashid*, he thought. *As long as Rania was free, he could still dream of his reward here on earth.*

"My Paradise, my dark-eyed *houri*." Nizar's breath stuttered, and his deep eyes bulged.

Khamis Zeydan slumped onto the sofa. "I didn't kill your father, Nizar."

The young man struggled to turn his eyes on the police chief. They were defeated and ready to believe anything.

"One of his articles portrayed the Syrian president as a coward and a traitor. So a Syrian agent assassinated him." Khamis Zeydan pushed his pistol into his shoulder holster. "The Old Man sent me to America to avenge your father's death. I killed the Syrian assassin. That was my operation in New York."

Nizar's eyes slid toward the ceiling. Omar Yussef felt the boy shivering. He held him tighter. "What was my father like?" Nizar whispered.

Omar Yussef caught Khamis Zeydan's eye and glared. "He was a brave man," the police chief said. He turned away.

Nizar shuddered.

"You can go now to your reward, my boy." Soft as a lullaby, Omar Yussef sang the refrain of the Lebanese song that Rania had listened to in the café: *Take me, take me, take me home*. He thought of the two lovers whose joy had been suffocated and crushed by the sinister presence of the Middle East in their family histories. It was the subject he taught at school—he ought to have known that it would surely kill them. In this, he saw, they were tragic.

Ala knelt in front of his friend and the woman he had loved. He tucked a strand of Rania's hair behind her ear and took Nizar's hand. He kissed it and wept as it grew cold.

Chapter 33

A heavy truck ran over a speed bump, rustling the two flags at the center of Dehaisha Street in its draft. The Iraqi tricolor, with its stars and its imprecation of the greatness of Allah, flapped across the lamppost toward the red, white, black, and green of the Palestinian banner. Omar Yussef grimaced at the din of the stones rattling in the back of the truck as it turned up the hill toward the limestone quarries. He waved to the last of the girls leaving through the blue gate at the front of the schoolyard and wondered when his budget would permit him to plaster over the bullet holes in the perimeter wall. It was his first day back at work since his return from New York. He felt at home behind his scratched old desk.

He wore a short-sleeved light-blue shirt in the warmth of late February. He loved the final weeks of winter, when the clear desert days were mild because the nights were still cold, but the sun was hot enough for him to detect the laundry scent of his shirt on the air, as though it were fresh from the spin-dryer.

By the time he reached the other end of the camp and came onto the porch of his gray-stone Turkish house, his armpits were damp, and he was glad to put down his mauve leather briefcase. His favorite granddaughter Nadia rounded the dining table in the foyer, setting a deep dish of broth at its center. The cool air filled with the scent of lentils and fried onions.

"A wife is supposed to cook this *rishtaye* when she makes a wish for something," Omar Yussef said, pointing at the dish. "What does your grandmother desire today?"

"Maybe she's hoping that Uncle Ala will stay for good and that you won't have to go to any more UN conferences."

Then I'm glad she cooked this, Omar Yussef thought.

His youngest son came out of the sitting room with Dahoud over his shoulder and Miral playfully punching his stomach. Ala pretended to wrestle with the ten-year-old boy Omar Yussef had adopted after his parents' death, then he let the thin child slip down his body to the floor and ushered him to his seat.

Ala smiled, and the exuberance in his face was a deep relief to Omar Yussef, who had worried for him so much. "Mama made *musakhan*, Dad," the young man said.

Maryam brought in a plate of chicken, fried and baked, served over flatbread with sautéed onions and purple sumac, slick with olive oil. "Sit down, Omar, my darling. I want to serve Ala first in honor of his return. I made his favorite dish."

"To your doubled health, O Ala." Omar Yussef took his seat at the head of the table. His eldest son Ramiz brought his boy, Little Omar, from the apartment in the basement, and Ramiz's wife laid out plates of green olives, parsley salad, and a cold *mutabbal* of eggplant and sesame paste. Omar Yussef rolled his tongue in his mouth, anticipating the delicate smokiness of the eggplant and the sesame's milky flavor.

Ala closed his eyes and groaned with pleasure as he ate, making the children laugh. Maryam piled more chicken onto his plate. "Americans are supposed to be fat," she said. "Why did you come home from New York so skinny, Ala?"

"He was pining for his mother's cooking," Omar Yussef said. "And so was I. I nearly starved."

Maryam patted Omar Yussef's little paunch. "The UN should pay for you to stay there another month, then."

When the meal was over, Ala tickled Nadia as she carried the plates to the kitchen and Little Omar fell asleep on his father's lap. *I may never see a houri*, Omar Yussef thought as he watched them, *but this family is the part of Paradise for which I would sacrifice myself.*

In the sitting room, he rested on the gold brocade sofa, waiting for his tea, and tuned the television to an Arabic satellite news station. During a report on the long peace negotiations with the Israelis, Omar Yussef's attention wandered. After his tea, he decided, he would pay condolence calls on the families of Rashid, Nizar, and Ismail. He would talk only of the days when he had been their teacher. Their relatives didn't have to know that they had planned to murder the president or that one of them had killed his oldest friend. He would reminisce about the days when they had been a gang of innocent Assassins.

The phone rang on the Syrian mother-of-pearl side table. Omar Yussef fumbled with the remote until he found the mute button and silenced the television.

"Greetings, *ustaz* Abu Ramiz." The hearty voice sounded distant on the crackling phone line.

"Hamza? Double greetings. How're you?"

"Thanks be to Allah. May Allah bless you, dear *ustaz* Abu Ramiz."

"His blessings be upon you. What time is it where you are?"

"It's six in the morning in New York, but I've been up all night. We've busted the Islamic Jihad drug-trafficking ring."

"Congratulations."

"A thousand congratulations to you, my dear friend."

"Why to me?"

"It was your discovery of the Alamut Mosque prayer time-table that led us to these men. You saw that every week there was one prayer time that seemed to be off by an hour and guessed that this was some kind of code." Hamza's voice was raw with excitement and fatigue. "You found the mosque's schedule in the apartments of Nizar and Marwan. Both men were involved in the drug trade, so I figured that the off-schedule prayers might mark the times when the drugs would be delivered to Marwan's café. Yesterday evening, three Lebanese guys came to the café with a case full of hashish, right on schedule, and I was waiting for them."

"My congratulations to you." Omar Yussef sensed that Hamza had something else to talk about. He waited.

"I'm still very sorry to have shot that boy, *ustaz*," Hamza said. "I heard the gunshot and—"

Omar Yussef detected deep contrition in the detective's voice. He had wished many times that Hamza hadn't shot Nizar, though he also felt the boy wouldn't have wanted to survive after Rania had been killed. His part in the girl's death troubled him, too. *Remorse is a heavy thing for a man to carry,* he thought, *but to give a little kindness will make my load lighter.* "I insist you feel no regret over that, Hamza. You were doing your job."

Hamza's voice became wistful. "By Allah, what is it like to be home, *ustaz?*"

"Praise be to Allah, it's wonderful."

"What's Bethlehem like now? How is my hometown?"

It's the same as it always was, Omar Yussef thought, *though I've changed. I've seen people I loved do dreadful things, yet I've also come to love one of them even more. I've seen New York, a city I never imagined I'd visit, and I've experienced it at its worst. But I also found people there to trust.* "Bethlehem has no policemen as dedicated as you, Hamza."

"Thank you, uncle. Let me reminisce about the old town with you a little. You've eaten lunch, I assume. Where will you go now for the afternoon?"

Omar Yussef glanced at the muted television. The satellite channel was broadcasting footage of the president's abortive speech at the UN. Over the politician's shoulder, Omar Yussef noticed the green windows of the translators' gallery. He caught the outline of a dark head through the glass of the last booth. "This afternoon," he said, "I'm going to visit the parents of a friend."